COME KNOCKING

COME KNOCKING

A NOVEL

MIKE BOCKOVEN

Skyhorse Publishing

Copyright © 2025 by Mike Bockoven

All Rights Reserved. No part of this book may be reproduced in any manner without the express written consent of the publisher, except in the case of brief excerpts in critical reviews or articles. All inquiries should be addressed to Skyhorse Publishing, 307 West 36th Street, 11th Floor, New York, NY 10018.

Skyhorse Publishing books may be purchased in bulk at special discounts for sales promotion, corporate gifts, fund-raising, or educational purposes. Special editions can also be created to specifications. For details, contact the Special Sales Department, Skyhorse Publishing, 307 West 36th Street, 11th Floor, New York, NY 10018 or info@skyhorsepublishing.com.

Skyhorse® and Skyhorse Publishing® are registered trademarks of Skyhorse Publishing, Inc.®, a Delaware corporation.

Visit our website at www.skyhorsepublishing.com.

Please follow our publisher on Instagram @tonylyonsisuncertain.

10 9 8 7 6 5 4 3 2 1

Library of Congress Cataloging-in-Publication Data is available on file.

Print ISBN: 978-1-5107-8344-7
eBook ISBN: 978-1-5107-8345-4

Cover design by David Ter-Avanesyan
Cover image by Kyle Laidig

Printed in the United States of America

This book is dedicated to Lee Jacobsen, who shoved me onto a stage and into a lifelong love of theater, and to Greg Ulmer, who did the same thing for my kids.

I'd also like to dedicate this book to "Captain Telstar" and the members of the BMMB that I've met IRL. The internet is not all bad.

CONTENTS

Reddit Post on r/ComeKnocking: I Finally Went to
the Show and I Can't Recover   xi
AUTHOR'S NOTE   1

INTERVIEW 1—Cole Gardner, Moderator of the
r/ComeKnocking Subreddit   7
INTERVIEW 2—Andrew Drebitt, Technician with
Come Knocking During Its New York Run   17
INTERVIEW 3—Sam Childs, Attended Previews of
Come Knocking in Los Angeles   26

Reddit Post on r/ComeKnocking: A Guide to the Nudity
in *Come Knocking*   34
INTERVIEW 4—C. S. Standish, Security Guard for
Come Knocking in Los Angeles   38
INTERVIEW 5—Bella Evers, Cast Member, *Come Knocking*
in Los Angeles   47
INTERVIEW 6—Bryan Barker, Prop Master for *Come
Knocking* in Los Angeles   56

Reddit Post on r/ComeKnocking: Something Is Wrong 65
INTERVIEW 7—Malcolm Rice, Bartender at *Come Knocking* in Los Angeles 68
INTERVIEW 8—Mazlee Hemple, Attended *Come Knocking* on March 13 76
INTERVIEW 9—Jagger Mora, Member of Who's There Community, Attended *Come Knocking* on March 13 83

Reddit Post on r/ComeKnocking: Going Tonight— Here's My Plan 92
Transcript of Voice Memos from Anna "Punky" Rodriguez: A Dancer at *Come Knocking*, to Her Boyfriend, Daniel Corona 95
INTERVIEW 10—Anders Petersen, Assistant Technical Director of *Come Knocking* in Los Angeles 102
INTERVIEW 11—Angus Schwartz, Cast Member, "the Knight," on March 14 110

Reddit Post on r/ComeKnocking: I Was There on March 14, Ask Me Anything 119
INTERVIEW 12—Rodrigo Giminez, *Come Knocking* Cast Member 124
INTERVIEW 13—Anonymous, Member of Who's There 132
INTERVIEW 14—Bella Evers, Interview 2, Cast Member, *Come Knocking* in Los Angeles 143

Post on the Who's There Discord 152
INTERVIEW 15—Talia Hills, Audience Member on March 14 156
INTERVIEW 16—Napoleon Gutierrez, Security for *Come Knocking* on March 14 166
INTERVIEW 17—Evelyn Sweet-Bachman, Stagehand at *Come Knocking* on March 14 176

An Excerpt from the Manifesto of Ethan Appleton	185
INTERVIEW 18—Franklin Hawley, Actor in *Come Knocking* on March 14	189
INTERVIEW 19—Brie Trulove, Audience Member on March 14	199
INTERVIEW 20—Malcolm Rice, Interview 2, Bartender at *Come Knocking* in Los Angeles	207
Excerpts of 911 Calls to the LAPD on the Evening of March 14	215
INTERVIEW 21—Dana Teller, EMT/First Responder to *Come Knocking* on March 14	221
Reilly Pegg, Administrator/Founder of Who's There	229
INTERVIEW 22—Clark Cardigan, Producer of *Come Knocking*, co-owner of Dumb Willie Productions	235
EPILOGUE	242

REDDIT POST ON R/COMEKNOCKING

I Finally Went to the Show and I Can't Recover

NoMoreVeins
Originally Posted January 17

This is an extremely painful post to write. I've been a fan since I first heard of the concept of the show and I've made some great friends on this sub but, as they say, "nothing beautiful stays that way." Please be kind.

When I got tickets to the LA production, I was over the moon. I saved for months, I booked a hotel, I took time off work, and I drove just over 300 miles to go to this show. I had my schedule all planned out—reverse story style. I was going to start at the Planetarium Garden, work my way down to the basement, and spend the third sequence following the story. I even dressed like some of you suggested—in black and red to match the decor of the Crypt. I looked cute, which isn't something I usually say about myself. When the handsome bartender handed me the mask, I was so happy I almost started crying.

The night started off better than I had hoped! The Garden was beautiful, more beautiful than I could have imagined, and I found Death, in his corner, just like you all said. He was right there! I was psyched through the fifth floor with the Desert and the Miller's Manor and all that. They weren't fighting yet, but I figured I'd catch that on the way up during the third sequence.

Then I made it to the Crypt.

When I said "please be kind" earlier, this is what I meant. When I was a kid, I caught fire once. I had gotten hold of one of my dad's lighters—yes, I was literally playing with fire—when some of the lighter fluid got on my arm and my hair and it ignited. I was old enough to where I remember what it felt like but also what it sounded like. The sound of the flames was so loud. It hurt, but I don't remember the pain. I only remember the sound. My mom told me that even after I had healed, I would crawl into bed with her and tell her I was afraid the sound was going to "eat me all up."

I hadn't thought about that sound for a long time. *Come Knocking* made me remember.

Guys, there is fire everywhere in one section for the floor. Flames shooting up, flames underneath the graves, flames around the giant Satan head. I heard the first "whoosh" and I was done. Terrified. Crying underneath my mask. I couldn't appreciate the work, the performances, it was all just "whoosh, whoosh, whoosh" and the feeling of heat on my skin. I ran, trying to find the stairs to go down to the floor where Judas is, but just as I found the stairs, the Demon Dancers come busting through the door. They're screaming and flicking their tongues and putting their legs above their heads. It was enough to trigger a panic attack.

Again, please be kind, guys. I can handle being scared and I can handle being traumatized but there was just . . . so much happening all at once, all of it bad. It came at me too fast and got on top of me.

I fell down and started gasping and gasping on the floor. One of the dancers stayed behind and helped me to the stairs where someone showed up to take me to the bar on the second floor. I remember the

Demon Dancer was painted red and she looked like she could've ripped my guts out, but she was whispering "it's okay" to me over and over, which was very sweet. I was in bad shape. I'm shaking just typing this.

Ever since I went to the show, I've been having nightmares—people on fire, people falling in graves, demons licking their lips as they come for me, the devil laughing as I burn. It sounds like literal hell, but that's what this show triggered for me. The dreams are so strong. Almost like a premonition. I feel like something really bad is going to happen to me. Or to the show.

Either way, I can't go back. I'm done playing with fire.

AUTHOR'S NOTE

Why fifty-six people died on the night of March 14th of last year is as complex a question as the location in which they died. But, to begin this investigation with a simple truth, over the course of five hours 372 people went into the Darnold Center near Los Angeles's MacArthur Park to see the interactive theater piece known as *Come Knocking* and 316 came out alive.

Hidden in that simple fact are more blood-soaked horrors than one investigation should contain—audience members bludgeoned and stabbed, performers shot and strangled, staff found and rescued many hours after the police were called, dozens of people trampled as they sought escape from the hellish maze in which they found themselves. But, before we get there, it's wise to set the stage, as it were.

Come Knocking is many things, all of them hard to describe. It's an interactive theater experience, a massive creative and technological undertaking, a show with a powerful and vocal fan base and, technically, a retelling of classic literature through a distinctly American lens. At one time, it was the hottest theater ticket in all of New York—and later Los Angeles, a town known for putting on a show—likely because it was a show that demanded much of its audience and even more of its performers.

It was also a show that, to hear its performers and organizers talk about it, was nothing short of a blessing that, thanks to time and several monumental misunderstandings, turned into a modern-day curse.

Opening in New York seven years ago and running for just under five years in the Big Apple, *Come Knocking* innovated in the theater performance space in a number of noteworthy ways. It was one of the first theater pieces to renovate a multistory building. Some of the technology used is cutting edge now, almost a decade later. But, most importantly, it was an experience that demanded certain things from everyone involved that set it apart.

Those who were lucky enough to get tickets in New York (the show ran a scant four days a week) were asked to show up at an appointed time, don a mask, and to remain absolutely silent during their time in the Netherworld. While the show mixed elements of Chaucer's *The Canterbury Tales* and Dante's *Divine Comedy* (with an emphasis on *Inferno*) into a "narrative about the inevitably of death and one's own hand in damnation," visitors were free to walk around the six stories of lavishly decorated and themed sets, explore the surroundings, find their own way through the show and even follow performers. The only official rules were to stay quiet, keep your mask on, and do not, under any circumstances, touch the performers.

From the official press materials:

A night you will never forget is just the beginning of Come Knocking, *an experience that smashes together dance, theater, movement, and special effects into a gory, unspeakable spectacle impossible to ignore. Explore six floors of designed space in an experience that is different for each and every member of the audience. From the depths of hell to the heights of sin, from the basement's decaying ballroom to the garden of immortality, no two experiences are the same and no soul is safe as the devil gets ready to* Come Knocking.

A robust community of theater fans spread the legend of the New York show, so much so that when Dumb Willie, the production company behind *Come Knocking*, moved their operation to Los Angeles, it was an immediate sensation. The delayed opening due to many societal factors only reinforced the desperate desire for some on the West Coast to experience the show for themselves, and by the time they finally opened, individual tickets were going for thousands of dollars apiece, with no shortage of those willing to pay to descend into the show's unique madness.

However, like any controversial piece of art, some saw the show as unwelcome, and others saw it as nothing short of evil. If anything, this is a story about how a small group of people can build a community around negativity and have that negativity curdle into hate and violence.

Over the course of my investigation, which you will read in the ensuing chapters, I heard from staff, actors, administrators, maintenance workers, and others who worked on the show, all of whom described a "dark feeling" in the months leading up to their "one bad night." This feeling followed the show, which ran successfully in Los Angeles for three years, until the night of March 14, when rowdy crowds, systemic issues, angry staff, and good old-fashioned poor planning led to one of the bloodiest nights in civilian American history.

Of course, *Come Knocking* had no choice but to close, with promises from Dumb Willie Productions that it will never reopen under any circumstances. But it bears repeating that the night in question wasn't special. The show was sold out like it had been for weeks. It was not the anniversary of the show's opening or a special promotion that prompted the events of that night. There was no terrorist attack, as was widely speculated by attention-seeking politicians. There are many reasons why the events of March 14 took place, but circumstance is not one of them. As I said earlier, this is a modern story that led to a night soaked in blood and suffering.

For this book, I was able to speak with dozens of those involved in the production, those who were there that night and, in a coup (if I can say so myself), Clark Cardigan, half of Dumb Willie, who had not spoken publicly about that night since it happened. All the accounts paint a strange picture, one of frayed nerves, ignored warnings, and terror. You will hear many different reasons that this show ended so terribly, but I urge you to make up your own mind.

Before we "get on with the show," as it were, there's something else I'd like to address.

After my book about the events of FantasticLand became a bestseller, I have been asked to cover any number of stories about mass death, though I was reticent to do so. Some of this was for my own mental health, some of it was that I felt I had lost my voice. While I still yearned, deeply, to connect with subjects and tell their stories, what I had experienced earlier in my career had left me in sort of a malaise. Was I going to write about blood on the streets of America for the rest of my career? Was that an existence I wanted?

But something about this story feels different. I ask your indulgence for a moment.

Mass shootings, for example, are a distinctly American phenomenon. You can argue that access to guns is a majority of the problem (it is) but I believe there's something deeper happening to us, as a county and as a people, that we have yet to reckon with. Something very near to the surface that the events of *Come Knocking* illustrate, almost perfectly, and that something is this: I think we are very, very scared and very, very selfish.

One need not look very far in the culture to see evidence of people who are one unkind word away from snapping. Search Reddit for "Karens" or "Tales from the Front Desk," listen to boomers complaining about millennials or millennials complaining about boomers, or, the next time you're at a restaurant, ask your server how their night is going. In any case, you will find fountains of entitlement, horror stories of mistreatment and anger, all of which seems to be happening everywhere. Whether it's in a big city or the country, people are eager to tell others how important they are, how they deserve certain things, and how much everyone else is terrible. But not them. Never them.

What you'll find in these interviews are stories of performers with a passion butting heads with an audience who, in some cases, feel as if they have the right to do whatever it is they want, including, in some circumstances, hurt and kill. You will find audiences approaching performers in good spirits only to be hurt in the process. And, most tragically, you'll find people in search of a powerful experience finding only horror in the hallways of the Netherworld.

Ultimately, that is what spoke to me about this story. It's not just about a tragic, bloody night. It's a story about how we got to the point where this tragic, bloody night was possible. And how we still live in that world and cannot seem to extricate ourselves.

A NOTE ON THE FORMATTING OF THIS BOOK

I have removed my questions, cleaned up the language, and condensed answers in some of these interviews, but only done so for the sake of clarity and/or brevity. I believe each interview accurately represents the words and thoughts of the interviewee, but feel free to visit my website and make up your own mind.

—Adam Jakes

INTERVIEW 1
COLE GARDNER

Moderator of the r/ComeKnocking Subreddit

Okay, I want to start by saying this is *very* exciting for me. I mean, it's one thing to love *Come Knocking*, and believe me, I loooove *Come Knocking*, but it's a whole other thing to be part of the history of the show. I get to be a little bit of the show's history by talking to you, so I'll try to contain myself. But it's very exciting! Don't judge me too harshly if I fangirl out a little.

So, I thought a lot about how I want to start, and I'll start here. Did you know the original title of the show was *Death Comes Knocking*, but they thought that was too obvious and gave away too much? I have to say, I agree, but there's very few things about this show I would dare disagree with. *Death Comes Knocking* makes the show sound more like a haunt or a spook house, something that's *just scary* other than what it was, which was so much more. What was *Come Knocking*? It. Was. Everything.

If I have to tell people what *Come Knocking* was, I'd take a deep breath and I'd say [*inhales*] *Come Knocking* took elements of classic literature including but not limited to *The Canterbury Tales*, specifically the Wife of Bath's Tale, the Knight's Tale, the Physician's Tale, and the Parson's Tale, depending on if you believe that section on Floor Four is part of the Parson's tale, which not everybody does . . . shit, what was I saying? Yeah yeah, elements of *Canterbury*, elements of *Inferno* by Dante, and other pieces of literature dealing with hell and the afterlife and throws it all into this blender of modern dance and creole culture and pyrotechnics and sex and murder and one-on-ones and smoke-filled rooms and, ahhh! It was just this magical thing, and the best part about it was it was never the same no matter how many times you went. **Not** once. I went ten times—I was hoping to make it a dozen, which is supposed to be the magic number to truly understand the show, but I ran into some trouble getting tickets—and each time was a unique, one-of-a-kind adventure that I will never get over.

How do they do it? If you ask me, it's a lot of things, but it starts with the mask. Once you put on the mask, the freedom you experience is almost absolute other than the two cardinal rules: No talking and no touching. Which is how all my dates tend to end. [*sighs*]

Let me dwell on the masks for just a second. The masks were the *thing*, okay? They were the very first step into that world. When myself and others who were big fans of the show put on the mask, we could feel a switch in our personality. Some people—and take this with a grain of salt because people who get really excited about interactive theater get *really* excited about interactive theater—but some people said they could feel themselves descending into the "Netherworld" when they put their mask on. It was like the lights dimming in a theater, but it was sort of like you were going onstage, too. And what a stage! Oh my f'ing God, there were so many amazing pieces of production design on the six floors. Just sumptuous and transportive and frightening and fantastical and scary and gorgeous. You go into the grimy ballroom on the bottom floor all the way to the Planetarium Garden on the top floor, and you might as well be in different worlds with a bunch of other worlds in between. Believe me when I tell you it was so, so good.

Okay, so I can sense my enthusiasm might be a bit much for you so let's pull back a little bit and let me tell you what it's like to be in the audience for this incredible show.

There are three things you need to know about *Come Knocking* to get the most enjoyment out of your time, according to me. But also according to the subreddit r/ComeKnocking, which is sort of *the* place to talk about the show. Luckily for them, I happen to agree with these tips, largely because I more or less ran the place for years.

The first rule is show up early. Your ticket will say you can "join us" any time between seven and nine p.m. with the show closing at ten, but what they don't tell you, but what should be obvious if you use even an itty-bitty bit of your brain, is this is a theater experience, not a club. And by that I mean if you show up at seven you get to roam and explore and see as much of the performance as you can for three hours as opposed to one. I cannot, repeat, cannot imagine showing up at 8:59 and to only get one cycle of the show. At those prices? Jesus, just throw money out the window, moron. What that line on the ticket does is separate out the normies from the real kings and queens who knew what the f they were doing.

Oh, I should have said, the show runs through three cycles a night, each cycle taking an hour, which is why you show up early. It's one of the most brilliant parts of the show, because there is a straight "story" where one thing happens and then another thing happens and it not-so-merrily rolls along. But I have been to the show so many times and I made an attempt, once, to catch the full story or "go story mode" as we say and . . . I guess it just doesn't work that way. Or it's very hard to do, I guess. People claim to have done it. I'm sure I've seen the story all the way through, but with the cycles it's amazing because you can watch the same thing happen three times in one night or completely miss it, and, I'm telling you, some of the things they do are big. Huge. Special effects and fire and blood and physically taxing dance and stunt work and a giant Satan that comes out at one point. And it's entirely possible to just miss it. I find that incredible.

So, long story short, step one, show up at seven. Step two, be open to anything. A lot of people who are new to the show will ask "how do I see the best stuff?" like the Demon Dance or the fighting or, if they're that kind of person, the nudity. And if they ask when and where they can see certain things they are completely missing the point of the experience. The point is not to set your clock and be somewhere at a certain time. Or . . . or, I'll do you one better. It's not about sharing an experience like normal theater. It's about finding your way to your own experience, which is a metaphor for death which is kind of what the whole show is about, unless you think it's a strict retelling of the end of the Franco-Prussian War, but I don't believe any of those really "deep" readings, myself. God, this is going to look so stupid in print! Oh my God.

But, before I move on to step three, I really do want to emphasize how each time you go through *Come Knocking*, your experience is your own if you're open to it. Some of the performers, they love breaking up couples and taking them to different parts of the building so they can have their own experience that they only get to recount to one another after it's over. Bachelorette parties, Jesus Christ, they don't stand a chance. The Demon crew descends on them, and they're scattered to the winds. Unless they're Ghouls, which is what we call people who don't buy into the spirit of the thing. Trust me, if you have even a little imagination it's easy to get whisked off by a handsome stranger into a strange part of a building, but some people are like, nope. Nuh uh. Not gonna happen. And anyone who crosses their arms and refuses to get into the spirit of the show, they're Ghouls, and they are left alone to their own experience, which usually consists of standing in the corner. And they're welcome to it. I'll be trying to get a one-on-one with a hot, barely dressed man with red glittery paint all over his body, thank you.

One-on-ones? Just one more thing that makes *Come Knocking* the f'n greatest show ever. Okay, so picture this. You've just seen the Human Jubilation parade on the bottom floor, or whatever. A big scene with a lot of cast members, okay? And one of them stops, mid-leap or mid-line or mid-whatever, and stares at you. Then approaches you. You can see their face, but they can't see yours. They can talk to you, but you cannot talk to them. They lead you somewhere. And you have a one-on-one. Maybe the performer will dance for you, maybe deliver a soliloquy that you have no context for, maybe they grab another performer and put you in a crypt on the fourth floor. You have no way of knowing what's about to happen but what you do know is what's happening is happening in the moment and happening just for you and it may never happen again . . . which is a metaphor for the entire show about living life before death inevitably makes fools of us all . . . just, you get it.

Just, real quick, I love to tell the story of my second one-on-one, if that's okay. It was my seventh time. Lucky number seven, and it was already a good night. I was in a new relationship so just bursting with that new relationship energy, I was a little high—you don't want to be too high or too drunk but if you hit it right, oh my *God!*—and each and every time I had gone before I had started in the basement with the Human Jubilation. It's a scene where, I'd say 70 percent of all the performers gather for this big, raucous sequence where everyone is full of joy and happiness and then one of the performers "dies" suddenly, it's a very moving scene. Anyway, six times before I had gone to the Jubilation but that night, I don't know what came over me, but instead of going down, I went up. My thought was I wanted to walk through the Planetarium Garden before it got too busy, because it's one of the most beautiful things I've ever seen. I mean, it's a set but it's a garden but it's a galaxy and the flowers are planets but they're not and it's dark but has this incredible open feeling. Anyway, I go up. And there she was.

If you haven't caught on yet, I like me some men, okay? Love me some dudes. But in the middle of the garden was this woman. She was wearing pants and a cape with a hood with an elaborate mask, but she was bare chested and gliding among the flowers. Just a vision that was . . . everything. Sexy and beautiful and spooky and transcendent, and it was just her and me, or maybe it just felt like her and me, there might have been other people up there but if there was, I didn't see them. I felt like I was in a trance, or that I had accidentally stumbled into someone else's dream but in a good way. She glided toward me, took my hand, and led me to the huge telescope in the middle of the room and wordlessly gestured for me to look through. I did. What I saw was an old painting. It was hard to make out and I looked at it for thirty or forty seconds trying to figure out what it meant, and when I opened my eyes, she was gone. I was alone in this gorgeous place and I felt an overwhelming fear at being alone. Not like someone was going to jump out at me or I was going to get assaulted but more like something existential. Something all the way in my chest and back to my soul. I was alone, and it was terrifying.

I think about that experience every single day and will think about it every single day until I die. That's what this show does to people. It changes them, if they let it.

Then, of course, people came in or someone moved too loud or something, and the spell was broken. I went to the forums and told them about it and no one had had that experience or anything close to it. It was just for me. So . . . yeah. Be open.

Then, we have the other side. So, have you ever seen that Reddit post about "if you could broadcast one idea to every living person at once, what would it be?" and people are like "be excellent to each other" or "climate change is coming for us all" or "Baba Booey Baba Booey Howard Stern's Penis"? Well, what I would say is, "If you go see *Come Knocking*, whatever happens, do not speak." Seriously, it's the cardinal rule, the one thing us fans want more than anything. Respect the show, respect the space, respect the performers. The best way to do that is to not. F'ing. Talk.

For some people, it's a bridge too far, and they can't handle it, and if you're one of those people, may I politely suggest *Aladdin* down the street, okay? If the show is too much for you, the show is too much for you. As I tell all my friends, this show isn't for everyone, but it's definitely for me.

So, those are the big three rules. If you show up early, are open to all experiences, and respect everyone by remaining silent, you are in for the time of your life. If you show up late and start screaming "What am I supposed to do?" because you were too lazy or too stupid to do even a little bit of research into your $250 ticket, then, like, how are you even getting through life at that point? What are you even doing? And, look, I know fandoms can be hard to get into, particularly on Reddit. If you don't know why you would follow the Porter from the lobby as he goes to the Demon Dance or why seven people are on a table screaming until blood comes out of their mouth, it's not my job to do that labor for you. But it is my job as moderator of the r/ComeKnocking subreddit, which is a job I take very seriously, to be welcoming, at least.

I'm sorry, *former* moderator of r/ComeKnocking. After March 14, I just . . .

I know why you're here. I know what "blank" I'm filling in for your story. I know I'm the person who is going to mourn the loss of this great thing, and yeah, I can do that, but before I do [*deep breath*] let me tell you about how I experience 3/14, as we call it in the fandom.

Truthfully, I had heard the rumors. I had read the posts. Some people would come to us looking for an explanation, and we certainly have explainers on subreddit, but some of them would come at us hard. Let me read you some of the messages I got.

"I don't know why you bunch of . . . 'gay f slurs' . . . go to hell and take your stupid 'experience' with you."

That one, that's kind of a common refrain. We had a special name for them, which was DDTR, or "didn't do their research." And, look, I get it. *Come Knocking* is *a lot*, and if you go in blind, you're bound to have a pretty strong reaction one way or another. And, what can I say? The internet is the internet. Here's another one. Please remember I'm quoting here.

"That was fucking dumb and a waste of money. I don't know why you . . . 'gay f slurs' . . . like it so much."

So I bet you're sensing a theme. So, you've got the people who don't know what to make of it, and then those who have a bad reaction to it and, trust me, as a moderator, I saw eight to ten of these messages come across a week. A constant stream of negativity like that because the internet is the internet, and this country is this country. But it was after the move from New York to LA when I started getting messages like this one:

"I would have enjoyed it a lot more had someone not shoved me down trying to get to the Devil's Dance."

Or . . .

"My girlfriend got a bloody nose last week just because she got too close to a performer. The 'show' was garbage and I'm going to tell everyone not to go."

I did a little bit of digging on that one and the woman tried to get on a table in the basement floor during one of the big dance numbers. Basically, they invaded the space of a highly trained dancer doing incredibly difficult and fast-paced routines. It would be like jumping onstage with a ballerina and complaining you got kicked in the face. Also, notice the last little bit. Everyone has to feel so important, like they have any power at all over this multimillion-dollar production. I see that all the time, too. Okay, last one:

"I used to love this show. I went twice a year in New York and my boyfriend surprised me with a trip to LA for the new show. It was different but the same. The biggest thing I noticed was the way people behaved. There was talking and when security would show up and try to stop them they'd just scream louder. Nothing breaks the mood of a powerful show like someone screaming about how they 'are going to call their lawyer and sue for your balls.' Needless to say, I won't be going back."

Those are the ones that really broke my heart, because I know there was love there. I know this person "got it," and if you're lucky enough to "get it," then *Come Knocking* is truly like nothing else on earth. It touches the heart and moves you in ways you didn't know you could be moved and to have someone come in and barf their entitlement all over it, it makes me angry. Angry and sad, which is what I seem to be a lot these days.

Okay. On to what you came here for.

I'm obviously not a full-time moderator for Reddit. I don't think those jobs really exist. But my job has a lot of downtime, and I'm able to do a lot of work on breaks and over lunch and things like that. There are two other moderators who can help handle the load, but the night after it happened, which was a Friday night, I called in sick because I knew things were about to explode. And explode they did.

While we usually have 450–600 active, regular users at any given time and posts that get a couple hundred or so upvotes, when it happened, we hit the front page of Reddit and stayed there for a week. Presidential elections don't stay on the front page for a week. Taylor Swift releasing a sex tape with Beyoncé wouldn't get the front page of Reddit for a week. But we got the front page and everything that comes with it. And, of course, I'm reading all this content in absolute shock and trying to work through my feelings as best I can, but the fire hose just will not shut off. Then, because the internet is the internet, the death threats started. And in between everything I had to be doing research on the current cast to see if people claiming to have worked on the show and were commenting on stories actually worked on the show, and then news organizations started calling and started taking me out of context—I swear to Christ, I picked up the phone and one "news" organization said their name and then hung up and then quoted me as saying a paragraph's worth of absolute horseshit—and trying to calm people down and locking threads and deleting threats to other members and it was just nonstop fire hose chaos from morning until night.

I used up all my vacation time, and for my trouble I get vilified and villainized and destroyed by the people I was serving. But I'm sure you could have figured that out yourself, so, time for me to do what you came here to have me do.

It really sucks. The fact that people died and died badly is, of course, tragic, and the fact that Dumb Willie was sued into oblivion means a pioneer of the theater scene and two titans of creativity have been cut down. All that is . . . lamentable.

But what I think about when I think of *Come Knocking* closing is the loss of something that everyone needed to hear. Remember earlier when I said the show was "everything"? Well, that was sort of a lie. There was one part of the show that you couldn't escape, that even the dumbest Chad and Karen or DDTR who walked through the Netherworld yakking the whole time were sure to at least partially understand. And that is that the end is coming. Mortality is the point of the whole damn show! From the Human Jubilation ending in death to the Devil's Dance ending in death to Death on the sixth floor, which, you guessed it, leads to death, it's all about the one universal truth, and that truth is We. All. End.

I think back to my one-on-one. My moment. Do you know what I saw in the telescope? Okay, you're going to get something out of me here because . . . well, not everyone is going to like this, okay? Somebody is going to be offended by this, and they're going to let me know it. But do you know the very ubiquitous Christian painting of Jesus standing at the door and knocking? It's Revelations 3:20, I've memorized it because of course I did. "Behold, I stand at the door, and knock: if any man hear my voice, and open the door, I will come in to him, and will sup with him, and he with me." It's a very famous painting. Anyway, when I looked through the telescope I saw that image, but Jesus wasn't Jesus. Jesus was shrouded in black and had no skin on his face and was carrying a sickle. Death was knocking at the door. Just like he always is.

God, I get chills just thinking about it.

INTERVIEW 2
ANDREW DREBITT

Technician with *Come Knocking* During Its New York Run

There's an old saying among us tech guys: There's a moment when just another show becomes just another show.

You can find different people who think different things about what it means, yeah? But me? I think it's pretty obvious that old saying is about the minute when a "show" becomes a "job." You can love the music or the dialogue or whatever, but you hear something eight times a week for fifty-two weeks a year and suddenly this thing you love becomes nothing more than pushing buttons. There's no art or excitement to it anymore. The actors, they do the same thing, the special effects, they do the same thing. And you? Just push the buttons then reset in time for the evening show, which is . . . just another show.

Come Knocking took a little longer than most to become "just another show," but it got there. Sure as anything, it got there. Part of it was the looping nature of the show—basically I was responsible for three technically challenging short shows each night and it was taxing, man, even if they were only an hour long. Taxing and, ultimately, dull. There are only so many times you can get a thrill out of hitting the lights in the "cold hell" section in minute forty-eight before the "work" of it begins to take a toll. It doesn't help that people don't, like, applaud, and that any reactions they have are stuck behind masks we have to clean and disinfect every damn night. It was like that. Started as a passion, ended up using Windex on two-hundred-plus masks, wiping God knows what off of 'em, when you should be at the pub. Nothing will make you fully recognize that we are all giant sacks of meat than cleaning out masks and seeing what kind of goo people left inside of 'em.

Yeah, I suppose there were moments when it was "magic," whatever the hell that is. Times when a bunch of people were in the right place at the right time and I got to really melt some faces. But mostly it was dull, dull work. It didn't help that the two guys who ran Dumb Willie were micromanaging assholes.

"And hit the smoke machine . . . now!"

Yes. I've done that literally thousands of times, thanks. Thank you for your expert direction. Twat. But there are worse jobs. I know that firsthand. I sold appliances for three weeks once in my twenties. Every time one of those mouth-breathing bastards were screaming about my timing, I think back to having to learn all about refrigerators, and my job didn't seem nearly so bad.

But yeah, I know why they closed the show in New York. More importantly, my friend, I know why they never should have moved to LA in the first place. It wasn't a curse, unless you count Clark Cardigan and Dan Darnold as a curse, which I do if you get the proper number of pints in me.

So, a bit of history before we get to the good stuff, because you need to know about the two micromanaging pricks before you can start to understand why everything went down the way it did. Clark and Dan met in primary school. There are conflicting reports to whether or not they were ever lovers, but I couldn't care less about that. Bugger who you want as long as they want it too is a core tenet of my philosophy. What was important is what they did when they were or were not fucking each other. Their work. I vividly remember the first time I went and saw one of their shows on the West End—that's in London. Sorry, but some of you Americans don't know the basics, so . . . sorry. Anyway, I went to see one of their shows, like, the first week it opened, because I had this girlfriend who got her tickets cheap through uni, and Darnold came out at the end of the show in a cape. A full-on cape like he was gay Batman or something. Like he was the Poofta of the Opera. And, of course, the place goes nuts for him because, and this is a theme in case you miss it, if someone talks big everyone will swallow massive amounts of bullshit from them with a smile. You add a flashy cape in the theater world, you might as well *be* gay Batman.

I'm off topic. Just . . . long story short, I am very impressed by them and, thanks to some mates I have, I get introduced, I offer a critique of the lighting in two scenes, Darnold agrees, offers me a job on a production he's working on, and I start off as a light designer and then to head of lighting design, and then more and more until I'm basically running tech. Not a bad career path, and it would have been boring, but I would have been happy to work in a few of those early shows they did and just run them until the wheels fell off. That's an asset of a Dumb Willie production. They run a long time.

Here's the part of the story where working for gay Batman becomes a liability.

Dan Darnold, or DD, as he was colloquially known, was always pushing. Never satisfied. Never "done." He tinkered with the tech constantly. "Can we get more sound here?" "The fill isn't dark enough." And, my own personal nightmare, "It just needs to be bigger." He would say that all the time and every time he said "it just needs to be bigger" it would mean a late night. Because what he was saying was "I don't even know what I want, I just want something." And his producer, Clark Cardigan, indulged DD every single time. So we, as the staff, had to indulge both of them, usually, because they had this amazing reputation in the theater community and a less-than-stellar reputation when it comes to . . . personal stuff, if you follow. They also have a reputation for employing extremely good attorneys, so I'm going to just leave that sit.

Darnold, who was the one I mainly dealt with as Cardigan was more of the behind-the-scenes guy and kept more to himself, came to me about *Come Knocking*. Called it the most "American" idea he had ever had, and I can't say I disagree. It was lavish and it drew on the southern part of the States, that look and feel. I knew nothing about it, but that was okay, because he came armed with books and magazines and websites and movies. . . . I'll skip a bit, because I know the sort of things you want me to talk about and you don't need some arsehole endlessly prattling on forever, but just know CC and DD had a way of getting everyone excited for their next thing. And I was excited. Until they told the part about the building.

The original idea was to use the entire theater to do the show. Everyone would wait outside, put on the masks—for the record I always hated the masks for more reasons than I can tell you—then the thing would start and people could wander backstage and into the balcony, and the performers would be in the theater but not confined to the stage. It was a logistical nightmare, but everything they did was a logistical nightmare, and I was along for the ride. But the more we pushed that concept and the more, as you Americans say, "the rubber met the road," it became clear the idea was just untenable. Not impossible, but Darnold would say, "It just needs to be bigger" more times than I care to count. I think I lost twenty pounds during that preproduction. Just a nightmare.

They wanted to go bigger, so they went bigger. I remember this clear as day. It was a Tuesday when they broke the news that they had secured a five-story building in New York and that we were all to go home, kiss our loved ones, and pack our bags because the show was moving across the pond. I almost didn't go, but . . . personal circumstances. You don't need to know about that. Not relevant. Just know that most of us who were working on the West End show followed those two crazy bastards across the ocean. I think of my entire crew, maybe three didn't get on that plane. And when we got there, well, we had a lot of work to do. Again, I'll skip to when we open in New York but just know, tempers were higher than I'd ever seen them, and I went up and down the stairs in that wretched building so many times I put on fifteen or twenty pounds of muscle in addition to the pounds I had lost during preproduction. As another aside, New York women loved toned men with accents. Again, I'll leave that there, but I was working hard and living the life. Not bad times, when I look back.

Opening night was great. Raves. Like always with those two. And the show kept going and then, somewhere along the line—poof—it stopped becoming this bohemian fever dream adventure and started becoming a job. For all of us.

I don't remember when it happened, but I remember feeling it happen, yeah? Like, CC and DD stopped coming around as much, though they were up my ass whenever they did. And the shows just rolled. I liked New York. And three years went by before I started to notice that other shift we talked about over email. The shift in the audiences.

That sort of shift is inevitable, I suppose. I've talked to other "lifers" like myself, and they all have seen it, felt it. It's why stuff like *Death of a Salesman* has a limited run and usually needs some movie star to get it off the ground. After a year, old Willy Loman looks pretty bad in comparison to rapping presidents and human cats and screaming genies and all of that. Something unique and beautiful like *Come Knocking* was eventually going to burn through the audience that "got it" and start dipping into those who came because their friends told them to or because they heard they might get to see a naked person or whatever the reason. I remember saying to Darnold once, explicitly, you need to figure out a way to keep the hen parties away, and he nodded and laughed, but I was dead serious. This was art, man, and with art, on occasion, some guy's cock and balls are invariably involved.

I'll tell you two stories to illustrate the sort of shift I saw.

The first big one I remember was clearly a tourist. She comes in with two other men. I got the impression from their whole "situation" that the men were a couple and this was their wine-drunk friend from Indiana or wherever. But she's a bigger lady, and she's in jean shorts and a shirt that says "New York Fuckin' City," and she's clearly been overserved, in the parlance of the service industry. I also remember she had a giant plastic chain around her neck like they sell in Times Square. Don't ask me why I remember that. So, security decides to keep an eye on her. She gets the mask on okay, and her friends are trying to keep her quiet, which is a good sign, but she just won't listen to them. She starts talking, loudly, about the set and how it's beautiful and how she's been to a place like this in New Orleans and on and on and on. She just would not shut her damn mouth, and soon other people are starting to shush her. This is right at the start of the show before they turn the audience loose, right? And she takes offense to the "shushing" and starts yelling.

The good news was her friends were embarrassed as hell, as was right and proper. The bad news was we had to "break the world," which was our code for bringing up the lights and bringing in the actual security who were in regular security gear. We try to not "break the world" until absolutely necessary because it ruins the experience for everyone else. Every stitch of fabric, every difficult dance number, the music, the extensive set dressing, the revolutionary lighting system we created was all for one purpose: Bring our audience into the Netherworld. Ninety-eight percent of the time, that's exactly what we did. But after that first fat woman from Indiana made us break the world, it was the like the floodgates had opened.

A week later we had a fight in the Gummar Bar, which is where you start and end the show and have a high-priced drink to talk about your experience with bartenders and who you came with. The fight was stupid—most of them are—and it wasn't in the Netherworld itself. An incident happened there the week after. One of the audience members touched a performer, sexually. Now, this was always a concern and the subject of considerable training and worry on the part of CC and DD. To their credit, they even hired an extra costumer/specialist to make sure everyone who had a sexual element in the show, be it nudity or dancing provocatively or whatever, was comfortable and felt safe, which was not cheap. But this fuckin' guy thought the performer trying to lead him from the Devil's Dance into a one-on-one was actually hitting on him and started trying to stick his tongue down her throat and grab her tits. We sent a costumed security guy out to try to get him away from her, but he started punching our security guy, and we had to break the world. It was a very bad night, I don't mind telling you. Several of the performers were on fire that night—figuratively, not literally—so that made it worse, that we had to break their stride.

It just sort of went like that for a few months. Eight or nine shows would go splendid, and then we'd have a bad night. When you have a bad night on a show like *Come Knocking*, it's worse than a lot of other shows, which is to say, it's a real bad night. And that's when we started losing performers.

Again, I'm a pro at this, so I know when performers start talking among themselves that a show isn't working, well, that's the fish rotting from the head, isn't it? Not much you can do after that. The writing is on the wall. Thing is, I know Darnold strongly felt like the show hadn't run its course for how much time and effort it had taken and, frankly, how much we had innovated. If I can congratulate myself for a second, this show was unlike anything anyone had ever done in a space no one had ever done it in. So, CC and DD went about trying to save the show.

They added an entire section about what was expected of you when you entered the Netherworld, making the implicit understanding between audience and performer an explicit part of the show. It worked a bit. People already had to sign liability waivers because of the low light, but they added a page about "not being intoxicated" and "any touching of the performers in any way will result in immediate expulsion." That sort of thing. And again, it kind of worked. Until the night the goddamn frat came through.

I don't want to get into too much. You can read about it if you search for it online, and, honestly, it was one of the worst nights of my professional career. These twelve boys came in with the intent of treating our show like a strip joint. It was disgraceful. Whenever we kicked one out, two more would show up on a different floor. Twelve of them! At $250 a ticket, you do the math. We had two dancers quit after that. Good ones. Then, the next night, a few more. Then our reviews on a couple sites dropped by half a star. Then the boys starting posting videos on TikTok and then response videos to those videos and that got picked up by the clickbait media and before we knew it we had an honest-to-Christ public relations problem on our hands. It was a bloodbath. I don't really want to get into the details, but nerves were already frayed. And, after that, CC and DD started thinking about closing the show. Given what the show was dealing with, I cannot say that I blamed them.

So, on to what I think about March 14th, yeah? The reason you called in the first place.

I'll start off by saying I have not been able to speak to anyone at Dumb Willie, including Clark Cardigan or Dan Darnold, since the night in question. I worked with both men for almost a decade, so I can make some educated guesses for you as to a few things, so as long as you keep in mind I don't have primary sources.

If I had to surmise what led to everything that happened, it's that the building in LA wasn't as suited to our purposes as New York was. The Crypt was smaller. The bar was on the second floor, not street level, which presents three problems I can think of just off the top of my head. All of what I've heard points to a space that worked worse than the one I ran for years, by bits and bobs. Again, I don't know that for sure, but I'd put money on that playing into March 14, at least a little bit.

But, truthfully, my professional analysis as a veteran of the stage is that people ruined the show. Yes, I will admit *Come Knocking* had some more dangerous stuff in it than other shows. There was a lot of fire and a lot of set pieces and, with the crowd having the freedom they did, more things could go wrong. But that's not why this happened. The audiences and, of course, those goddamn nutcases online, they were the ones who made it happen. No show thinks "I need to design this set to deal with active shooters" is what I'm saying. I don't completely absolve the show, but that's my professional take. I wish I had more in-depth analysis for you, so let me say this before we finish.

I say this with all the love to Clark and Dan, I think they should have let it go when they saw what was happening in New York, particularly with the audiences. I told them this . . . well, Dan anyway. CC never really hung with anyone but Dan and, by and large, everyone was fine with that arrangement. Dan and I were both night owls, and there was this bar three blocks away from our building that stayed open insanely late, three or four in the morning or something. So, one night I took him for a late drink and laid it out for him.

The show had made money. The audiences were starting to deteriorate. You could walk away and do something else, I told him.

Opening this thing in Los Angeles was a whole different beast. A different building, a different crew, a different audience that might not be primed for what you were bringing them like a London or a New York would be. I told him "consider London." I told him "consider your next thing." I didn't beg him or anything like that. Our relationship was not that type. But I told him that moving a show did not mean the show moves with him, if you understand. You're creating a different thing.

He listened, bless him. Dan, he can be a cock, but he listened and took it in. And then he said to me "I understand. And I'm going to do it anyway."

And that, sir, is why March 14th happened, in my opinion. Because that was CC and DD in a nutshell. "It just needs to be bigger." From what I understand, *Come Knocking* in Los Angeles was, indeed, bigger. Certainly more infamous. It's a shame.

I'd like to tell you one more story, if I may.

The way we liked to handle people who didn't "get it" or the Ghouls, as we called them, was to use the bartenders as go-betweens. We understood a largely silent, movement-based retelling of classic literature with considerable horror elements, nudity, and the requirement that everyone be masked was not everyone's cup of tea. To that end, if someone was confused or anxious or just not in the spirit of the thing, the bartender would, ever so lightly, break the world and give them a hint or two. "Go to the third floor and look for Judas trapped in ice," which was one of my favorite effects, or "Want to see something amazing? Head to the top floor as soon as you can." This was enough to calm and reassure 95 percent of the audience.

But more and more I saw people affronted by what the show was. It's challenging, and some people react badly when challenged, not to put too fine a point on it. One woman was separated from her husband and came out crying, just great sobs, because of what she had seen. We had a security guard go get her and bring her to a quiet place, but this show, and it was just a damn show, was so angering to her that she had a breakdown and then sued Dumb Willie for emotional distress.

To me, I would have seen that as a bright, blinking red light to reassess what we were doing.

CC and DD had posters printed up the day after the lawsuit was filed.

"*Come Knocking* is depraved, satanic, angering to normal people, and should not exist in this day and age."

We sold out five weeks in advance based on that ad.

INTERVIEW 3
SAM CHILDS

Attended Previews of *Come Knocking* in Los Angeles

I didn't get it. At all.

I better start by telling you how I ended up with early tickets to that "show." My employer, who I'm not going to name, is very famous. She *needed* to be at the opening night. Everyone important was going to be there, and she was definitely one of the important people. She was going to take the other very famous person she was dating at the time and they were going to see and be seen. You get it. It's kinda my job to make that happen for her in a bunch of different ways, and this was just one of those things. Call the publicist, get tickets, make all the arrangements. Once I drop her name, it's usually not that hard.

So, I called and got tickets for the very famous person I work for. Obviously. But their people asked if I wanted to come and see the show in previews and that was something new. Usually I'm a very tiny piece in a very big puzzle that includes her publicist and agent and drivers and everyone, so to get any attention from a group like this was very flattering for me. I was flattered, but I thought it also made sense to go to the preview, so I could brief her about what she and the very famous person she was dating were in for. Win-win right? Of course, I had to ask my boss, who said "fine," which can mean many things, but in this instance I took it to mean, "You've wasted twenty seconds of my day. Stop doing that."

So, I got the tickets and I read through them as best I could, but I could not make any sense out of this show's material. It was all over the place—all "devil" this and "Satan" that, which set off some alarm bells for me. So did the location. I can tell you from living in LA for two years that the building on the ticket was *not* where plays usually happen. It's not where anything usually happens. It's in sort of a shitty part of town, out by MacArthur Park, so that should have been the first red flag. Lots of homeless people on the way there. You get it. The second red flag was I missed the part about the masks when I was reading the tickets. Yeah. That would have been a giant red flag for me because, first off, the very famous person I work for does not like doing anything that's going to mess up her makeup—I mean, it costs between $200 and $400 for good hair and makeup to a mid-level event for someone of her status—and also I don't know if you guys have ever been to, like, a haunt? A big space where people jump out in gooey outfits and yell "boo"? Well, the second they put on the masks they're ready to scare you, in my experience, so why was the audience putting them on? Like I said, I didn't get it. It seemed like a bad idea. I was totally surprised when I got there and got their speech about Underworld or whatever it was and they mentioned the masks.

I will give them this—the masks, themselves, were pretty great. Like, have you seen *Eyes Wide Shut*? They were like that only scary, so elegant and scary is what I'm saying. That's a tough thing to do, be creepy and also, like, "those are some really nice lines." But they pulled it off. And I will give them this, too, before I talk about my experience: The set design was some of the best I'd ever seen in a live show in LA. I was completely surprised given the outside looked like homeless people used the inside as a toilet. Sometimes a lot of LA stuff either tries to be too big and over the top or too minimalist, like, they go too hard or too soft. This went hard, but it went hard in a way that made you go "cool" and not "you're trying too hard." Again, a fine line to walk, but for sure they walked it beautifully.

This is the last nice thing I will be saying about that show, in case you're curious.

So, I get there, and I put on the mask, which I know is not going to go over well with my boss or her date, and then I head into a bar. And my first thought is, *how are we going to order a drink if we have masks on* but immediately I see they have straws and they tell us we can lift up the mask to take a sip but only in the bar and drinks aren't permitted anywhere else but the bar and that explains that. And then they open the doors and . . . what? Like, they said you can go anywhere you want but it's a six-story building. But, like, what's part of the show and what isn't? On top of that, as an aspiring storyteller myself, I'm sorry but it's your job to tell me the story not my job to walk through and what? Make up my own story as I go? The stuff I read said there were world-class dancers and artists throughout the space, and I immediately had a hundred questions. Where were they? What if I missed them? What if I got wrapped up in something else and missed the story? Would I have to come back? It just struck me as really pretentious and not very practical. But that was just the beginning of my night from hell.

The bartender, thank God, sees that I'm struggling a bit and takes mercy on me. He's like "maybe start in the basement" and I'm like "thank you!" Was a little direction too much to ask for? I mean, I don't think so. And he's in character, which is nice, but he's not the greatest actor, if you feel me. You get it. Nice looking, though. Anyway he gives me directions and I go down the stairs and that's when things start getting really uncomfortable for me.

First off, it was dark. The whole thing was dark. Just dark, dark, dark. And you're wearing a mask which means you're just bumbling and stumbling around and, while the masks were pretty comfortable—I told you I liked the masks—they limit your vision a little bit so I felt like you couldn't see very much. And then they throw a parade at you, which is what's in the basement. So, you're trying to figure out what way the parade is going and who's in the parade and what is even happening in the dark and someone starts screaming. Like, terror, murder, emergency type screaming, which I don't think has any place in theater. How are you supposed to know what's a real emergency, right? So, the screaming starts, and my heart starts beating so hard I can see it in my eyes, which the mask doesn't help, and I don't even want to figure out what's going on. I just go back up to the bar to talk to the bartender again.

He sees I'm in some sort of distress and says, "How about this, try the third floor. It's a little calmer and they'll be fewer people up there, but it's worth checking out." I thank him, while, at the same time, noting the parade was something my very famous employer would probably like because . . . I don't know, I just know what she likes, and she would like that stupid parade. Anyway, I go up to Floor Three. There are stairs in some places and those, like, exposed elevators in other places but if you want to change between floors that's, like, what you really have to focus on doing. It's not like there are signs saying "stairs this way, this way to the naked people" or whatever. They're trying to "build a world" and, if you ask me what my biggest problem with that show was, it's that I don't want to be in a different world where I don't know what's going on. I have enough trouble figuring out what's going on in the world I live in anymore.

That's beside the point. But it's true.

There is a staircase right by the bar that takes you to whatever floor you want to go—not wheelchair accessible by modern standards, I guess, but whatever—and when I get up there, I get why that's where he sent me. The second you go through the door, you are met with the word "Treachery" and everything is in very vivid whites and reds. Somehow, through the lighting or set decoration or LEDs or I don't know, they were able to make it both a cool, icy vibe and a hot red devil vibe at the same time. I remember coming out and being very impressed, and calming down a little bit because, while it was still darker than I like but more brightly lit than the other places. But it highlighted something else that just made my stomach drop and my anxiety jump—it's impossible to know how big the space was. Like, you're walking around, and you don't know if there's a football field in front of you or you're about to walk into a wall. I get it, they're creating an effect and making you feel uneasy, but I didn't like it. As a woman living in this town, I like to know where my exits are but also the dimensions of the space I'm in! That's just basic . . . basics!

And there were other people who had made their way up here and were wandering around with the masks. Were they performers? Were they audience? What was to stop one of them from grabbing me or robbing me or hurting me? What if someone snuck into the place and wanted to hurt people? Nothing would stop them because it's dark. I'm good at my job, I knew I had to keep going, but part of my brain was screaming "*run!*"

The last straw on that floor for me was when I heard even more screaming and saw a bunch of women dressed like stripper whores just destroying everything around them. They were loud and throwing their bodies everywhere and their asses were out, and I was just not in the headspace to be in an angry strip club at that moment, so I turned around to go the opposite direction of those dancers and ran straight into a guy with a mask on. I screamed and the guy I ran into laughed at me—Laughed. At. Me. From behind his mask, which made me feel about two inches tall. Then the dancers were all around us and I shoved my way between them and found the stairs to another floor.

Needless to say, I was not having fun, but I needed to be able to tell my employer more about what she was in for, so I, obviously, went back to the stairs. I didn't need any part of that mess. You get it.

I'm not going to give you a floor-by-floor breakdown because, honestly, I couldn't even if I wanted to. Parts of it sort of feel like a dream, which is what I bet they're going for. But I do want to tell you about the part of the show that legitimately had me fearing for my safety, and no one on any damn subreddit is going to tell me I had an "amazing, one-of-a-kind experience." I felt like I was in danger, and when you feel like you're in actual, real danger, "I'm-about-to-die" danger, your body doesn't care if everyone around you is pretending. So, please keep that in mind.

After the third floor, I decided to go up to the top and work my way down. I remember really liking the top floor. It was a lot less . . . angry than the other floors. Does that make sense? All the other floors had this constant sense of movement. Even if nothing was happening, there were chains swaying like some goddamn Hellraiser movie or people in the background that I always figured were waiting to jump out at me. But the top floor, the sixth floor, was perfectly still. No wind machines, very little noise although I do remember hearing the sound of the ocean. Maybe I smelled it, too? Other than the bartender who gave me bad advice, it was my favorite part of the whole thing. I think about it a lot.

The fifth floor I don't really remember, but when I got to the fourth floor, that's when it happened. I was already freaked out. I had seen dead frozen people doing trapeze acts and parades full of bloody shit around most corners . . . it was already too much. So, when I got to the fourth floor, I was already dreading it, and when the room opened up into a giant crypt/cemetery thing, I dreaded it even more. And rolled my eyes, because, like, how obvious can you be. Just put a fucking Spirit Halloween in the space and call it good, am I right? But as I got farther and farther into the fake-looking graveyard, I saw what they were doing, or what they were trying to do. Each one of the graves was its own little show. Actually, I will compliment them on that, because while some graves were just set dressing—skeletons and other macabre stuff—some of the graves were active with people in them undergoing all sorts of torture. One guy looked like he was buried in chunky mud, and you could just see his eyes and the top of his head, another guy was screaming as lava dripped on him. It was a vibe.

But here's where it went south. It started getting kind of crowded, like everyone knew something was about to happen, and then there was this giant chime, a sound so loud you feel it in your chest, and everyone who was in their graves started climbing out. They did this little dance number, and at the end of the dance they all pointed at one spot in the cemetery, and this woman descended from the ceiling. She was naked, I think, or had a leotard on and it was cold out. You get it. But she was painted head to toe in the most elaborate paint and she had this massive headdress on. It was kind of like a Día de los Muertos sort of vibe with the black paint and the white bones but also super glamorous so I made a note to tell my employer about it as she would really dig that aesthetic. And the cool part was this actress commanded that graveyard. You could feel everyone there, actor and audience, were both scared and in awe of her. Then she started directing all the people who were in the graves to start grabbing people in the crowd.

Okay, "grabbing" might be a strong word. More like "very convincingly pulling them into a corner" and, of course, I was one of them they pulled into the dark, which I was not happy about. I tried to let them know I wasn't cool with this but . . . how? You're not supposed to talk and you're wearing a mask. You can't use a facial expression because, again, you're wearing a mask. So, I shook my head but apparently that wasn't enough because this guy who looked like he had been whipped to death—his clothes were in tatters and there was blood everywhere—starts herding me into the dark. I wish I hadn't gone with him, but at this point, I wasn't completely melting down, so I allowed myself to be taken. He takes me about twenty feet away to this lighted alcove. I honestly don't know if it was a lighting effect, because I didn't know how big the room was, but when we got there he starts to moan, which I do not like. Then he reaches in his shirt and cups something in his hands so I can't see what it is. And he gestures to it, like he wanted me to lean down to take a closer look.

When he opens his hands I lean down just a bit—my heart is just jackhammering, by the way—and I'm able to see that he's holding this small, wet baby. Like, a fetus, I guess. Or something that just came out of a jar like in those science classrooms? And the worst part? The fetus is moving! It's sort of wriggling and slowly stretching around like it doesn't like the light. And that moment, with that scary guy showing me a dead baby he's protecting in hell, that's when I finally say, "Fuck this show. I'm out."

I mean, how did he know that I haven't had an abortion? How did he know I was ready to see something like that? He didn't! And how am I supposed to feel about that? Disgusted or grossed out or sad or terrible? Because I felt all of those things. Why would they want to make me feel like that? What kind of art says, "Here's something terrible, now you deal with it"? Shitty art, that's what.

After that, I try to find my way back to the stairs, but I'm all turned around and things are moving everywhere and then, when I think I've found the stairs, the Demon Dance starts, which is an entirely different thing and it just . . . it got to be too much. I made it to the stairs and sat down in the stairwell and had a panic attack. I took my mask off to get more air and, not thirty seconds after I took it off, someone from the show was there with a bottle of water, making sure I was okay. They took me back down to the bar and that was it. That was my show experience.

Since you contacted me, I've thought a lot about what I wanted to tell you, and I've got two things.

The first thing is I don't want to make it sound like the show was cheap or terrible. I think I've been very kind to it and they do some cool things, but the whole format of the show is broken as far as I'm concerned. Some of the stuff in there was very cool but very hard to understand, so I did some reading and, as it turns out, there's a lot of layers to the show, or so they think. But how is the audience supposed to know that? I had to spend two or three hours of intense, online research to "get" the show and, like, who's going to do that? OCD people, that's who. You get it. I don't want to watch forty-five hours of content to understand every reference in some comic book movie, and I sure as hell am not going to read a dense piece of literature from the 1600s or whatever to "get" a play I go to. There should be rules about that.

The second thing is the show is very intense. Very, very intense. When I heard about what happened, truthfully, I was shocked but not surprised. I mean, the body count was extremely high, yeah, but people are wearing masks in the dark. What did they think was going to happen?

Did I recommend it to my employer? I told her my experience, and she went anyway. She told me she had fun, but I've never seen her away from her phone for more than ten minutes so I'm sort of skeptical that she went at all. She's the sort who would make up the fact that she went for a story. And, like I said, she wouldn't put on a mask. She probably went, got the photos taken in the new, fancy place, and went off to do other things. I did hear the famous guy she was dating at the time loved it, though. Like, really loved it. And he was the one who told me where to go online to learn about the show and I did, but I'd never go again.

Not like I have a choice at this point.

REDDIT POST ON R/COMEKNOCKING

A Guide to the Nudity in *Come Knocking*

FreeTheNurple

I understand that *Come Knocking* is a complex, powerful piece of theater that both innovates, inspires, and asks basic questions about the nature of being a human on this Earthly plane . . . but did you know it also has lots of boobies and dicks on full display!?

Below is a guide to when and how you can get the most naked people out of your *Come Knocking* experience. Remember, the show runs three times, or loops, in the three-hour period the "theater" is open, so if you miss one of these opportunities for some nudity, you can always catch it on the next go-around. Also, while this guide is pretty accurate, as near as I can tell, the actors have a lot of freedom in this show and have been known to move around. I can give you time frames and general areas but, unfortunately, I cannot be super specific about where the goodies are at.

Let's start from the top floor of the building and work our way down. And to those of you who are going to comment that this is "gross" or drag me in the comments, you're the one who clicked on the headline.

6th Floor—Not every night but there have been reports that early in the evening, a topless woman will be walking in the Planetarium Garden area. Again, this might not happen every night, only the directors, cast, and crew know for sure, but each time this hot mamacita has gone shirtless through the flowers, it has happened early in the night and it does not repeat. Those lucky few who have seen it say she has the best tits in the entire production, bar none, but that might be because of how rarely she's seen.

5th Floor—Divided into two distinct areas, the 5th floor offers ample chances to see some ample boobs. The first area, widely known as the "Desert of the Damned," features a dance number anywhere from 35 to 40 minutes into each hour-long loop. During the dance, reports of nudity vary, and those who have reported positive nipple viewings say it largely depends on how raucous the dancing gets. The Miller's Manor, which is the second part, is styled like more of a "Meow Wolf" sort of exploration area but, if you take two lefts and a right you can find two men fighting toward the beginning of the loop, and one or both of them is nude. The first guy is hung like a horse with a 5-inch flaccid penis, uncut, and has a physique that will stick with you long after you exit the area. The other fighter is not as well-endowed but has a good body and I've been told he puts on a great show. Confidence is sexy!

There have also been reports of the woman in white from the 6th floor appearing on the 5th floor, though not enough reports to be credible.

4th Floor—Reports vary on Floor Four as it's, by far, the darkest of the areas in *Come Knocking*. I've heard reports the leader of that floor, often referred to (but not confirmed) as the Wife of Bath, is naked. But it may be the low light on this floor that leads people to believe that's the case, my own close inspection is that she is in an ultra-tight bodysuit. While it leaves little to the imagination, it is not nudity. I repeat, she is not nude. But that doesn't mean there aren't goodies galore on floor number four! Several reports of one-on-ones on the 4th floor have involved both male and female nudity. The only dependable spot I've been able to find is the fourth crypt on the right when you first enter the floor from the main stairway. There's a guy in there and, if you watch him long enough, you'll see some schlong. And nice schlong at that!

Finally the Demon Dance comes through the 4th floor at the 22-minute mark and, as any good *Come Knocking* participant can tell you, those female demon shirts often do not cover their breasts completely. If this is hell, sign me up!

3rd Floor—Judas and his friends, who are in the ice toward the middle of the floor, are in various stages of undress which can change from night to night. I've had very credible reports that at least one of them has been fully nude on occasion, but that was not my experience any of the times I've gone. This floor doesn't have a lot more to offer in this "sins of the flesh" area, I'm afraid. The sacrifices are really something that needs to be seen and are erotic in their own way, but everyone keeps their clothes on. They take place at the 30-minute mark, if you're into that sort of thing (no judgment).

2nd Floor—Aside from your chances of picking someone up at the Gummar Bar, the second floor is one of the least populated by actors, meaning less chances for the "no clothes" set. The Demon Dance does go through here and usually attempts to pick up some masked patrons along the way, and there are tales of some people allowed to be a little more rowdy than maybe they should be. Either way, have a drink and head downstairs to the . . .

1st Floor/Basement—The Human Jubilation kicks off the show and is a party-and-a-half, however, it is a fully clothed party-and-half. But don't give up. I tell people if they are at a loss of where to go, for whatever reason, the 1st floor is a great place because there's always something happening. Based on many reports, here's the nudity I believe happens down there nightly:

3 minutes—Again, the dancers are clothed but, in my experience, some of the sexiest dancing I've ever seen happens at the Human Jubilation

and it happens very close to you. On some nights, you can join in. That happened to me once. I danced with one of the hottest guys I'd ever seen (I don't swing that way but can appreciate beauty when I see it) and I found the whole thing sweaty and very erotic.

11 minutes—Right after the bodies are carried away from the Human Jubilation, there's a mourning scene where women and men rip their clothes in an old-school funeral type of scene. Some get carried away and you can see nipple.

18 minutes—If you head to the right and head about two-thirds of the way down the main room, you can see two women engaged in an erotic dance. It's so hoooot, well worth your time.

19 minutes—A love scene between a man and a female demon gets very hot and semi-naked until she kills him and starts to consume his body. This scene moves around, as far as I can tell, and has been spotted on Floor Four and once on Two by a very reputable source.

27 minutes—A naked man, covered in blood, wanders around the place and occasionally screams. Circumcised, less than three inches flaccid, from what I can tell. It's sort of difficult as they will change actors on occasion and the fact that he's covered head to toe in blood makes it hard to get a good look. It could be a prosthetic penis as well, but I'm not sure.

:2 minutes—Not every night, but some nights the demons will return to the first floor and torment the man most consider to be the Knight. Through dance they tempt him with many different offerings, including their bodies. I've heard of this happening on other floors but have never been able to confirm it.

And that's it! If you have a spot that I missed or better descriptions than I have put together in this post, please add it in the comments. Happy hunting, my horned-up homies!

INTERVIEW 4

C. S. STANDISH

Security Guard for *Come Knocking* in Los Angeles

I was a bartender a long time before I worked security. Seven years. That's a long time. People see me, about 5'4", 150 pounds or so, kind of soft-spoken with the Southern accent I got, and ask "How did a girl like you get into security?"

I tell them it's 'cause of my brothers.

I was the last of five kids and the only girl from a rural Kentucky family, and my brothers and my dad didn't hold back with me. Not at all, not that I would have let them. They tackled me, and they tossed the ball hard at me, and every time I passed one of them, they'd punch me a little. Kind of a little "love ya" thing. I was the sort of kid who'd run up and show Momma all the bruises I got that day, and she'd roll her eyes and go back to whatever she was doin'. I tried to play football for a year, but I was no good at it but was proud of myself for being tough like that. I didn't mind being hit, but I just wasn't that fast or big, and when you're a defensive back, that matters a bunch.

Being a bit rough-and-tumble worked for me as a bartender, too. I could be very sweet when I wanted to. Very sweet because I like tips. But I had a line and if you crossed it, I knew enough to put you on the ground before you realized what had happened to ya. But I don't need to tell you working at a bar can lose its charm pretty damn fast, and the pay ain't great. Which is why I applied for security at *Come Knocking*.

Once I got the job, I was very surprised to find out a lot of the performers were tougher than I am. Dancers who were as physically strong as anyone I've ever seen, people who could endure pain like no one I've ever met. Real artists and real badasses. But the show itself? It wasn't for me. I get why it was so popular and why it was as big as it was, but it's nothing I'd ever go to myself. Especially not after what I saw working there and what people would do to the performers.

But the people and the operation, they were all professional and they knew their stuff, I don't mind telling ya. Knew it forward and backward and forward again. I went through a two-week training course with actual cops to learn how to handle people, kind of to get the basics down. It was nothin' I didn't already know, but it was a nice time. The production wanted to know that everyone was on the same base level and could handle themselves if it came to that. And I'll tell ya, I had an amazing time during those two weeks. Basically you wake up, roll into work not having showered, and then proceed to throw dudes around for a couple hours. Then you go have lunch and spend the rest of the time punching a dummy in the face. It was the best part of any job I've ever had. That, and I will say there was a real energy about the show. Like I said, I'm not a theater girl, and I had never really experienced that sort of creative energy before. It was very cool. Very cool.

But it didn't take long for the cracks in the show to start, just like any job. You have the basics—it's dark, the actors really don't want to "break the world" which I thought was a stupid phrase—the technical stuff was very present and, while it was well done, it was tech stuff, and tech stuff breaks down sometimes. All that meant is that for every one time we interacted to help an actor or helped someone who had hurt themselves in the show, we had five cases where we had to go kick a smoke machine or hide a screen that had fallen out of place. Far less glamorous than I thought, but the money was good, and, my goodness, did it introduce me to some interesting people.

I thought I had stories from the bar. Let me tell you, three nights drinking with actors gave me more stories than two years slinging Busch Lights to guys wearing flannel shirts. I fell in love with the way these people talked and acted and drank and fucked, to be honest with you. And there's very little that they wouldn't do. Shots off a naked ass, stripping on the table down to their underwear, pretending to be from Australia and convincing everyone in the bar that's where they were from. And loyal! These people had each other's backs to the point where security people, like me, only heard about the worst stuff that happened in the show after it happened.

An example? Sure. So, if you're in the fourth-floor Crypt at a certain time, you'd see people fighting to get out of their eternal punishment. It's straight from Dante's *Inferno*, so I later learned. One person is treading water in a sea of blood, another was buried in human shit. But one guy, if you looked down into the grave you would see him in these wooden stocks—those things that hold your head and arms, only this one held his arms and his legs out—and he was getting roasted alive. The guy, Cedric, who did that bit, had this really sweet face and this amazing flop of gold hair, and he could really have you believe he was in severe and everlasting pain. Well, one night this audience member who was way into the show, bless him, he sees Cedric screaming and it triggers something, and so the guy tries to jump into the grave and save him.

What they don't tell you is there's a hard to see but very strong plastic barrier between the actor and the person, so when Mr. Hero jumped into the grave, he hit a barrier he didn't know was there. This is usually enough to make someone break character or laugh or react, but each and every one of the cast who interacted with the guy didn't just keep it together. They used it. Cedric only ramped up his suffering more and pleaded to the guy. Rose, who played the Wife who oversees the graveyard during the first part, she wandered over in her very elegant way and just stared at the guy, and he quickly climbed out of the small hole he had jumped in and ran off. I overheard him later at the bar saying it was one of the scariest things he'd ever seen in his life. He couldn't stop going on about it, the way the Wife's eyes "burned into him." That was the case of a possibly bad thing having a good result.

See, the actors, they got to have a lot of the fun. Me and my crew? We dealt with most of the assholes.

Oh my goodness, the assholes. So many assholes. Again, I thought I had stories about assholes from working in a bar, but I didn't know assholes until I knew the assholes who came to this show. Now, as I've said, I'm not an expert on theater. I've never studied it, I don't know the theory or anything. And, from talking to the actors, I got the sense that *Come Knocking* is what we used to call a "hard sell." It wasn't for everybody and when something ain't for everybody then there's gonna be some strong reactions. My main job was never to protect the actors. My main job was the deal with the people who didn't get what was going on or, worse, were actively trying to break it.

My team, which was led by a guy named Jacob who died on March 14, we had a lingo. Let's see if I can remember all of them.

A Statue was someone who was at the lowest level of understanding. Like, they didn't know what interactive theater was and so they would just stand there, unsure what to do, like a rock. The bartenders could usually take care of Statues, but if they just stood in one place too long, it caught our attention and we would come escort them somewhere else.

Freakers were the opposite of Statues. They didn't know what was going on and their response wasn't to freeze, but to explode. Those were very much our problem and something that happened at least once every three shows.

Ernies were drunks. Like Ernest Hemingway, I was told later. Some people would pregame or some people would do the show on psychedelics, which was a terrible, terrible idea. But if someone got too drunk or high or stoned or whatever, we'd have to fish them out of "the Netherworld" and let them hang out in a quiet room until it was all over with.

Broheims were always cocksure alpha male types. Too cool to get into the spirit of it, so they'd try to break stuff or get the actors to laugh or get mad or whatever. It was part of our job if someone was talking a lot to shut them up, and the Broheims were the worst at that. Some people, when confronted by something uncomfortable, need to talk out of insecurity or whatever and that was how you could spot a Broheim from a mile away.

Let's see, Karens. Obviously. Everyone knows about Karens, and we got our fair share.

But when someone on the radio called in a "Jester," that's when everyone came running.

Jesters were there to break the show. Sometimes they were protestors or religious types. Sometimes they were exes of an actor in the cast. Sometimes they were confronted with nudity and blood and decided everything needed to be shut down. And . . . how did they put it in that movie . . . some people just want to see the world burn.

The reason everyone would come running when someone said "Jester" was because they could really get somebody hurt. I almost saw it happen a bunch of times. Once, on [Floor] Two at the Depot, one guy unscrewed a bunch of light bulbs from the train car down there, crunched them up and then went down to the basement and laid them out for the Human Jubilation. Some people are near naked and barefoot in that part of the show. Of course, we had him arrested. And the actors took it pretty well. Cedric just told me, "LA, right?"

Another time I saw a woman get so mad at the show she took off her mask, pulled out a knife, and tried to stab one of the actors. God knows where she was hiding a damn knife! When I went back and watched in video, it all happened so fast that it was a miracle that Shawn—he was the security guy who watched all the monitors—anyway, it was a miracle he caught it before something worse happened. That woman, she was arrested, too. But that's not the worst. The worst Jester I ever saw before things got real bad was a protestor who, somehow, managed to get a couple of live snakes into the show. He was an "animal welfare" guy and, trust me, the irony is not lost on me that he took a couple snakes and threw them at the actors while screaming about how humans "deserved everything that was coming to them." That was mental illness, but ya still gotta deal with it.

That's the worst I saw until the start of this year.

Yeah, as the show went on, it got worse. I'd say that, no question. You'd start to see fewer people who were overwhelmed and needed help and more people who wanted to outright mess with ya or fight. I know that got to the actors more than the other stuff. I . . . okay, I told you I hold stuff close to the vest, but Angus, one of the lead actors, and I dated for a minute-and-a-half, and one night he told me that, as an artist, there's always a moment when you ask yourself, "Am I just out there humiliating myself every night?" And not just him, but he meant like, the whole thing, the whole show. Was the whole thing dumb? That's something you don't want the actors to ask themselves, because some of them are doing really complicated, high-risk sort of stuff and because they're actors. They're known for being dramatic, so the more folks you have out there saying, "I see what you're doing, and I'm here to take it down," the worse the actors feel about it, I think. And we ended up getting that more and more, and the actors started getting madder and madder about it.

Angus, he started gettin' frustrated, which is why I eventually stopped seeing him. But I remember, just after he and I stopped our thing together, that the actors all found this website called Who'sThere.com or something like that. Knock knock, who's there? That was the joke. Very funny. But the whole point of the site was for people who wanted to mess with the show and they had a forum on how best to do it.

One of the big, big things about *Come Knocking* is it's a "no phone" experience, and we take their phones before they head on in to the bar area and put them in those little bags with the magnets on them, right? Then people get their phones back after the show. But this video on that site or forum or whatever had cell phone footage of the show and, like, maps and times that told you when certain characters would be hanging out and what to do to best get under their skin. Turns out there were a group of people, and one of them was a former actor, I think, who had dedicated far too much time and far too much effort to figuring out how to "break the world." When the actors caught wind of that, it was a four-alarm fire for all the actors. Lots of anger, lots of accusations. Lots of stalking social media to see if they could figure out who was behind this. It wasn't just that there were people out there actively plotting against the show, which, to be honest, not one of the actors had experienced before, it was that there were videos and photos with commentary about their performances. It was all terrible, worst stuff on the internet type shit, you understand? And no one took it well. There were tears and threats and vomit.

Like I said, actors are dramatic.

That was February 2 or 3, maybe, that someone first discovered the site. No, it was the third, because we're dark on Mondays and this was early in the week, I don't remember exactly what day. I just remember there were whispers that something was going to happen that night and to make sure to check everyone extra well for any contraband or phones or whatever that they might bring in. I noticed a few potential Broheims hanging out but nothing that really caught my attention, though I did notice Shawn pulled another security person off the lines to help him watch the monitors. Shawn is pretty tight with some of the actors. *Was* pretty tight with some of the actors. Anyway, he would know what was up better than anyone. Just a fella in his position should know what's going on better than anyone.

The crowd seems fine, no alarm bells are ringing in my head or nothin'. And the first loop, the first hour, things go fine. The latecomers are coming late, the demon dancers are dancing like demons. We had one Freaker, but even the Broheims seemed to be behaving. Then, during the first part of the second loop, I see Shawn and whoever he had pulled off the line sprinting, just dead ass sprinting toward the stairwell. I had a position and an area to watch, so I didn't follow them. I was supposed to follow the Human Jubilation and make sure everything was orderly enough, but I heard something come over my radio, which is breaking the world in a major, major way.

"All security to 5B" which meant whatever was going down was going down in the Miller's Manor area. I moved as fast as I could, but nothing happens fast in the Human Jubilation, so by the time I made it up to Five all was said and done.

There's two really great guys named Rodrigo and Hao, and they had worked out this fight that looked exceptionally real. They showed us once, during training, and showed us what parts of what they did were fake and, if they were really fighting, what we'd have to look out for. I'm babbling, but, anyway, when the mood strikes Rodrigo, he does their fight naked, and the mood strikes Rodrigo pretty often, so I've heard. He's Ecuadorian and they are supposed to . . . well, he had a lot of reason to want to parade around nude, if you catch me, and I'm giving you all sorts of detail you don't need, I'm sorry.

So, a group from Who's There had taken off their masks and had tried to hold Rodrigo down. One of them had a metal rod or something. I don't know what the deal was at the time, but they had these little cameras and they had three guys who kind of snuck up on Rodrigo and Hao as they were doing their detailed fight. They caught old Rodrigo and held him down. But he managed to kick one of them hard enough to turn the bones in his nose to powder. Again, since I'm off the reservation here, part of me gets a solid chuckle that the last thing that guy sees before his nose is shattered is where the sun don't shine on poor Rodrigo. Got what he deserved, if you ask me.

So this guy is screaming and bleeding and everyone else thinks it's part of the show, right? Why wouldn't ya? And it was about that time that Shawn and crew showed up and tackled the other fellas and got them out of the stairway and downstairs before they could disrupt much of the show.

I asked around to other security after the show to try to figure out what happened and Napoleon—he's a guy who really marches to the beat of his own drummer and is supercool because of it—he told me. Nappy said a couple of the Who's There guys had snuck in with a butane lighter and a branding iron. Like, an honest-to-God branding iron. When Nappy came up on them, they were heating the lighter and he said it was glowing red and they had poor old Rodrigo's pants around his ankles and one of them was holding Hao down and he was screaming as loud as he could. Nappy said the best-case scenario was they were going to brand his ass and the more likely scenario was something a lot worse for poor old Rodrigo. Either way, he was able to yell real loud and throw a punch or two and that's when Rodrigo got the upper hand and naked kicked that dude into next week. That was the story anyway. As any story, it got crazier the more it got told.

I asked if he had slept with one of their wives or something and was told no one knew and no one cared to know. Didn't matter. What mattered was no one was going to break into our show and assault our performers, no matter what state they were in or what beef they had with anyone else in the real world.

I'm not gonna lie, I kind of saw the writing on the wall. Things were only gonna get worse, and I thought about how, exactly, things could get worse and it always left me with this pit in my stomach. The last couple shifts I worked, that pit only got worse. I felt like things were gonna get bad. There was a lot of talk about a curse or people feeling like some dark cloud was hanging over the show, but one thing I learned as a bartender and that I carried with me to this show is that's a bunch of bullshit. You can predict when something is going to go south by the way people act, the way they move, the things they say. It's real rare that violence just—boom—happens. There's a buildup, and that's what that pit in my stomach was. I saw it coming.

It doesn't matter how rough-and-tumble you are. A bunch of people trying to hurt each other in the dark is nowhere you want to be.

INTERVIEW 5
BELLA EVERS

Cast Member, *Come Knocking* in Los Angeles

Where do I want to start? Easy. Dungeons & fucking Dragons.

I was thirteen the first time I played Dungeons & Dragons, and it kinda saved my life . . . or put me on the path that would save my life, however you want to look at it. My dad was a deadbeat asshole, and my mom had a revolving door of guys who would pump her and dump her—I could see that by the time I was ten, but she never was able to figure it out—so I was a feral kid. I wasn't that smart. The kid who'd show up and ask what you were having for dinner and if I could stay. The kid who was smoking cigarettes by the time she was twelve and "dating" eighteen-year-old boys by the time she was thirteen. That kind of kid. I'm sure you knew her. But one day, I was at a classmate's house so I could get a free meal, and we ended up hanging out in his room where he and two other nerds introduced me the wonders of role-playing games, specifically Dungeons & Dragons. It changed my entire fucking life, and I am eternally grateful.

These boys, and they were all boys because of course they were, they were doing voices and moving their bodies differently and becoming other people. That moment, something in my brain—*snap*—woke up. I was like, "Where has this been all my life?" Why are we these gross, hormonal, loser kids with absent fathers and idiot slut mothers when we could be wizards and elves and shit? Why are we all being ourselves when we could be something, anything else? If I've got a "mission statement," something that drives me as an artist and as a professional and as a person, that's it. "Let's all pretend we're someone else."

I moved out to LA when I was seventeen on kind of a whim and with no real plan . . . again, I'm not that smart. Before you say it, no, I never ended up in the San Fernando Valley, okay? I know why you would think I would end up in a mansion somewhere pretending I was a nympho high school student who was stuck in a dryer and only my buff "stepbrother" could save me, but I never took that path. Could have. Of course I could have, still could if I'm being honest with you. I mean, look at me! I'm still tight as fuck. But never did. I used my body in different ways after I met Carolyn.

God, she was great. Carolyn ran a dance studio, and I don't remember how, but I made friends with her. She was an old dance maven who smoked like a chimney and took in strays. There aren't too many like her, but to a wayward kid, a woman like that is gold. She'll treat you like shit and blow smoke in your face but knows who you are and what you need and, goddamn, I loved that old bitch. She was how I learned how to dance and not just dance, she made me understand that dancing was an art and a craft and through dance you could . . . say it with me . . . be someone else. Plus, even though she was mean as a dog and it made me want to be mean as a dog when someone deserves it.

I know I'm going on and on and you want to get to the part where everyone kills each other in the dark and I get that, but before I talk about how *Come Knocking* was a death trap waiting to happen, I need you to know a few things about the culture of interactive theater. Shit, that sounded like the opening to my TED Talk. Trust me, this won't be a lecture. There are far too many bodily fluids for it to be a lecture.

"Interactive theater" is basically an umbrella term for anything where actors and audience get to interact, and it can mean all kinds of things. I mean *all* kinds of things. Once you get into the world, you get offers from every weirdo with a weirdo-ass idea who needs actors, and there are a ton of them out there, so many more than you think. I've done extreme experiences where we shave people's heads and fake waterboard them for an entire twenty-four-hour period. That "extreme" shit is no fun, but it pays really well. I've done interactive theater in a forest where

I'm hunting men and when I find them, I make them take off all their clothes and get into an ice bath. I've seen so many naked Chinese businessmen, you don't want to know. I've done interactive comedy shows that for the sake of time I won't go into. I've done religious stuff—the less said about that the better. I bring this up for two reasons. First, "interactive theater" can mean just about anything you want it to mean. And two, once you've done it and proven yourself good at it, like I was because of all the time with Carolyn and my Dungeons & Dragons mission statement, you become part of that community. The work is pretty steady as long as you are willing to do whatever is asked of you. And trust me, man. I really, really was.

Why tell you this fucked-up stuff you probably don't care about? Because very single actor in *Come Knocking* knew these set of facts and felt it in their bones. This is a cast who have pretended to be vampires for goth weddings, who have run through the city chasing people, who have gone out into the middle of nowhere and dressed up with no guarantee that some psycho with money hasn't hired them to kill them and fuck their corpses then sell the videos online. They play pretend anywhere and they do it harder than you. These are high-wire walkers, vicious performers for whom fear is not a thing that exists when you're performing. When you're not performing, yeah, there's anxiety and depression and bipolar disorder and drug addiction and attachment disorders and terrible relationship track records with just about all of us—we're a fucked-up little group in my experience, but when we're on . . . we are fucking on!

Make sense? You know who you're dealing with? Good, because it plays into everything that comes after. I mean everything.

I got the job at *Come Knocking* through other work I had done. Carolyn, that amazing bitch, put in a good word and I auditioned like a demon on angel dust, and I showed up for work every day sober and my performances were consistent and powerful. In other words, I'm not just a weirdo, or even a dedicated weirdo, I am a professional dedicated weirdo, and so were most of us who worked at *Come Knocking*. And it was fun! There was room to interpret and improvise. The director never breathed down our neck. We did our job and, at the start, it felt like the sort of gig that could continue indefinitely.

But time wears you down, doesn't it?

My job, yeah. My job started off as a member of the Demon Dance which means, in order, it was my job to be part of the Human Jubilation—almost everyone was part of the Human Jubilation if you weren't put into a rig or needed a bunch of special makeup—then to head to the Depot of the Departed and fuck with a few of our main actors who were heading through the Depot and into the Netherworld. The director always told us "try to represent a sin you have in life" while you were harassing the other actors, which was a bitching little piece of direction. I always liked trying to embody gluttony and lust. I don't mind telling you, when I go to hell it's not going to be for any of the lower-level shit like greed or treachery or heresy . . . well, maybe heresy, but I'm a lust and gluttony girl all the way down. Anyway, I start in the basement and move to the Depot . . . "in the middle of the journey of our life, I came to myself in a dark wood" . . . and then the dance started.

The Demon Dance was one of the highlights of the show, and if you were on Floors One, Three or Four, or Five, if we felt like it at the end of the night, you couldn't miss it. We stomped, we screamed, we were terribly physical with each other, we did everything possible except to touch the audience. No touching, both ways. That was one of the sacred rules, do not assault anybody, which goes against the spirit of some interactive theater projects I've been a part of but, again, I'm digressing. My point is it's a big-ass fucking line of demons painted red, screaming and dancing our faces off and getting all frisky and showing everyone with a mask on what their sin looks like reflected back at them. The dances were individualized, and each person was supposed to imbue their demon with a character through their movement and to try to really connect the audience with the idea of sin in a visceral way they were not used to. At least, that was the artistic intent.

In reality, one night in the Demon Dance meant the next night off or in a different spot because two nights of the Demon Dance meant your voice was gone and you were likely past the point of physical exhaustion. Most of us started off painted bright red and would sweat off most of the makeup by the time we got to the Crypt in time for us to get ready for the finale in the Desert. It was taxing as fuck, and we did it three times a night! You have to really watch how hard you push yourself or bad things can happen. I heard they learned that the hard way in New York where, depending on who you believe, one of the main dancers passed out and got trampled on because she was pushing herself so hard. The rumor was that she got trampled and then sued the company, but I don't know if that's true or not. The way I see it, it's what we signed up for. Professional dedicated weirdos.

But anything with that level of . . . aggression, I'm going to call it, comes with a certain degree of risk. And that's where our show got into some trouble.

When the show was working perfectly and you had an audience who was "into it" and "there for the right reasons," as the director used to say, what would happen is the Demon Dance would both repel and attract, right? The dancing and the moves we were asked to perform were more than enough to draw attention, but our appearance and the ferocity in which we were supposed to move would, when everything was working, seem really intimidating. Plus, the lighting, plus the effects, plus the music, plus the tone of the show, yadda yadda. It was all supposed to work together to say "these dancers are dangerous, and, hey, we told you not to touch them, so don't fucking touch them."

But some people are just gonna do what they're gonna do, you know?

There were between eleven and seventeen of us as part of the Demon Dance at any point in the show—some would drop out to go get ready for other parts of the show, others would bow out at certain points for reapplication of their makeup—but I was one of those who did my level best to go all the way through. Floor Two to Floor Four, three times a night in front of hundreds of people. I didn't notice it right away, which I felt stupid about, but some of the other actors would intentionally protect the Demon Dancers from certain members of the audience. What would they do? Not a whole lot of variance, actually. They'd either try to touch you or they'd try to screw you up, both of which are not optimal if you're doing a flying spin off a five-foot table and landing on concrete wearing nothing but pointe shoes. Every, I'd say, two weeks we'd have an incident where someone would touch, because the Demon Dancers were mostly women and, woman or man, we weren't wearing a lot. My costume was basically a sports bra, a thong with a tail attached which I fucking hated, and a series of headdresses representing the sin I was embodying that I'd lose about halfway through the dance.

It didn't take me long to get good at spotting when things were going to get hairy. At the start, it would look like this—I'd notice an audience member paying particular attention to me on one floor. Then I'd see them again on another floor. If they followed me to a third floor, I knew I was going to have a problem and, nine times out of ten, by the time I was done on Floor Four he had tried to grab a piece of my costume or my ass or my tits or assault me in some other way. It's hard to describe how you know someone is going to be a problem but as a performer, you know it when you see it. And, when that happened, security was on it. I will say this—security at *Come Knocking* was good for some things. I've been in shows where security was good for absolutely nothing or just simply nonexistent and you had to handle everything yourself. But our security was okay. My favorite times were when I would notice a creeper and another one of my girls or fellas would notice it and then, between the cast it became kind of a game. We'd adjust the choreo ever so slightly so the guy, and it was always a guy, wouldn't come in contact with the dancer he had decided he was going to harass. And it wasn't anything formal, we didn't talk about it. We just protected each other. Professional dedicated weirdos.

But about four months into the run, I noticed something shift.

This was before Who's There, you heard about them, right? The loose organization of people who had nothing better to do than fuck with our show and one douchenozzle, Reilly Pegg, who had made it his life's mission to fuck with our show? I could go into a very long talk about how to handle people who don't "get it" and how interactive theater is incredible partially because it forced the disengaged to engage with art, almost against their will in certain cases, but I won't bore you with that. I'll tell you about the bad stuff. Always with the bad stuff.

What was I saying? The shift, yeah. It started about four months into the run of the thing. Personally, four months was the longest I had ever held down a job by a wide margin, so when people stopped being grabby and pervy and started being intentionally cruel and ugly, part of me figured, "Oh, that's why everyone who works at places for a long time hates going to work." But the other performers set me straight. This was not normal by any stretch. I remember the first time . . . okay, in the show there's this part on [Floor] Four where the music switches from this sort of Creole/rock thing to a much heavier, industrial rave sort of vibe. When that happens, the dancers are suddenly backlit by red light and, for some people, that's the moment when it goes from "creepy" to "scary" for a lot of people because there's less light than before and the idea is dancers are supposed to pop in and out of the light at what seems like random intervals. It's choreographed within inches, by the way, not that that's important. But the point is we're supposed to move closer and closer to the audience until, at one point in the song, the lights are supposed to come back to normal and we had all disappeared. Then the lights go out for no more than two seconds and we're back. Truthfully, we just fall to the floor and stand back up but the effect is badass.

So we're at that part and I'm doing my bit and I "disappear" and when I reappear, there's this Broheim standing far too close to me and he just whispers "you're a cunt" loud enough just for me to hear it. Then the lights came back on and, by then, he had faded back into the crowd like the brave little guy he was. I mention it backstage and four of the other cast had experienced the same delightful interaction. He had a mask on, so it's hard to say for sure but I'm betting that was Reilly Pegg or one of his douchebag, murderous boyfriends. It sounded like him, in the interviews I've heard since then. I can't be certain but I'm pretty certain. After that, it started happening each week. People would try to say the worst possible thing they could think of during that one moment in the show.

"Die in a fire."

"Your mother is ashamed."

"Whore."

"You're nothing but a hole."

"Cum dumpster."

"Filthy gash."

It was all sexual, because of course it's all sexual with those guys. And the male dancers, they got it too. You'll have to ask them what was said, though I could wager some pretty accurate guesses. These people aren't creative. My point is that was the beginning of my awareness that people were intentionally fucking with us and then they started finding other points where they could get away with doing it to other performers. And, shortly after that, the sabotage started.

I know you're talking to Bryan the props guy, yeah? He's a dork, but he can tell you more about the sabotage than I can. And I didn't get the worst of it. I got the penny-ante shit, the pieces of twine they'd string through areas, the sticky shit they'd pour on the floor. Truthfully, if you think twine and glue is going to stop me from performing, I don't know what to tell you. Actually, I know exactly what to tell you and it's, "I gave more than forty Chinese businessmen ice baths in the woods and got paid for it, you don't scare me even a little bit."

I'll tell you what did scare me, though. And that was the way it made everybody feel.

I've thought a lot about how to say this, because it's not an easy concept to get across, so here it goes. Ever since, I don't know, seven or eight years ago, does it just sort of feel like something's coming? Like people are nervous and scared and they have this innate sense that something really bad is right around the corner? Something no one is going to be able to escape? Personally, I think it's climate change—we have fucked our planet so hard it's actively killing us—but other people have different ways to explain it. Like, income inequality, a system that can't sustain itself, selfishness, which is a good explanation, or just general entropy reaching a point where we can't ignore it anymore. The system is breaking down in a big, bad way and people get it, they sense it. You know this feeling, even if you don't know this feeling, even if you haven't let yourself feel it, right? You are experiencing it and feeling the consequences of it even if you think everything is fine. Now, take that big, macro feeling and put it on a small micro level and crank it up to eleven. That's what it was like to be in the cast of *Come Knocking*.

Actors and dancers would say things like, "Hey, I got another paycheck," like they weren't sure another one was ever coming even though we were wildly successful. Or "Made it through another one," that was almost a greeting after a show when we were peeling off our levels of makeup. Of, just, more drinking and more war stories and more commiseration, all with the understanding that we were on a sinking ship no matter how hard we danced or how well we performed or who we connected with. I'm not describing it well, but the audience was turning on us, or at least part of them were, and we had to ride it out. Jordan can fill you in on the specifics of how that worked but I'm a professional dedicated weirdo, and I'm telling you we felt it. The artists were the canary in the coal mine and knew we were taking on water well before March 14, to mix my metaphors.

But what do you do? No, seriously, I'm asking. Do you throw a fit? Do you file a complaint? With who? Do you write a letter? Schedule a fucking protest? Against who and to what end? Truthfully, being a Dedicated Professional Weirdo, I had been in rooms full of misfits and drug addicts and sex maniacs and the broken and those desperate for attention and we all formed sort of a fucked-up family, but the one thing I'd never been in was a room full of performers who felt defeated.

I had seriously considered quitting a week before March 14. One of the Who's There assholes had taken it a bit too far. They found this spot in the stairway between [Floors] Two and Three and pushed me down a flight of stairs. In the stairways we're basically a tumble of bodies but, somehow, no one caught me and no one ran after the dude, so I busted my mouth on the concrete and lost a few teeth. Spit a bunch of blood, but that was a common occurrence in the show, so no one really noticed until after I ran backstage. Still, the audience had turned, and no one had stopped them. I mean, they caught him later, but, at that point, the damage was done. It was time to go. It really was.

But I didn't go. Because, like I said, I'm not that smart.

INTERVIEW 6
BRYAN BARKER

Prop Master for *Come Knocking* in Los Angeles

No one, I repeat, no one pushed poor young Ms. Bella down the stairs, no matter what she tells you. I know because it's my job to know.

There's a line I often think of from *Star Trek VI: the Undiscovered Country*—or maybe it was *Galaxy Quest*—regardless, the gist is that "the captain knows every weld and every rivet in his ship." By no account was I the captain of the SS *Come Knocking*, but it was my job to know every inch of the space my actors inhabit and make sure everything has a place and every place has a thing. If there are smudges on the glass or a hat has been moved from one room to another as the masked hordes tear apart the carefully prepared space, it's my job to know and fix that room or to usher that hat on the long journey back to where it belongs. That's how it's been since the show opened, and that's the way it was until everything went to shit the week of March 14. For almost eight months, I knew every weld and I knew every rivet.

With that context, when I say I know Ms. Bella fell down the stairs, Ms. Bella fell down the stairs. Given the large amount of substances she ingests on any given night, as reported by many of the performers and, to a lesser degree, backstage staff, it's no surprise.

That doesn't mean things were going smoothly. I would say the opposite, actually. I am, as we say in the business, a seasoned professional in that I have been prop master for many, many staged productions here in Los Angeles. *Come Knocking* was a challenge unlike anything in my career. Take my hat example from before. Think, in your mind, of all the time and effort it would take to locate a single hat on six floors of heavily decorated space that an audience has been encouraged to pick up and interact with, and, once that hat is found, getting it back to where it belongs for the next show.

Now, take that amount of effort and do it nine hundred times.

In any one night of *Come Knocking* there are nine hundred items that, in one way or another, can be picked up, interacted with, moved, destroyed, damaged, smudged, smeared, knocked over, spilled, hidden, removed, or left alone. Nine hundred potential trips up and down those cursed stairs. You should have seen my calves at the height of the show. Nine hundred chances for me and my team to make a mistake and for some important prop not to make it to where it needs to be. That's why I was in the booth, every night, cataloging how the audience interacted with everything, taking detailed notes about what went where and how. So, yes. I knew every rivet and weld in my ship because, if not, my job was impossible.

Add to that a very picky group of performers who are their own props, in a way, and you start to get a sense of what my job looked like.

That's my long, long way of saying that Ms. Bella fell down the stairs three weeks before "the incident." And that Jack and Anastasia on Floor Three would often duck into an alcove near the Judas on Ice section and have sex when everyone was supposed to be at places. And that a lot of performers seemed to have a ton of energy and an itchy nose right before the show. And that this, frankly, amazing thing that had been constructed was a giant turning wheel in which I was a vital and irreplaceable cog.

And it also means I can tell you exactly how terrible the audiences were. In painstaking detail.

When the show first launched in sunny California, the audiences started off quite receptive and interacted the way we'd hoped they would. They would touch and explore, they would follow performers, and they would follow the story being told to them. Quickly, has anyone spoken to you about the story? Oh, it's fantastic, very complex if you're into that sort of thing. If you start at the bottom and go to the top in about ten-minute intervals you will follow the virtuous yet arrogant Knight as he explores the terrors of the Netherworld and comes to grips with his own mortality. I know this because it's my job to know this—if we had three hundred audience members a night, fewer than seventy-five of them would ever make it to the sixth floor, where the finale of the "story" takes place. I could go on, but there was a story, I assure you.

The first time I remember realizing that an audience was rotten, not just a single bad actor but the majority, was when a group of twenty or so went to the bottom floor on the recommendation of our bartenders and stayed there, waiting for the show to start. It was a complete and utter misunderstanding of the show they'd purchased a ticket to watch. To which, I said, we can do all the pre-roll and send all the emails in the world, but we cannot read the material for the audience and certainly can't understand it for them. We can hold their hand for a long time but, eventually, they have to go and have their own experience. This insight was not met with much positivity by management. They had a hot property and were extraordinarily reticent to cancel a show or shut down or, really, make any changes that might have improved the experience if it meant sacrificing possible ticket sales. It's typical. People like money. Like I said, I'm "seasoned" and have seen this sort of behavior from management before.

But there was a bigger problem—whenever someone didn't "get" the show and then ignored all our prompts and suggestions, they tended to get angrier and angrier as the show went on. It was as if they knew something remarkable was happening around them, but they lacked the ability to access it. Which would frustrate me! I'm a *Star Wars* fan, and I've felt that way since Dave Filoni took over. Then, and I saw this many times, in their search for any sort of connection there might be someone on the fence about the show and these negative people would pull them over to their side.

"Can you believe they're not telling us where to go?"

"Where's the show? I'm missing the show!"

"If something doesn't happen soon, I'm demanding a refund."

I heard all these things from my perch in the control room. And I would keep an eye on these people. And then the moment would come.

Frustrated, lost, angry, they would break something. Almost every time.

Usually it was something small like a glass in the bar or they would find some piece of decoration or furniture and destroy a bit of it. Sometimes it was something more integral to the show. The Depot of the Departed was rich with props, just stuffed with them from paper coffee cups left on the train to a secret door which led to a records room to piles of shoes left outside of the gates to the Netherworld, and all those props were a popular spot for a little unhappy destruction. They would tear up the coffee cups and scatter the records or stuff them in their pockets. It was all out of frustration, you see. Frustration and, if you'll forgive me, entitlement. No one was explaining the show to them, on purpose, and that is something that makes some people dangerously uncomfortable.

Which led to my accidentally escalating the situation.

You see, I enjoy the internet and am part of many communities and forums and Discord servers in my spare time. By the looks of me, I'm sure you can tell I don't attract women at quite the rate as some of our more in-shape and conventionally attractive artists. I spend a lot of time online, is what I'm saying, and because of that, I was able to . . . infiltrate, if you will, a couple of spaces where Angelenos were talking about the show. It was a lot of Facebook, unfortunately, because that site has been damn near unusable for the past five to seven years, but it's where a lot of groups tended to congregate and spill their bile. This group, when I first came across it, was called "*Come Knocking* Sucks," befitting the level of sophistication of most of the posters, and they would complain about the show and they would feel left out of the conversation and then, invariably, one of them would say "I destroyed a coffee cup on the first floor." And that person would get flooded with compliments and praise. And the next day, someone would say "I wonder what would happen if someone stepped on one of the dancer's tails" and everyone would speculate.

And, since the internet is the internet, things got darker very quickly.

I guess, in a certain way, it's a testament to what *Come Knocking* was. These people knew they had "missed" something, knew they were on the outside looking in on something grand. And it stuck with them and angered them and spurred them to seek community. If the measure of art is the reaction it creates, that's a very real and fierce reaction, if you ask me.

So, I played along. This was, I'd say, early into our Los Angeles run. I pretended to be someone who agreed with them. "Oh, the show was horrible." "What a bunch of pretentious nonsense." "I bet they're laughing at us in the dark." Which we do, sometimes, but I digress. Then I took it too far and went to coffee with one of the posters.

Her name was Joanna, and, yes, it was a "date," not that I'm proud of that fact given what happened. At the time I had no companionship, and one of the women in the Facebook group seemed articulate and interesting. And she seemed to be interested in me. I am an old prop man, but I am also very human so, I will confess, openly, that I was romantically interested in this woman. And, yes, I lied to her about what I did for a living, sort of. I told her I was in theater production and that's why I was so upset at *Come Knocking* and that it wasn't real theater and . . . yes. I did all of that. Not great to talk about, really, but I need to be open with you about that since I've been accused of so many things since March 14, almost none of them true. But to get at what is "true," I need to tell you all that happened, the ugly parts, too, I'm afraid.

The date goes well and turns into a second date. And then a third and then, things that happen on third dates happened and I began to feel quite ashamed of myself. I was in too deep. I was starting to develop feelings, and I had lied about who I was. So, in my infinite wisdom, I decided to end things with Joanna. I chose my job over my burgeoning relationship. I took her to a nice, busy restaurant and told her our relationship wasn't going to work. I did not plan on telling her why, just leaving, but when we got to the restaurant, she spoke first. She told me that a smaller group from the "*Come Knocking* Sucks" page were going to go back to the show. She was extremely excited about it. She said that they had done their research, and that they had a plan. So, instead of stopping her, I let her spill her guts as she laid it all out—there was going to be three of them and they had done their homework. They had found r/ComeKnocking on Reddit and had gotten a map of the building and when and where everything took place.

Their plan was, actually, quite good, as far as disruption goes, from an insider's standpoint. As near as I can tell, their goal was disruption, not to engage in any violent acts, but I can't say that for sure, particularly considering what happened later. They were going to start in the Depot of the Departed, where there was a whistle from the train that, if you pushed the right button in the front of the subway car, would blow quite loud. It was one of those interactive things that we could turn off from the control room if it was being abused, but no one knew that. Their plan was to take the whistle off the train, take it to the entrance to the Netherworld, and blow it continuously, interrupting the story. Remember when I told you the Knight would travel through the Netherworld? That was where his story began—technically it began at the Human Jubilation, but that is less obvious, and you really have to be looking for it. Many people will follow the Knight all . . . night, ha, and their plan was to follow that actor around with a train whistle until they got kicked out. One of them had a small camera that, likely, would have evaded our security. By Joanna's thinking, it would ruin the show for at least a few people and, as she said, "it serves them right for giving that damn show their money."

I feigned excitement, didn't point out that her solution to being angry at the show was to buy several expensive tickets, and in the spirit of being a slimy piece of shit I have been accused of being, slept with her again. Then I "ghosted" her, as the kids say, and made sure I was working the night she had mentioned. I wanted to see if she'd go through with it.

She didn't just show up with two other people. She showed up with six.

Immediately, I was concerned. I had not been on the forums for a moment, because Facebook has that damn feature that lets other people know when you are online, plus all that useless AI, but that's another matter, and I didn't want to risk a confrontation. I was out of the loop! Six people meant they had changed the plans and, likely, expanded them, so I drew the attention of the director right to them. I told them I had seen them fidgeting with something that looked like a camera. They got "extended" security attention, and they found a camera on one of the six. This isn't enough to kick them out, particularly at our high price point and particularly not if the person seems apologetic, which this person faked quite nicely. But still, I told the director, if you have an eye to spare, keep it on these people.

This is not an uncommon occurrence in the control room. If *Come Knocking* is a hurricane of dance and smoke and screaming and bodies, the control room is the eye of the storm, keeping everything nice and neat and in control. Everything runs through the control room, from the effects to the lighting to the security. Like any good show—and believe me, *Come Knocking* was a well-run show for the most part—if something happened like a medical emergency or someone making a scene, it could often be dealt with in a way where 95 percent of the audience would be unaware that anything actually happened. Even if the group's plan had gone perfectly and they had paraded through the second floor with a loud, honking horn, you could still keep most people from having their experience disrupted.

So . . . I watched them. They started off downstairs, like they said they would, but then skipped the Depot and went higher, to the Crypt on Four. I didn't know what they were up to for sure, but the opportunities to make a mess on Four were a lot higher than they were on Two. I abandon my usually meticulous note-taking and watched. They stayed pretty tight, but our cameras are very good and I could tell they didn't have any illicit material. Or so I thought.

Can I stop for a moment and say this might have been one of the most exciting days of my life? I'm sorry, but intrigue, double crosses, spycraft, sex. Throw in a martini and a tuxedo and I'm pudgy, socially awkward James Bond. Apologies, no more digressing.

It became clear pretty shortly what their plan was. When the Demon Dance makes its way up to the Crypt level, there are a few scenes where several of the dancers all climb on a table and use it as their launching pad for some near acrobatics—flips and kicks and such. It's very athletic and requires everything to be in its place. I saw them cluster around the table, and the second they did, I alerted security, and it's a good thing I did, because they wouldn't have seen the glue before it was too late.

The glue? Yes, it was serious stuff. Professional-grade cyanoacrylate. Super crazy glue, if you will. It would have made the staging area quite unusable if they had succeeded. It might have even hurt someone. Luckily to smuggle it in, they had to sew it into the linings of Joanna's dress, so it took a bit of tearing and effort to get it out and, once they did, they had a little trouble getting the lid off. It is glue, after all. It gave security more than enough time to swoop in and stop them. They were all summarily kicked out, but, and here's where I might have made quite a blunder, I made sure I was at the Gummar Bar when they left. I let Joanna see me as she was being escorted to the street. I made sure to make eye contact. I made sure she knew. Why? I've given it some thought because of what came next and the best I can come up with, sadly, is it felt good. It felt good to feel superior. Also, I didn't have to break up with her, now. So there was that.

The next day I woke up to several dozen death threats. It hadn't taken anyone very long to do the barest bit of research and find out where I worked, and Joanna helpfully provided my email and phone number. I still get threats, on occasion. But I'm a child of the internet, so that does not bother me. Threats and harassment are part of being online. What bothered me, gravely, was when the leaders of "*Come Knocking* Sucks" decided to pull their activities from Facebook and start their own website and Discord server. Which is where Who's There came from, which is where the trouble really started, which led to . . . well, I've got a whole different story when it comes to March 14.

Before they went offline and before she disappeared from my life forever, Joanna did send me a few messages, if you'd like to read them.

Author's Note: The following are four text messages sent to Mr. Barker between the dates of September 18 and September 21:

I slept with you out of pity, you absolute pile of shit! I never liked you and I hope you die in a fire. If I ever see you and your tiny dick near me ever again, you'll be so fucking sorry.

You know what you are? You're a pig. A giant, fat pig with a tiny dick and no soul. But we know who you are, now. All of us do. You're going to suffer, pig boy. Suffer and bleed. Bleed like a pig. Bleed like the swine you are. We'll dance in your blood, pig. See you soon.

God, I hate you. Motherfucker. Go die.

We've been planning, pig. We've got this figured out. You were an insider with us? We've got insiders with you. People you'd never imagine. You're never gonna see us coming.

REDDIT POST ON R/COMEKNOCKING

Something Is Wrong

Canonical Candy

This is my first time submitting to this sub, so I apologize, in advance, for going on too long.

When I saw *Come Knocking* it was in LA already. I didn't really know anything about it except that the building was in a weird/bad part of town and that it was a hard ticket to get. I hate to be *that* sort of LA person, but if a ticket is hard to get and I get one, I'm going. Even if the show sucks, maybe you'll see someone famous, right?

And holy shit, I was totally blown away. After that, I fell down the rabbit hole of the "Netherworld" and, thanks to everyone here, I started to understand a lot more about the show when I went back a second time . . . and a third. I've seen the show like five times now (I've spent a lot of money I don't really have), which is why, I think I can say with some confidence, when I went last night, something felt off. Like something not good is going on. I know I'm going to get a lot of hate for this because we all love the show, but I want everyone to know what I'm about to write comes from a place of love and concern, not trolling.

On my last trip, instead of going bottom up, the way the show progresses with the Knight's story, I went from the top down as suggested by some of you on here. It started off fucking great. This sub mentioned that a lot of people don't even make it to the Planetarium Garden on the sixth floor, so when I started there, I had it basically to myself and got to appreciate the space in a way I hadn't before. It's the most well-lit of all the rooms, but in some ways the most grim. It's the only place where there's really "life," you know? And then there's death in the middle of it. There wasn't a lot happening, but I found it beautiful and spent more time than I should have up there during the first cycle.

It was when I started heading down that I noticed a problem.

In the Desert and the Miller's Manor, they had had that disturbance a few days ago, and you could tell. The fight, that well-choreographed one that everyone raves about so much, wasn't as great as I'd seen it before. Maybe they had new people performing that piece, I wasn't sure, but it was a lot slower and less impressive than I remembered (plus, everyone had their clothes on). Then I went to the fourth floor, and there was the opposite problem. Everyone in the Crypt was going nuts! Just screaming and flinching whenever anyone got too close. I'm not a mystical sort of person, but the energy of the performance seemed almost like they were panicking, like for real. And before anyone starts telling me "that's what the Crypt is supposed to be like," I have been there on nights where the anguish of the dead felt more real and less frenzied. I don't know what was happening the night I went but everything was just turned up to 11 or higher, and it didn't feel right or good to me. It felt threatening, which was new for this show.

I ran into the Demon Dance during the second cycle when I made it to the third floor, and that's when I saw something I'd never seen before. I saw someone break character.

The Devil Dance was moving toward the end of the space, and the lighting was getting really frenetic. I was over by the far side of the room and heard one of the dancers struggling. I'm not sure how to describe it other than they were grunting and I heard someone else grunting and when the lights stabilized, or whatever, the dancer was standing over an audience member and yelling at them. She was saying stuff like, "How do you like it, you pervert?" and "I hope you liked my foot in your balls," or something like that. Again, there is always so much going on it's hard to remember exactly what I saw and what I heard, but, from what I could tell, one of the dancers had kicked or squeezed or done something to an audience member's junk and was yelling at them afterward.

But that wasn't the only thing! In the Depot, there were parts of the train that were torn apart and not replaced, I saw security for the first time—not people dressed in character but real security guards who were just messing up the entire vibe of the scenes. When I finally got to the basement for the Human Jubilation at the beginning of the third cycle, the mood was ruined for me. It went smoothly, but I was looking for something to go wrong, you know?

Has anyone else ever seen something like that at the show, or is it just me?

Finally (and I know this is long already) but before you comment, please know I love *Come Knocking*, unlike a lot of people who post on this sub (I will not mention names), and I only hope that this remarkable bit of theater can be saved from whatever is happening. Because if people are misbehaving and the actors are kicking guys in the junk and security is visible to keep people from making a mess of the show, I'm really worried *Come Knocking* is going to end when someone gets hurt.

Then, of course, that's all anyone is going to be able to talk about.

INTERVIEW 7

MALCOLM RICE

Bartender at *Come Knocking* in Los Angeles

I have a reputation of not getting out when the getting is good.

I was late being born by like a week, so Ma tells me. I stayed after school too late a couple times so when the bad guys came around, there I was, all nine years and eighty-five pounds of me, just waiting to get my ass kicked. I've stayed with toxic girlfriends so long that they start, literally, asking me what the hell I am doing. What can I say? I stick around places too long.

You can see how this plays out in terms of the situation we're talkin' about, right? 'Cause I was there on March 14 long past the point where I shouldn't have been anywhere near that fuckin' place. Things had already turned bad. Man, it's a shame, too, because I have had jobs, but I've never had a job that played so much to my strengths as a performer and as a person. And, shit, as a bartender. 'Cause I was a damn good bartender, and in that place, there were nights when I was something special!

One time, right, this guy and girl came in, and they were clearly together, and they were fighting. Like, having a knock-down-drag-out, like you do. I pick up on the vibe and ask them what they're drinking—this is before they put the masks on and "descend into the Netherworld"—and they each know what the other one is drinking. So, okay, longtime thing, on the rocks. I feel you, and, brother, I can help with that. I tell them both that part of the magic of this thing is everyone gets their own experiences. They can try to stick together if they want, but most people end up alone, which is part of the point of the show, right? You can die surrounded by your friends and family and you still, basically, die alone. But, yeah, I told them maybe explore the space and debrief with each other afterward, but, like, I did it in character. I got this deep, Southern thing I can slide down into if the mood strikes and I did that and could see the lady in this couple kind of smile at me, so there's a little flirtatious energy there. Then I find one of the cast and spread the word to break this couple up. Do it early and do it fast. That couple was in there nearly the whole time, and when they got back to the bar they were drinking and smiling and laughing in the kind of way that says, "We're definitely gonna go back home and fuck tonight." And that was me. I was the magic that made that happen.

Then you got the Karens and the Broheims and all the other assholes comin' through this place. But, you think, the good ones make up for it. At least, that's what I told myself. That's why I stuck around despite getting called every name in the book, even the ones where you're legally justified in punching a guy in the face, right? Those words? I got called those words and I stuck around 'cause I'm the guy that sticks around too long. But I always get a feeling, right? Before the shit hits the fan and I'm there too long, I always get a feeling that I've overstayed my welcome.

I never felt that feeling more in my life than I did on March 13, the night before it all happened.

Oh, I was working March 14, too. I'll get there. But you gotta understand, the 13th, that was just as bad in a lot of ways, just not as bloody. Just a nasty-ass night, top to bottom for us bartenders, backstage, actors, you name it.

So, real quick, I'm in the Gummar Bar on the second floor, right? Got my bow tie and my fancy shirt and my sharp vest, and I'm looking pretty damn good four or five nights a week. I worked at the show longer than a lot of the other bartenders. If we were open, chances are good you'd get me. The Gummar Bar, that's where everyone starts their experience, gets the rules, flirts with the handsome young bartender, puts on their masks and, as the show puts it, "descends." That's a good night, when all that happens in that order with a minimum of issues. On a bad night, security is up everyone's ass and everyone is pissy about it, and no one is drinking and no one is listening, and the people who are gonna hate it already hate it, and the actors are already starting to bitch about what's going on. And March 13 was all that shit and more, right?

You could definitely tell from the vibe that it was gonna be a rough one, but I can tell you some of the concrete things that made March 13 a bad night. First off, like I said, no one was drinking. I ain't one to tell you what you should or shouldn't be doing in terms of the chemicals you put in your body, but before this show if you've had a drink or two you're much more likely to get into the spirit of the thing. That's just a fact. Second thing was people were over at some of the tables and in corners, and you could just tell those motherfuckers were up to no good. Lots of whispering, lots of chuckling, you know, and not the good kind. The kind that says, "I'm laughing at you and what you're doing." Then, and this was the bad one, someone started messing with me at the bar.

Like I said, I'm a handsome guy, and I'm a part of this show, even though my job is to make drinks, so I've had a lot of conversations with a lot of actors, and they told me all kinds of stories about people fucking with them. I believed it and saw, like, the impact of it, but I didn't "feel" it, ya know? No one had made it their job to mess with my night up until that point. Who wants to give the handsome bartender a bad time? But that night, one guy just . . . walked behind the bar. White nerdy-looking dude just walked right up and started chugging a bottle of very nice rum before I could stop him while his buddy filmed and laughed. I gotta back up a second—I was working that night with my boy Renaldo. Together we were a pretty dynamite team, so, technically, this guy got behind the bar on Renaldo's side as he was working hard mixing his drinks, and he didn't see it right away so I had to, like, tap him on the shoulder, right? And we walk up on the guy on one side, and I clock security paying attention on the other side, so this guy isn't long for the show, you know what I mean?

Renaldo and I, we both come up on the guy and he pulls out a lighter, flicks it, and spits the booze he was chugging into the air in a big fireball! This became a story later so I want to tell you, on the record, the dude aimed his fireball toward the crowd and where his boy was filming with his phone—remember me telling you his buddy was filming? This guy wanted the fireball on camera and wasn't looking to hurt nobody, I don't think. The story got around that he was trying to set me or Renaldo on fire, and I honest-to-God don't think that's the case. Regardless, we can't have some punk amateur circus performer blowing fireballs behind our bar, so Ronnie pins the guy's arms behind his back and I am able to give him a pretty good shove out from behind the bar and security took it from there. While that was bad enough, the scary part for me was that was right after the unauthorized fireball was the only time that night where people came and ordered drinks. They thought it was part of the show, which was really scary to me. I mean, you get behind a bar and blow a fireball in any other joint in New York, and you're getting arrested or at least getting the shit kicked out of you. Here you get applause, your dude filming it gets some great shots for your socials, and everyone moves on with their night. Crazy.

That was the first time I got messed with, but it wasn't the only time that night. After that, it was crystal clear that something crazy was going to happen once folks put the masks on. Again, I'd heard the stories. Not to tell tales out of school, but I had myself a little on-again, off-again thing with one of the dancers, and she was always telling me about how some people messed with you on purpose but that gave other people permission to mess with you and others and the rest of the show. And that makes a ton of sense, based on what I was seeing from my little part of the show. While I ain't got no one blowing goddamn fireballs before March 13, I did run into a lot of people getting angry about the show, telling me it was too loud or too confusing or too whatever. And sometimes they'd get angry and take it out on the cast.

How it's supposed to work is everyone puts on their mask when they "descend," and they take them off when they get back into the Gummar Bar. After the second cycle that night, just at the point where the bar is truly empty like usually happens about that time of the night, this dude comes up to me with his mask on and starts talking to me.

First, it seems like he's excited about the show and wants to know more. Like, he's going on and on about how technically impressive it is and how interesting he finds the staging and all that. He even ordered a drink, so my guard was way down. So, I told the dude, "The Netherworld is really something. It takes a lot of people to put it together," or something like that, right? I acknowledged what he was talking about but don't break the world. And he goes "the control room is behind the bar." Which it is, but that's sure as shit not his business, so I politely serve him his drink, and he repeats himself. "The control room is behind the bar."

I'm not quite sure how to navigate this guy, so I sort of nod at his drink. And he says it again. Third time. At a loss for a way to deal with this weird-ass dude, I busy myself cleaning glasses. And he keeps talking.

"You know, you should have hid the control room better. If anyone can just walk in there, imagine the sort of problems they could make."

He's behind the mask, so I can't describe him, but he sounds like he's dropping his voice to try to be intimidating, you know? Then he starts listing off exactly the sort of trouble someone could make. What was it? It was like, "You could drop the Queen of the Damned from the ceiling and break her face." "You could change the fire settings in the crypt and burn an actor alive." "You could turn off the cameras and murder someone on the fifth floor and no one would realize it." And as he sat there, listing all of the terrible things that could happen to my coworkers, I realize he's reaching in his pocket for something.

I had never pushed it before, because the "handsome bartender" can talk his way out of about any situation. But this guy was intentionally being threatening and then was reaching for something, so, yeah, let's let the professionals deal with this. I push the button and nothing happens, not right away. I push the button again and nothing, but this time the dude in the mask notices.

"Calling for help?" he asks me. And he gets what he wants out of his pocket and it was what I figured it was. It was a knife. The knife itself wasn't that big, but it looked . . . tactical is the only word I can figure to use. Like, it was slick and the blade was black and it was intimidating as hell, and this asshole just starts playing with it, like touching the tip with his finger and twirling it around a bit. How he got that knife past security, particularly on that night because they were really hassling people, is beyond me. But he managed it and then he showed it to me.

Now . . . I'm not sure I wanna tell you this, but I'm gonna. I deal with the people in the masks and the spooky shit in the Netherworld and spooky dudes and spooky chicks, and I've had more than one customer come up to me and tell me they were actual vampires and pour blood from a vial into their drink. I mean, it's fucked up and all, but it comes with the territory with this kind of gig. This is a spooky show, and while I'm not a spooky dude myself, I can get along with pretty much everybody. That's my superpower, you know?

When the dude asked me if I was calling for help and pulled out his pigsticker like he did, it was the first time at that job I ever felt scared.

It's a weird-ass thing, being scared. Like, I'm not a small guy, and I'm fit. Well, fit enough. My point is I could have taken that guy every day of the goddamn week, but in that moment I was scared, and I felt the whole thing closing in on me and . . . what do they say, "fight or flight"? I was all about the flight, man. I wanted out of there. But another part of me, call it the part that grew up in a shitty neighborhood where I got my ass kicked for being where I shouldn't have been more than one time, that part of me knew if you ran, they're only gonna chase you. So, my only choice was to do what I always did in that situation.

I turned on the charm.

"That's a nice knife," I told him. "A little slick for my taste."

And he asks me "What kind of knives do you like?" like we're two cool guys just hanging out.

I tell him I'm not really a "knife guy," but my daddy had a knife with a pearl handle that he carried in a leather holster every day he went to work. Now, keep in mind I am totally making this shit up. Improv, baby, nothing true about it except what you make people believe. I never knew my dad, and if there was a fella in my life who carried a pearl-handled knife my mama would have stuck that knife up his ass and twisted it around a little bit. But Mr. Stabby took the bait and asked me why he carried it. "Yes, and," you know what I'm saying?

"He worked construction and used it for his job, sometimes," I told him, lying my ass off. "But he had also been on a few rough sites and said it was nice for 'the guys' to know he could take care of himself if he had to."

And Mr. Stabby considers that for a second and then he goes "Can you take care of yourself if you have to?"

Dude, I swear to God I don't know what came over me, but I put both my hands palms down on the bar, spread my fingers and said "I try to never let it reach that pitch. But yeah. If it comes down to it, I can handle myself."

Please bear in mind I am three seconds away from filling my drawers at that moment. I'm literally shaking but tensing the muscles in my body so that Mr. Stabby can't tell. Then, real quick, he takes the knife, stabs it into the bar between my pointer and middle finger. The knife just fuckin' stuck into the bar, and I feel pain so I know he'd cut me a little. But when I looked down, I saw the knife had just ever so finely cut into the webbing between my fingers. I looked at it later and it was like a paper cut but as hard as he stabbed, he could have gone through my entire hand. . . . The bar is laminated wood, but he stabbed so hard it went right through the laminate and into the wood itself. But he does it all real quick and then grabs my shirt and pulls my face close to his mask and he whispers something, then books the fuck out of the bar. And then, a few seconds later, all hell breaks loose.

The third cycle . . . well, you know what happened to the third cycle that night. And if you don't, get someone else to tell you, because I'm not the person. Talk to Dominick or Tavis or Charlotte or Bella or Cristobal or Stern or any of the actors. They saw it. They know what's up. I just heard things and I ain't telling you their story. I'm telling you my story about almost getting stabbed by some fucker in a mask on a power trip.

Do I know who it was? Not for sure. I mean, I'm pretty sure it was Reilly Pegg. It just makes sense, don't it, him knowing so much about the show? Where the control room was, where the panic button was? He was never the guy doing the dirty deeds, he was the guy pulling the strings. And, if what I hear is right, he's exactly the sort of asshole who would threaten the bartender while everything else was going on in the dark. He doesn't seem like the kind of dude who would get his own hands dirty when he could be twirling a knife and acting like the world's biggest douchebag. You can tell him I said so.

What did he whisper to me? Some real Reilly Pegg bullshit, if you ask me.

He pulled me in and said, "I was going to stab you tonight but I changed my mind. I wouldn't come in tomorrow night if I were you." And he left me a tip. Twenty bucks, the biggest tip of the night. By far.

Getting was good, man. And I showed up to work the next night anyway like the dumbass I am.

INTERVIEW 8
MAZLEE HEMPLE

Attended *Come Knocking* on March 13

I had been saving to go to that show for months. I'm still paying for it.

That's not a metaphor or whatever. I still am paying off the hospital bills from that night. Turns out even if you are hurt in a high-profile way and even if someone is clearly at fault and even if all your friends and family know your story, the American health-care system is still going to find a way to fuck you. They're always going to find a way to extract the most they can out of your bank account. I've lived in this sick country long enough to know that for sure.

That's neither here nor there, but it fucking sucks. If you want to start a GoFundMe or whatever when this book comes out, that'd be great. As it stands, I'm financially drowning.

So, I'm not, like, a dummy. I knew what *Come Knocking* was. I have two kids and I'm not the sort of mom who sits them down in front of the *Texas Chainsaw Massacre* and then gets all upset that they're exposed to scary shit. Like, not even close. I do my research, so I knew the show and I wanted to go to the show. I was there for the rare, elegant night where I get to experience some adult art and, hopefully, spend the night not covered in one of my kids' varied and abundant bodily fluids.

The night started out great. Dev's parents were visiting, so they had the kids. We had a nice dinner booked and, not that you need to know this, a hotel afterward. We eat, we drink a little, we get to the place on time. Given this is LA, the fact that those three things went well were pretty incredible. We were a little worried because the neighborhood where the show is isn't good, but when we get there, we walk into a beautiful bar. Low light, decorated all the way with this gorgeous sort of Southern Gothic thing. Honestly, it was better than I'd hoped. Immediate immersion. Then they handed us our masks.

My husband, who works like a dog, is also a bit claustrophobic, so he was none too thrilled when I told him he had to put on a mask for this show. But the masks were high quality and stood out from the face a bit, like they had taken that into consideration. It was well done. Then we got our instructions, which I had already read online, and we started our "descent." So far, so good. Not for long, but it started off great.

Like the people on the internet told us, we started in the basement. Now, here's my first complaint. To get up and down the floors you have to go up and down stairs. There is an elevator, one of those old-style elevators with a wire mesh doors that you could see people going up and down in. I read later that they are for VIPs and to meet OSHA requirements, which makes a bunch of sense. What I'm saying is the stairs are the only part of the show that I saw that were well lit. The rest of the show was dark. And I get it, it made sense. The show's subject matter was dark, all the sets looked better in the dark, the performers could sneak up on you in the dark. Other things can sneak up on you in the dark. . . .

Sorry. I am going to get through this without being emotional, if you don't count anger as an emotion. Which I fucking don't.

Once we make it to the bottom floor, it's chaos. Apparently the "start at the bottom and go up" plan had made the rounds, and it was shoulder-to-shoulder people in masks, which just about made Dev shit his pants, not to be too graphic about it. He was already doing something he didn't like so I could do something I liked on my birthday and now he was in a nightmare situation, unable to move with a mask strapped to his face. He held on though, and we saw the Human Jubilation, which was cool, but that's when the first thing went wrong. There's a point in the parade, just as the dancing and the music and the lights hits its crescendo, that a shot rings out and people scream. Strike that, the actors scream, and you're supposed to look at where the screaming is coming from and see the dead people and ponder your own mortality or whatever. But when they started screaming, people started pushing. And pushing. And pushing. And what was a nightmare situation for my husband turned into a dangerous one.

He started hyperventilating. Now, when he started breathing heavy, I stopped being impressed by all the lights and the dancing and the acting and whatever the fuck and my one and only focus was getting him back to the stairway. Which I did, because I can throw a mean elbow when the situation calls for it.

Turns out, based on some of the threads I've read, Dev isn't the only one who has had this problem. Seems like something that the production company would want to fix, but what the fuck do I know, right? I'm just the customer whose husband was in danger of suffocating during a show he bought me for my birthday.

I get him to the stairway and take off his mask, and he's able to get a bit of air. And, like a good wife, I ask him if we want to go back to the bar or if we can find something different to do and he's like "we paid all this money, we're here, let's do it." Reason number 212 why I love that goofy bastard. Plus, he's right, we paid an assload of money for these tickets. So, I think about it and figure if everyone is going down and then up, let's start up and go down and see what we can see, so we hike up four or five flights of goddamn stairs and open the door to just . . . incredible beauty. The garden part on the top floor . . . it was everything I wanted. Just lush and kinda sad, I guess. It made me feel something. See? I've got nice things to say about the show. Until "she" showed up.

Apparently, reading the forums, we were able to come across the "white ghost," which is a topless woman in a huge, ornate mask dressed all in white. Except for her tits, which were also white . . . never mind. But Dev, he's interested again, the little perv, particularly when she comes over and, wordlessly, tries to take him away. Now, again, I did my research. I knew that "everyone is supposed to go have their own experience" but he was in danger about fifteen minutes before, and I didn't want to leave him, which I think is reasonable. Also, a little more selfishly, I wanted us to have this experience together, you know? Like, this was the time we bond and remember that we're not just parents or employees or roommates or fuck buddies but a couple who goes out and does things and bonds over shared experiences and loves each other. I wanted that. But the woman in white who was allergic to covering her boobs was insistent that she had something to show him and that I wasn't invited. And, look, I'm not some insecure bitch saying, "Some big-tittied actress ran off with my man," but . . . I mean, kinda? You could definitely describe it that way! Anyway, she took him away and I didn't see him until I was being taken away on the ambulance.

While he's off having his own little big-tittied adventure, I decided, fuck it. I was going to the Crypt. Why? Because I was a little pissed off, and apparently Dev thought we needed some time apart. I do love him, but I wasn't happy with him at that exact moment, so I went down.

Everything I'd read said the Crypt was both really cool and really individualized. Like, if you were a bit salty and wanted to go on your own adventure, the Crypt was the place to head to. And . . . it was dark. Because of course it was, and my mask was making it darker yet, as I'm sure they intended. So, I moved toward whatever light I could find, and that's when the Crypt sort of opened up, like a song that starts slow but gradually picks up, and soon all the instruments are playing at once. There were colorful graves with hands reaching out of them, people being tortured by other people in the corner but, like, in a beautiful way; there were things creeping out of all the shadows and, in the center, was the woman. She was one of the most beautiful things I've ever seen, with this huge headdress and stark, white makeup, and this flowing gown that was both there and not there, it's really hard to describe but, for a moment, I "got it." Not just the appeal of the show, but what it was trying to say—that we're all already in the grave and beauty does not last which is why you need to grab it with both hands while you can.

Then some piece of shit broke my nose.

I don't know who or how. I don't know if it was a foot or a fist, but I bet it was a fist. Now that I think back on it, I'm amazed that my teeth didn't break, because I was just standing there with my mouth open, but it sure as hell broke the mask I was wearing. I was also not braced for it, at all, so it knocked me square back on my ass. I didn't make any noise because my voice was caught in my throat, but I just remember the pain in my face and then the pain in my tailbone as I hit the pavement, which was pretty unforgiving, I gotta tell you.

I expected someone to, ya know, help me up. But nothing like that happened. I just heard the sounds of the show, the music and all that. I whipped off my mask and sort of held my nose like it might fall off or something and tried to find my way back to the stairs, but I was all turned around. I had no idea where I was or where I was going. No idea. I had one hand out in front of me and I bumped into someone and, before I know it, I'm on my ass again and this time someone's attacking me.

I . . . okay. Just a second.

It's hard to put into words what, exactly, I felt or when I felt it. It's like the whole experience was compressed. I remember everything and, at the same time, it's like it all happened at once. I know I'm not making sense, so here's what I can tell you. Once I hit the ground, I started getting feet to the upper body and face. Just kick after kick. Don't ask me how, but I could tell the feet weren't, like, wearing shoes. Not naked feet, but feet without boots on. Dancer's feet. I remember, distinctly, thinking that, which was a weird thought to have. My next thought was, *they're not going to stop.* So, as my last resort, with my nose gushing blood and an unknown number of nearly naked feet kicking at my head, I jumped up and started throwing hands.

Anything I could vaguely see, I hit. Anything that looked like it might be a person, I hit. I screamed and I punched and then—I'm on the ground again and my hands are behind my back—then the kicking started again. That was the worst part.

I remember a good kick to the ribs and having trouble breathing. I remember, and this is so fucking stupid, someone grabbing the back of my leg and twisting the skin. I remember getting hit so hard in the back it was like someone was sitting on me and not letting me breathe. The last thing I remember, was the kick to the face that knocked me unconscious. When I woke up in the hospital, I was in more pain than I've ever experienced in my entire life.

All told, I had four broken teeth, one broken jaw, bruised ribs, a sprained ankle, possible internal bleeding that didn't amount to anything, and a $282,000 hospital bill that, along with my $3,000 fucking deductible is going to run me just shy of eighty grand, which is about sixty grand more than I have in savings. I missed a bunch of work. I had a bunch of dentist appointments to make. I have scars in places I wish I didn't have scars. So, yeah, pretty bad fucking night.

Dev didn't find me until the ambulance was, literally, about to pull away from the building. They have sound systems all over that damn place but aren't interested in using that expensive sound system to tell anyone that there's been "an incident." I didn't hear from anyone from the show until, like, four days later and then it was through a lawyer. And, look, I get it. This country fucking sucks, and health care is irrevocably broken, and the first thing they have to worry about is getting sued out of existence, which, spoilers, I don't have the money to do. But, at no point, was my humanity acknowledged. At no point did anyone say "Hey, sorry our staff beat the ever-loving fuck out of you in the dark. Please talk to us about it." I still don't know why it happened, not officially anyway. But I've done a bunch of research, particularly after everything that happened at that place twenty-four hours later, and I think I can make an educated guess.

Let me do this. Let me tell you a completely fictional story and see if it's something you like. Let me tell you a story that I made up out of my head so I don't get sued for money I don't have for saying things that aren't true. Let's try that.

Let's pretend there's an interactive theater show, right? And that show is under attack from a small section of internet trolls who have decided that this is their stupid project for this period in their sad little lives. As part of this project, they get to feel all big by harassing the staff and threatening people in a way that makes them feel legitimately scared for the safety of their workplace. And this happens every night for a while and people start to get paranoid. Then they start to get really paranoid. Then their paranoia bleeds through to their performances and they start doing little things here and there to take back their power. These theoretical artists I'm talking about, they escalate. Then the trolls escalate. And then, one night, some poor woman, let's make her a thing of stunning beauty and taste, maybe call her Princess Marleen, is stumbling around in the dark is in the wrong place at the wrong time. She's mistaken for someone who has just assaulted one of the dancers, which is easy to do because it's dark and everyone is wearing a fucking mask.

Princess Marleen got caught in the cross fire. She is beaten very badly and is never the same after that. Princess Marleen has nightmares about being attacked out of nowhere, constant dreams of masked demons coming for her from the shadows. She is fighting to be the mom she was before "the incident" and trying to reconnect with her husband, who feels guilty and probably should, at least a little bit. And then her insurance pulls a "we're not going to pay for nearly enough of your obvious medical needs," like they always do and . . . end of story, I guess. It needs work. It's kind of depressing, as it stands.

INTERVIEW 9
JAGGER MORA

Member of Who's There Community, Attended *Come Knocking* on March 13

You're gonna hate me.

You're gonna think I'm the asshole. Maybe worse, you're gonna think I'm the kind of asshole who wants to hurt people. I'm volunteering for that, which is fucking stupid, but here we are. The only thing I can say is I didn't do anything illegal. I don't think I even did anything immoral. Either way, you may think I'm the asshole but I'm not. I didn't do anything wrong.

I can already hear people rushing to their keyboards to type "but you told this person to die in a fire" or "you told this person you hope she gets raped." Talking shit about someone or something isn't wrong, okay? You've been on the internet, right? It's 60 percent shitposting and 40 percent ads. Big fucking deal. Get over it so I can get through this.

I was nineteen when I first started posting on Who's There, and it wasn't for any specific reason. I found a link to it and thought the whole thing was super niche, which made it fun. I didn't hate the show—I barely even knew what it was—but there were people who really fucking hated the show and that made it fun to read. It's like, have you ever seen those shirts that have a picture of Jean-Luc Picard and it says "'Use the Force, Luke'—Gandalf." This guy I know used to wear that shirt to cons and one guy got so mad about it, and we laughed about that for a while. My point is, people come to the internet to get mad. They sure don't come for valuable information to help them make life decisions.

The Who's There group was just another version of that shirt my friend wore, but a little meaner and a little more conspiracy theory–based. Which is fine. I can roll with that. I don't think the Earth is flat but watching people get mad that other people think that is hilarious. Which isn't wrong. I didn't do anything wrong.

What was I saying? Right. The earliest I remember hearing about Who's There was on a TikTok post. Some woman does this series called "Internet Drama You're Not a Part Of" and tells you all about other people who are having drama. She featured Who's There and how they were organized against one show, which seems stupid and petty until you really dive into it. I joined their Discord to see why the show, which seemed cool enough even if it was only for rich people, was making everyone lose their collective minds. I didn't get it. It only took me a little while to get red-pilled.

They had it all laid out. There were five reasons why the show shouldn't exist, according to that community. I wrote them down, just a second.

1) It's stupid. I know that sounds, like, juvenile, but there was a whole thing about it. Their interpretation of classic literature was stupid. The interactive part of the interactive theater was stupid. Interactive theater itself is stupid. They had a whole intellectual argument behind it that was really long and detailed. They even had a two-hour podcast about it. That was the first reason.
2) It's dangerous. This was the most popular one on the Discord. They talked about how low light and fire and flailing dancers were a bad combination. Stuff like that. There were stories of people getting hurt, but I don't know if they're true or not. Moving on.
3) It's pretentious. I think that's pretty self-explanatory.
4) It's making LA worse. This was an interesting point because I wasn't entirely on board with it when I first joined. The idea is that the show isn't in the arts district. It's a little off the beaten path because that's where they could find a building to, like, retrofit. And because they were there, the neighborhood became

more expensive and priced some low-income folks out of their homes. There was this one guy who had a whole honest-to-Christ PowerPoint presentation about it. I have it burned if you want a copy.
5) "The incident."

You know about that, right? If you're any sort of reporter, you know about that. About the spy they sent to seduce one of our members and then shut us down? This was the big one in the community. Huge. The woman it happened to, she was, like, a rock star in the group and put all the receipts up for anyone who wanted to see. It was kind of amazing because she didn't look that great in the text messages, she came across as needy and a little bitchy, but the dude who seduced her looked worse. It seemed legitimate to me because it didn't seem like she was hiding anything, if that makes sense. It was real. It was honest.

I mean, what sort of messed-up fucking play conducts espionage about a group that is making fun of them online? Is there a more pathetic thing you can think of? I can't. It still kind of bugs me when I think about it. I mean, why would they do that?

I can also tell you "the incident" was the key to everyone taking everything to the next level. After it was clear they were willing to send some dude to spy on us and plot against us, it's hard to know what else they were gonna do. It goes downhill from there, right? If someone is sending spies, there's obviously some shady shit happening with that show. If someone's, literally, after you, then you can do whatever is necessary to defend yourself. That's, like, basic. Everyone could have just left everyone else alone, I guess. But it was funny! It was a community. There were hundreds of people on that fucking Discord posting every day about this shit. If I had to tell you what was different about it, it was that we had an enemy that had actually engaged. We didn't have to make them up, you know? It became fun to guess at any other super shady stuff they might have been doing, and we had all sorts of these theories—that they were tied in with the government, that they were a secret Chinese spy agency. A small group of people actually thought they were part of a bigger cabal and that they were a front for a child sex ring. Crazy stuff but, seriously, what isn't plausible at that point?

The most popular section of the Discord was people who had been to the show and started sharing intel. From that intel we would come up with plans on how to fuck with the show. I mean, most of it was speculation. There was a lot of "wouldn't it be cool if a light fell into one of the graves and actually caught fire and burned the actor to death." We didn't actually DO that, and we didn't want to actually burn anyone alive. It's the internet. I once got told to "hang myself" because of my opinion about a *Star Wars* trailer and then later the commenter sent me my address over DM. And, to answer the question I know you're going to ask, yes, we realized that giving *Come Knocking* money in the form of ticket sales was against the entire thing we were trying to do. We weren't stupid. Mean, but not stupid. The way we got around that was one of the moderators, I remember which one but I'm not going to tell you, worked at a radio station in the advertising department and, I don't know how, but he had access to tickets. Not a ton, but access. So, if someone had a good idea, chances are good the mod in question could hook you up. Which is how the pranks started.

I've got no problem calling them pranks, because that's what they were and anyone who tells you differently is being a fucking drama queen. Like I said, I didn't do anything wrong. Since I live in Glendale and a lot of other people in the Discord didn't even live in California, it made sense for me to go "test the waters" and see what I could get away with. We weren't doing anything illegal. At most, at absolute worst, we were being bad audience members, which, like, whatever.

The first time I got sent to the show, they told me to just get a sense of the place and to take pictures. They take your phone when you first get in there, and we knew that, so I had a GoPro and I cut a little hole in my pants pocket so anytime I wanted to get some video or a photo of something, I just walked up to it, put my hand in my pocket and pushed the button. Easy. And it worked pretty well when I put it on the "low light" setting. There were certain things they wanted me to take pictures of, all of it technical stuff. It wasn't "what's the show look like," they wanted pictures of the exits and if there was any sign of the control room, or if you saw places where the cast entered and exited the space. Truthfully, that sort of stuff is really hard to find because, even though I hate everyone involved, the show was pretty good. It had some talented people in it, but I wasn't there to watch the dances. My GoPro worked great, I kept my eyes open and got the Mods what they wanted, which is why they sent me back. That felt really good.

The Mods told everyone I did a good job, but they didn't share my photos with the group, which should have been a red flag. Then they sent me back a few weeks later to get video of some of the dances to get their timing and location and how they worked in the space they had set up. Again, the mods didn't share my photos or video with the wider group, which was . . . bad. But I didn't have too much time to think about it, because we had moved on to the next phase—fucking with the dancers.

"Fucking With" is the wrong wording, because it makes it sound like we were grabbing their tits or something, which would have been illegal. One of the only reasons I'm talking to you is because I *didn't* do anything illegal. The police came and talked to me after March 14, and I spilled my guts. It was my first run-in with the cops that wasn't a speeding ticket and . . . it was a trip, man. It's way different than I expected, and I told them about Who's There and showed them all my posts and told them all the stuff I did. They didn't arrest me. Like I told you, they couldn't, because I didn't do anything wrong. I want to make that really clear.

The thing about the dancers that caught everyone's attention was first, they made the biggest noise in the show. The Demon Dance they do is loud and athletic and in your face, so it makes sense that they were the big players in the show, right? The second thing was their information is just . . . out there. Like, if Jennifer is a dancer and I want to talk to Jennifer, I google "JenniferComeKnocking," email her agent, pretend to be interested in hiring her for some private job, and eight times out of ten you have her phone number in less than twenty-four hours. I mean, protect yourself a little bit! I am really careful about putting my personal information on the internet. It's crazy out there, but if you can't stand the heat, stay the fuck offline.

This is the part where I don't come off looking so good. The part where I'm worried that I'm talking to you. Whatever. Here we go.

It was my idea to fuck with the dancers. There are three different dances that do this, admittedly, pretty cool thing where it seems like the dancers are popping up in different places. If you don't know what you're looking at it's a cool effect. If you do know what you're looking at, it's a trick of the lighting. "Oh, I'm over here." Then they shut off the lights in one spot and you go there and then "Oh, I'm over here now." It's dumb if you know the trick. My idea was to know where they were going to be and just . . . be there with a little message for them. Since, by the look on your face I can tell I'm already the bad guy here, I'll go further and tell you it served two purposes. The first was to scare and insult them. The second was to let them know that we had studied them and that we could do worse if we wanted to. I want to stress the word "could," because I didn't do anything wrong.

So, yeah. I led the groups who did the first couple rounds of fucking with the dancers. And it was a blast, man. So much fun. More fun than it should have been because the dancers are trying so damn hard not to break character and to keep doing the stupid little dance that they're doing but they're human, too, so they can't help but have some kind of reaction. Some of them would scream, some of them would jump. One of the dancers actually started crying. It was fucking awesome! She disappeared right after she started crying and may have come out somewhere else after she got herself together, I don't know. All I know is she had a real bad night which was good enough for us.

What sort of stuff did we say? We called them names. We made loud noises. My line, our line, was to never touch, right? Never do anything where they could play the victim because they weren't the victim. At all. We were the victims because they had spied on us and who knew what else they were capable of. The other great thing about messing with the dancers was we couldn't do it every night, only certain nights where we could get a group together and get tickets. But we knew the result was that they were always looking over their shoulder. They never knew what night we were going to be there to call them names and mess with their routine, so they were always on alert. If we weren't always there we *could* always be there. Kind of beautiful, if you think about it.

I did it three times. The last time was March 13.

I can't tell you what happened that got that poor woman beaten so bad she ended up in the hospital. But that's really funny. I mean, yeah, it sucks for her, but they were so freaked out that they beat the teeth out of some poor woman's head. Head shot, man. Better than we thought we could do. It means we were taking up a lot of room in their collective head. Like, a lot. I can't tell you what led up to the beating, but I can tell you what I saw.

I'm not going to lie, it was exhilarating, and it felt like we were making a difference, that we were hurting this evil empire that had moved into my neighborhood. March 13 was a Thursday, I think, and we had already been there on Tuesday. We had gathered some momentum so it felt special, it felt like something was going to happen soon and this was the lead-up to it. I can't give you any reason why that was besides that we were messing with the dancers and anyone else we could with more and more frequency, and the Mods were asking more and more of us, and we were happy to oblige.

I wasn't on the crew that went to the show on Tuesday, but I was with the one on Thursday, like I said. Our plan was a little different than the last few times—one of the mods was coming with us. I just know everyone's screen name, so when the mod didn't find me or introduce himself or whatever, I thought that was kind of weird, too. But I had my crew of two other guys and we were there when they opened the doors. The plan was always to let the first cycle pass, so we had an hour to be seen walking around and acting like good little audience members. Then, during the second cycle is when we'd start and, if we didn't get kicked out or leave, do it again during the third cycle in a different place. One of the guys in my crew was talking about how he was going to try something "different" this time, but I didn't have a chance to ask him what that "different" thing was before they opened the doors, and then we obviously couldn't talk.

When the second cycle came around, we got into our positions on Floor Three, waiting for the Demon Dance to come through. Floor

Three has this weird "fire and ice" theme with one side of the room being fire, the other being ice. We were going to wait in the "ice" side, but the tech people had moved the lighting around so when the Demon Dance got there, we weren't in position. The lights flashed and the music played, and we were about twenty feet away feeling pretty stupid, honestly. Plus, chances were excellent that the guys in the control room had made us at that point, and we were probably on our way toward getting kicked out or at least watched really closely. That really pissed off one of the guys I was with, and I remember seeing him bolt for one of the stairways. I followed him, and my blood was really pumping when we got to the Crypt on Floor Four. I remember this guy, who I'm not going to name, telling me "those fuckers aren't going to get away with it." He said some other things, too. I thought that was a little . . . aggro. I mean, they weren't doing anything to us, specifically, but he was . . . let's just say he wasn't going to let the opportunity to mess with the show pass him by again.

We get into position and, even though it's dark, I can make out what's happening. The dancers come through, the lighting started to change, and we knew now was the time. That's when I saw the crackling blue light.

Asshole brought a taser and hit one of the dancers with it.

This was over the line, clearly. I'm looking you right in the eye right now and telling you I had no idea that a taser was in play, and if I did know that, I would have tried to stop it. I would have stopped it. But, at the same time, I knew where he was coming from. Like . . . everything was escalating, right? They were moving lights and avoiding us . . . look, I'm not endorsing it. I'm just saying I know where he was coming from, though I would never go that far myself.

The thing was, in the low light, I noticed sort of what happened. After the guy on my team zapped the dancer, she fell and it looked like she hurt herself. I don't know or really care if she did, but my guy threw the taser at the feet of someone else. I don't know who because everyone looks the same in there with the masks. But . . . okay, it went like this. Light, shock, the dancer falls, my guy throws the taser, the dancers look and see the taser and then proceed to beat the shit out of the person who the taser was in front of. I'm sorry, but what assholes. What complete and total assholes they are. I mean, they just saw the taser and went "that person," and beat the teeth out of their head! What absolute moron assholes they are.

I told the police this. I told them everything and, shortly after that, my parents told me I wasn't supposed to go on that Discord anymore. They had a point. It had sort of taken over my life and gotten me all amped up and almost gotten me in trouble. I eventually went back on a few months after "the incident" and had hundreds of messages from people calling me a snitch, which I get.

But, the way I see it, at the end of the day, I didn't do anything wrong.

REDDIT POST ON R/COMEKNOCKING

Going Tonight—Here's My Plan

VideoGameCock
Posted January 12

I've followed this sub for a long time and I finally have something to post!

I'm a transplant to LA and I work a terrible job doing meaningless work but I've managed to save enough money to get tickets to the show this Friday. After watching videos and reading almost everything this sub has recommended, I think I have a plan on how to attack this thing. Please let me know if I'm missing anything big.

First Sequence: Start at the Desert of the Damned and see if the fighting has progressed. Someone said it's not as great toward the end of the night as they get tired (which is understandable!) so I want to see it at full strength. I'm also really interested in how the actors interact with the sand at the beginning of the night versus the end of the night. I would get sick of going home with sand everywhere!

I want to then move down one to the Crypt and catch the Queen of the Damned descending. I understand that happens around 25 minutes into each sequence, and I want to spend some time in that space. I hear it's amazing.

Second Sequence: This is going to be my traditional run—see the Human Jubilation and follow the Knight all the way to the top. This will be my story sequence.

Third Sequence: I want to follow the Demon Dance. From there I want to pick up anything I've missed or want to spend more time with. I want to end the night on Floor Six.

Here are my questions:

> How can I increase my chance of one-on-ones? I know they can seem random but any tips would be appreciated.
>
> Aside from my watch (which I will be wearing) is there any way to know when one sequence ends and another begins? I can totally see a situation where I get caught up in something and my plan goes to hell.
>
> Is there any truth to the rumors that the show is getting dangerous? I don't mind a little danger (I'm bored as hell and could use a good story) but some of the stuff on here is making me a little nervous. Is it true? And is there anything I can do to avoid the worst of it?

Thank you for any answers you can give me! I have been looking forward to this show for so long. I hate to say it, but it's the thing that's been keeping me going for the last few weeks. I finally get to go to the Netherworld!

Replies:

ErrybodyPantsNow: You'll want to adjust when you see the fight. It takes them until the second sequence to really get rolling (and if they're going to get naked, they don't do it right away). One-on-ones happen randomly. I've never seen a good bit of "advice" for making it happen.

TonyAlto: You're right that the Desert of the Damned is underrated. Spend some time there but be careful around the graves.

SamSang2242: To me, the show gets worse the lower you go. Or better as you go up, depending on how you look at it. The Planetarium Garden is second to none in terms of sets.

LowBatterySmokeAlarm: I thought the talk about the show being "dangerous" was overblown. I had no problems at all. I never felt danger, just awe.

TRANSCRIPT OF VOICE MEMOS FROM ANNA "PUNKY" RODRIGUEZ

A Dancer at *Come Knocking*,
to Her Boyfriend, Daniel Corona

March 14

11:02 A.M.
Hey, baby. I'm awake now and I need to talk. This is way too much to text, and I ain't sending an email in this day and age so . . . I need your help. I need you. I'm not doing okay. In so many ways. I know you're working right now. Just give this a listen and we can maybe have coffee or something tomorrow morning? I'd just really like to see you soon because I need you. I can't talk to anyone at work and, I know you told me not to complain about work so much 'cause I can always find a new gig but I don't know if I can right now. Even if I quit my rent is through the fucking roof and I almost missed it last month. . . . Sorry. I'm doing exactly what you told me not to do. Just, give me a call if you can before my call time at 4:30. I'd really love to hear your voice. I need to hear your voice. Call me, please, baby.

11:33 A.M.
It's me again. I was thinking about Lake Tahoe. That was a great trip. We . . . [*sighs*] we really just got away. Turned our phones off, which I know was hard for you to do with your job. I remember that loft bed and we got so drunk the second night we almost couldn't climb the ladder to go to bed, so we just camped out on the floor and talked for

an hour until we sobered up and could get up there. That was one of the best conversations I ever had with anybody, baby. I told you things I've never told anyone. I love you. Call me if you can. I want to tell you something. Something that's scaring me. I need that guy from Lake Tahoe. I need him. Sorry to be so needy. Love you.

12:04 P.M.
Okay, so I was hoping you saw my messages or had them translated or whatever your phone does. I thought you'd see them and call me right when your lunch hour started, but, apparently, you didn't do that. Apparently you're busy today, so I guess I need to lay this out for you without you on the other end to hear it. I asked for your help. This is what I get?

    Look, baby, I know I'm acting out of my mind right now but . . . shit, I'm just gonna say it, I might be going out of my mind right now. I swear, my fuckin' blood pressure is up and my anxiety is up and the meds ain't doin' shit and I can just feel like the show is trying to kill me. And I ain't the only one. All the dancers feel the same way. We're getting attacked every night and you know how I don't take shit from anyone? Imagine seventeen dancers who feel the same way. Some of them are talking absolutely crazy and I'm agreeing with them. Bella said she's gonna smuggle a knife in her hair and I believe her. The thing is, I feel like she's right. Like, we need to defend ourselves and that's why I need you to talk me down. Talk some sense into me you big, sexy motherfucker. Call me. Okay.

12:28 P.M.
Sorry, babe. Thought you called but it was someone else. Seriously, even if you get 10 minutes free, hearing your voice would be the best medicine for me right now. Come through for me, okay?

1:11 P.M.
Okay, fuck you. I waited by my phone for your whole lunch hour. I know you ain't that busy, but your "crazy" girlfriend is messaging you and messaging you and you just don't want to deal with it. Is that it?

Were you lying to me the other night when you told me the pussy was so good it was worth the crazy? Are you a fucking liar, Daniel? Because it sure seems like it.

You know what? Don't call. I'll deal with all this shit myself and maybe you and I have a talk about what, exactly, we've been doing for the past year and change. Maybe we have a good long talk about what our future looks like, huh? You like that? That crazy enough for you, you sad little man bitch? I don't fuckin' need you anyway.

1:20 P.M.
I'm sorry, baby. See, this is why I need you to call! You can talk me down for doing this crazy shit like yelling at you or feeling like I feel right now. I'm scared and I'm angry and I'm sorry to take this out on you. I still need you to call, okay? Okay? I'll make it up to you. Sorry. I just suck so much sometimes . . .

1:53 P.M.
It's obvious we're not gonna talk before I go to the show tonight. So this is what you get, Daniel. A long-ass voice memo where I say what I gotta say. Maybe it'll help to know you're gonna hear it tonight if you're still listening past that message where I went all crazy on you. I'm still sorry about that. That was uncalled for but, honestly, if you don't know why mom called me "Punky" yet, I don't know what to tell you.

So, here's what's up. I think I'm either going to get hurt or I'm going to hurt somebody tonight.

I know how that sounds and I can almost hear you saying "don't be so dramatic" in that way you do, but it's the truth. And I can hear you saying "are you on your meds" and I am, though I missed a couple days earlier this week because things are really stressful right now and I just forgot. The audiences and that one group of assholes I told you about has been getting really bold and really scary over the last few weeks. Last night something happened. Something bad. One of the dancers got tased in her leg and it caused her to crash through part of the set. There was blood everywhere after. . . . I don't know if she's dancing tonight. And some of the dancers, they took matters into their own hands and kicked the shit out of the person with the taser and then the security guards joined in and it was just a huge fuckin' mess. I wasn't there. I didn't do nothing. But if I had been there, I would have kicked that bitch so hard I'd have broken my foot. And that's what I need to talk to you about. I'm violent, Daniel. I feel it in me. I know that's a stupid thing to admit to on a voice memo, but I feel like I'm not just capable, I'm, like, eager. I'm either going to get hurt or I'm gonna hurt someone and you know what, baby? It feels like it's time. It feels like it's time to make a little noise when, just a few weeks ago, all I wanted was to just want to do my thing and make rent.

Remember when we first met and you asked me why I became a dancer? I didn't want to scare you away and tell you the truth but you want to know the real reason? It's not just because I'm good at it, which I am, or that everybody likes watching me, which they do. It's because it felt to me like the best job in the world. Like, I could just move my body and do my thing and just sort of go into the "dance trance" and think about beauty and artistry instead of filling out fucking documents or spreadsheets or whatever. I could be a person doing a thing and not a cog in a wheel. Plus, as you've told me a lot, I probably am not cut out for the nine-to-five sort of gig. I got a little bit of crazy in me, that's what you say. You're right, baby. More right than you know.

This already feels too long. I hope I can send it to you and not have to use Google Drive or some shit. Just a second.

2:06 P.M.
Like I was saying, it felt like the best job in the world, dancing did. You know how you're always going on about the assholes you work with and the bosses and the control freaks and all that? Almost every show I've ever done it's been the opposite of that. Yeah, there are assholes, but when it's all said and done you either do your thing or you don't do your thing. No one is like, "you didn't fill that report out right." Show up. Do your thing. Dance like a fuckin' maniac. That's what I do and you know what? I felt like I had a secret. Like . . . like I'd beaten the system a little bit. Like I was special.

And now? Baby, you ain't never dealt with the shit like we're dealing with. And it's dangerous now. And it's scary now. And this secret thing I thought I figured out turns out to be just like everything else in this fucked-up world. It's falling apart. This secret of mine is a curse.

I gotta tell you a story then I'm done. Three nights ago, or three performances ago, I don't remember, it all blends together, anyway! Three nights ago this dude made a grab at me. First time it happened. All the other dancers have had it happen to them and not me, which I was thankful for but was also, like . . . never mind. I ain't even going there. But it happened, and it was worse than I thought it was going to be. A lot worse because I think it's the same thing! I think I had this special little space and the man literally reached out and grabbed me in a way that only you grab me and when you grab me like that you know, you *know* how horny it gets me but it was like, the mirror of that. And I had the mirror reaction. Instead of wanting to pull you close and let you into my world and my body, I wanted that motherfucker out of my world and as far away from my body as possible. I was ready to fight to make that happen.

Since then, I've felt like I wanted another shot. Like, part of me wants someone to try something so I can break three of their fuckin' fingers, or I want someone to try to tase me so they can understand what it's like to get electricity shot up their ass. Maybe I want to do it first. My coworkers aren't helping.

They're in war mode, baby. Every time before the show they're talking about darker and darker shit. Maybe it's the show, right? Maybe it's all the death and gross stuff in the show that's making them talk that way but maybe it's not. Seriously, there's this one girl, Amber, who you met I'm pretty sure but I don't expect you to remember, she's got the darkest shit in her head, man. Taking about cutting them and using their blood in our dance. Talking about her "final show." Like, "for my final show, I'm cutting off one of their balls and eating it" or "for my final show, you'll be able to dance on the trail of bodies." She comes from the other side, the "theater" side, not the "dance side."

Shit, this message is longer than the last one. One sec.

2:19 P.M.

The thing is, everyone is absolutely ready to throw hands at a moment's notice and terrified that they're going to lose their jobs. And some of those girls are tight. Like, I never feel excluded, exactly, but I get that some of these girls have been around each other for years and really care about each other. I pick up on that vibe. I feel it. But that ain't the real shit. The show and what the show's about and the job and the dancers and the Karens and all that, it's not what I'm worried about. Daniel . . . I'm worried about me.

I don't know how much you remember from that night. The one in Lake Tahoe. But I told you something that night I ain't never told anybody and you never said anything so I don't know if you even remember it. Given all we had to drink that night, you can be forgiven if you don't remember but you acted like it was fucked up at the time. Because it is. But now . . . I feel it again and I feel like I gotta tell you about it.

It feels like it's all going down, baby. The show and my job, yeah, but it's deeper than that. It's hot out. It's March and it feels like June and in June it's going to feel like the surface of the goddamn sun in this city. I make more money now than I ever thought I'd make as a little girl and I can't buy shit with it. I love "me doing my little thing" but I can't . . . it feels like every time I do it is going to be the last time. Like everything and everyone is just burning everything down and nobody cares or can stop it.

When I was a little girl I heard about all the problems in the world and I thought *I don't have to worry about that. That's someone else's problem.* It's my problem now and I just feel the weight of it. Every day I feel this weight. Being a brown girl doesn't fuckin' help, but you know all about that. But it's like, if it's all over then why do my thing? Why not . . . take a knife and carve the balls outta some motherfucker and make him eat them before the cops show up? If they're showing up at all. Why not make everyone bleed just a bit, give 'em a scar so they remember you? If we're all about done anyway, if we're cooked the way it looks like we're cooked, I think it might be time to figure out who I'm taking with me when I finally go down and how I'm gonna do it.

I shouldn't send you this one. This is a new level of crazy, ain't it? This ain't me "doing my thing." That was . . . scary. Which is why I really hoped you call, baby. I really hope you could call and talk me down because me and the girls, we're going to do something. If not tonight tomorrow and if not tomorrow than soon. We ain't taking this anymore because *why*!?! Why fucking take it and take it and take it everyday for it to mean nothing!? For it all to mean some rich prick gets a little richer? For it to mean you're replaced the second you're gone. Why would you do that? Why?

That shit ain't me. That ain't me. That ain't none of my girls in the Demon Dance either. I love you Daniel. I love you, but I got this thing inside me, and I'm about out of ways to tell it to calm down. I'm all out of excuses to give it. Ain't nothing more to say.

I gotta get ready for work.

INTERVIEW 10
ANDERS PETERSEN

Assistant Technical Director of *Come Knocking* in Los Angeles

My job is high stress. Because of this I need you to understand that I speak plainly and am not given to hyperbole. I say exactly what I mean out of necessity. Part of that is my Dutch upbringing. Part of it is my analytical nature.

With that in mind, March 14 was a shit show, and it was a shit show the second we opened the doors.

Being in the control room and only occasionally on the floor does not mean we are immune to what the performers think and feel. Far from it, actually. We are in consistent contact with the performers based on need. They are our eyes on the ground. We are the eyes in the sky. My point in telling you this is I understood some of the actors and performers had been dealing with rowdy elements. This is not uncommon on shows of our caliber and complexity. I would point you toward a recent incident where a high-ranking government employee was caught in minor sexual congress with her boyfriend during a touring production of some sort or another. Again, my point is I was aware of the problem, as was our director.

What we were not aware of was the extent of the problem. To put it simply, we underestimated what was happening. Please believe me when I say if we had any inkling of how terrible this situation could have become, we would have shut down the show in an instant. We are partially at fault. To a piece, we accept that fact.

Before I go into the specifics, which is what I have been brought here to do, I want to assure you that I take my job very seriously. I also take the incredible loss of life very seriously. I want to express regret, I want to express immense empathy with those who lost loved ones. Finally, while I am not in jail as I broke no laws, I do want to speak to the fact that, despite a lifetime of high-level technical work in the theater, I realize my legacy is forever going to be *Come Knocking* and the events of March 14th. This is my burden, though it is far less than others who will go without their loved ones for the rest of their lives. Now, as is often said in my side of the curtain, let us please proceed.

My first hint that something was amiss on the night of the fourteenth was quite abrupt. My job during the first cycle is to visually confirm most of the major effects over the course of the first hour. From there, I typically split my time between the performance space and the control room. I am able to do so because of a series of elevators, scaffolds, and the fact that I am also wearing a mask and can pass through the audience undetected. While I have been asked not to by our director as I have many duties over the course of the night, I have also served as confirmation for security, which is on the same channel on the headset. *Come Knocking* is an atypical show in that there is so much more space to cover and so many things that can go wrong. As a result, while my job, ostensibly, is to report on what's happening on the floor, I am part of a team. As part of a team, the technical staff often use the phrase "other duties as assigned" which translated to "you will often be asked to do a task for the good of the show." This was a nightly occurrence and not at all out of the ordinary.

On March 14, I had donned my mask, I am wearing my headset, and roughly fifteen minutes into the first cycle, the line goes dead. We have three reserve channels, which were also not working. This made me sprint to the control room. Why? Because a dead line of communication is nothing short of catastrophic.

We have six floors, seventy-two cast and crew, over eighty individual effects, and a crowd of roughly three hundred people, give or take some stragglers, whose entire experience and, to some degree, their safety relies on our staff's ability to control what is happening. If there is no way to dispatch security, no way to alert actors or audience, and no way to control what is happening in the room, "catastrophic" seems the correct word. At this point, I was also unaware whether communication was down, which was its own significant problem, or if the entire control room was down, which would be considerably worse.

As an aside, the wiring in the room was fantastic. I saw early speculation after March 14 that part of the issue might have been a poorly wired control room. I was part of the team overseeing the construction of many of the show's elements, and that was not the case. I assure you, utmost care was taken in that element of construction.

I do apologize, I do not remember where I was, exactly, when I realized the communications line had gone silent. But I do remember where I was when I heard a voice I did not recognize on the other end. I also remember, vividly, what was said.

I had just rounded the corner of the stairwell on Floor Two and was about to enter the bar when someone said over the headset, "That was harder than I thought."

I wish I could tell you I had a vivid realization of what was happening, but I did not. Instead my only thought was *you need to get to the control room* and, by the time I rounded the corner into the bar—I should have mentioned the control room was behind the bar, which was the subject of many jokes but worked very well for our purposes—the intruders had the door locked and barricaded. Security had yet to arrive, which was dispiriting. They should have realized what was happening before I did, but they did not. They would not arrive on the scene for another five to ten minutes by my estimation.

The bartenders, however, were good men. One appeared to be injured, but I did not take that into account as they were already trying to get back into the control room, as were several other employees. Everyone seemed fit and of the appropriate level of concern, trying desperately to open the door. But the door was made not to be opened. When the entire premise of the show encourages the audience to explore, "a locked door must remain locked," as the thinking went. They quickly told me they had been bum-rushed and that four men had forced one of them, on threat of severe violence, to call for the director over the headset. I knew Phillip, our director, well and he was a solid craftsman. I give him high marks on everything I had seen him accomplish and on his technical acumen. I do not know what was said over the headset, but it must have been very compelling to get Phillip out of his director's chair at the front of the control room. Very compelling.

Once inside, they released the bartenders, I presume, took over the control room, and barricaded the door. It was, at this point, that I must admit to a bit of panic. Aside from everything that could go wrong with the show when communication was down, we now had players likely intent on mayhem. I am not telling you, at that point, I could predict the spectacular loss of life that was to come. But I had a fairly strong premonition at the time that *Come Knocking* may be in the midst of its final performance.

My first order of business was to attempt to get the door open. I had a key—I was one of the few who did—but the door was barricaded, as I had suspected. I also deduced that Phillip was inside as I cannot imagine anything that would have kept that man from the other side of that door given that strangers were behind the controls. It never occurred to me that he could be somewhere else and I was proven correct. He stayed in that room until they murdered him, but, again, I had no idea that was in the offing. Failing to get in the control room, my next action was to try to make contact. I called and texted Phillip on my personal cell phone and, when he did not answer, I put on the headset and began to speak to whoever was in the booth.

I must address an issue before I go further. There were reports, that were accurate to my knowledge, that the police were not called until roughly thirty minutes after the control room was taken. I wish to confirm and explain. I did not call the police. I did not ask anyone to call the police. It was my assumption, and I don't believe it to be irrational, that the police had already been called. The bartenders had roughly a minute to two minutes between the time the handset went dead and my arrival. I do not believe it a "stretch" to say they had called the police during that time. I wish I had double-checked, as I am accustomed to doing on so many of my duties but, given the extreme circumstances, I did not do so. I was very focused. I do not mean to be aloof and say "I had more important things to do," but that would not be inaccurate to my thinking. Had I been thinking more clearly, I would have realized it would take more than two minutes to retrieve a cell phone from a locker and make that call. I cannot justify my action further, though I wish I had been more responsible.

Back to the headset. I pushed my "all call" button, which speaks to the control room, security, backstage, and to several key actors for whom communication was vital. The "all call" included the bartenders as well, so when I began to speak and saw them shaking their heads, I realized communication had been cut off completely. This was one of several times I felt panic that night. No communication means there is no warning when the Queen of the Damned falls, which was due to happen any moment. It meant security would not know anything was wrong. It meant the effects in the Desert of the Damned, some of which could severely injure if deployed inappropriately, were behind a door to which we had no access. I could list a dozen other severe injuries, a hundred potential problems, and several situations, all leading toward the spilling of blood, not to be melodramatic.

To put it simply, panic seemed appropriate.

I spoke harshly to the bartenders. I told them to "get that door open at all costs," and they looked blankly at me. I called them names. I regret that. Their faces, which conveyed their rising panic as well, snapped me out of it. I grabbed each of them by a shoulder, apologized, and said they needed to help me. I told one of them to wait for the police and continue trying to get the door open. The second one I told to start on the bottom floor and run, *run* to all the actors, letting them know we had lost the control room. They agreed. They were strong, young men. I hoped they were up to the tasks I had given them despite one of them appearing to be injured.

My main objective after giving the bartenders instructions was to get to the fourth floor. I remember running to the stairwell, pushing masked patrons out of my way, and looking at my watch and realizing I wasn't going to make it. The Queen of the Damned was likely to either going to plummet to the concrete or not descend at all, which was the better other two scenarios. I had hope, at that point, that whoever had taken the control room was more mischievous than malevolent. That hope vanished when I rounded the corner on the fourth floor in time to see Penelope fall, unencumbered by safety equipment, and smash onto the floor.

I have been told by experts in trauma that there are small details you will remember during traumatic experiences that seem small but take up much of your recollection. Since this is my account, this is my minor detail but it looms large in my mind. I remember applause. Slight, faint, but identifiable applause as I ran to the actress whom I had worked with since we opened in Los Angeles. My momentum carried me to her before any of the dancers who were part of the Demon Dance realized what had happened. I blame the low light and the intricacies of their performance, not malice, as some had ascribed, to why I was the first to try and help. "Try" is the operative word in this situation.

My first aid training is not up to par, but it was clear that Penelope was in serious medical distress. She had lost consciousness, which was a blessing, because given the angle of one of her arms and the amount of blood pouring from her head, she would have been in an incredible amount of pain had she been with us. As it stands, her eyes never opened again. Her main wounds, I remember, were coming from her mouth, likely due to most of her teeth being destroyed in the fall, and her right arm which had a compound fracture. I will remind you, as I had to remind others later that night, that a compound fracture is one in which the bone sticks out of the skin, and the bones that had made up Penelope's forearm had splintered and penetrated through her skin. Later I learned many of her other bones were broken as well.

Some of the cast who had seen what had happened looked at me as I came up on her. I heard someone whisper "Dance! Anders has got this."

On one level, I appreciate the dedication and confidence in my abilities. On another level, this one interaction was indicative of the attitude that led to mass slaughter on March 14. If everyone had just . . . stopped. Just stopped and manually brought up the lights and communicated with each other, we would have saved so many. But that's not what happened. The dance continued. The dance always continues.

One of the cast, whom I was not able to recognize because of her makeup, lingered a bit and got a very good look at Penelope, who was dying. This cast member tried to spit out some words, but I didn't recognize what she was trying to say. My adrenaline was high and I might have muttered "this is bad" or something to that effect. I am not a writer. English is my second language. I did not have the words. The cast member disappeared and I was left with the broken, bleeding, dying woman on the floor. It was then I realized I had an audience.

A group of masked figures were standing above me, watching intently. Watching for my reactions. Watching for my performance. I have given this some thought and have come to the conclusion, why wouldn't they? This was another spectacular stunt. The dancers were dancing. The lighting said "the show is happening." There was nothing to indicate that this woman's fall was, in any way, out of bounds as to what should be happening during this show. I have described to you my emotions, which I am not used to doing, nor particularly interested in doing, but I will tell you that my panic gave way to dread. It is a very different emotion. Panic is "something is going wrong." Dread is "many things are about to go wrong."

And many, many things were about to go wrong.

In my heightened state, I froze. This is embarrassing for me to admit as the one thing you cannot do during a performance is freeze whether you are a performer or behind the scenes. But I froze. I was fixated on Penelope, and how she had gone from a vibrant, attractive and capable performer to the terror in front of me. I had never seen anything so terrible. By the end of the night, I would have seen worse. But my brain froze on Penelope, how her breathing was slowing, how I could see her heartbeat as it pushed blood out of her broken forearm. I fixated on how things could end so quickly.

In retrospect, my actions only made it seem more like a performance. As did what I did next.

I knew the best chance of getting her to any sort of help was to get her offstage, run back to the bar, and check on where the police were. Possibly we could add medical rescue to the scenario. I needed to get her off the public portion to the backstage area, and I knew there was a backstage area only a few steps away, hidden in the shadows. Though ill advised, my plan was to move poor Penelope offstage and then run for help. I can barely count the lapses in judgments on two hands, I realize, now, what a terrible idea it was, but I cannot justify my actions other than to say I was in considerable shock. I hope Penelope and her family who is reading this can forgive me.

I picked her up in my arms and heard "this is beautiful" and "how symbolic" and similar talk from the crowd. She was harder to pick up than I had imagined, because she was coated in elaborate body paint that made her slightly slick. It wasn't until I picked her up that I realized most of the blood was not coming from her mouth but from a large hole in the side of her head. My theory is the elaborate headdress she wore must have . . . I'm sorry. It must have cut into her head when she landed. The thought of the dull, decorative headdress being pushed past her hair and skin and skull and into her brain is too much for me to imagine. I don't like thinking about it but the reason I mention it is when I picked her up, it caused blood and other contents of her skull to leak out on the floor. And it was then some people realized this was not part of the show.

And it was then, as I started walking with Penelope, that the screaming finally found my ears. Screaming all around me. Screaming as if hell had opened up on all sides. Screaming that meant blackness.

The last thing I remember was dropping Penelope and then following her down to the floor as the lights went out around me.

I had been hit from behind. Hit with something quite blunt and heavy. Possibly a stage light or a candelabra. It was not a situation where I saw it coming or knew I was going to pass out. It was simply one moment I was conscious, the next moment I was not.

I woke up covered in blood, still staring at Penelope's closed eyes. She was pale and was not breathing, and around me, everything was on fire.

INTERVIEW 11
ANGUS SCHWARTZ

Cast Member, "the Knight," on March 14

Yeah, man, I've seen my share of the wild side. I've been backpacking through Europe and came upon what I thought was a real satanic orgy. Bunch of naked people in a field, man, just going to town on each other while animals looked on. Turns out it was a regular orgy, but you see my mistake, what with the goats. I've seen lights in a dark field float around and move in ways I've only ever seen in the movies. I saw it with my own eyes. I went to the Philippines and got a tattoo from Whang-Od, that hundred-year-old lady who uses a small rock hammer-looking thing to pound in the needle. I could go on. I've lived a life and I'm only twenty-eight, so I've got a lot more life left in me, brother.

But when I close my eyes, I don't see the orgy in a field or floating lights or the face of that beautiful, old woman and her needles. I see the masks.

Did that sound dramatic? I think it did. If you want to use that in the trailer, and, like, "whoosh," zoom in on a shot of one of the *Come Knocking* masks, that would be bitchin'. You don't have to credit me. Just an idea.

Seriously, though, those masks are super fucked up from a performer's perspective and if you have to look at nothing but masks three hours a night, six nights a week, they work their way into your brain and stay there. I started working at *Come Knocking* when it came to LA. I was out here, trying my hand at the whole acting thing, and had a couple of credits to my name. Didn't have my SAG card yet, but I was doing okay. It was mainly on the stage but some film work. The stage connections were how I hooked up with Dumb Willie and their crew. Good people. I've worked in some pretty sketchy conditions, and *Come Knocking* was not sketchy at all, despite what the tabloids say about Clark Cardigan. I never dealt with that with Dumb Willie. For me, it's class all the way down, man. Class and professionalism. And money! From where I stood inside the Knight's outfit, which wasn't really elaborate but had a lot of leather so I was always soaked in sweat by the end of the night . . . what was I saying? Oh yea, truthfully, I don't know how this happened. But when things went sideways, they went fuckin' all the way sideways!

My job, each cycle, was to carry the story, though the director made it clear to me that I wasn't the "star" of the show, the show was the "star" of the show. Whatever that meant. My job meant starting at the bottom of the building and moving toward the top of the building, hitting a few key scenes, and basically being the good guy going through hell. I used to tell females when I talked to them at a bar or the gym that my job was, literally, to go through hell three times a night. Sometimes I'd say "knight" and explain the joke and, man, LA chicks loved that. But yeah, bottom to top. I had a more important job and that was to be the "Everyman," and what I mean by that was I was the easiest story to follow and, if you followed me, you got a highlight reel of the entire show. Every show, people would follow me, and it was my job to lead them. Lead them and look good doing it. And let me throw this in there, man—the show was a hard sell for a certain type of people. If you're the type who is anxious they are missing something, this show is your worst nightmare, because you're going to miss something, like, by design. If you were that sort of person, the bartenders usually just said "follow the Knight," and I gladly took it from there. My point is I can see how people would get frustrated if they missed me, which happened here and there.

On a good night, or knight, heh, I would have thirty people glued to me as I "traversed the Netherworld." On March 14, it was a little anemic, maybe twenty people. Still a good crowd and, listen, I give a goddamn *performance* each and every time I put on that costume, okay?

I don't care if it's three people or thirty people. I always leave it all out there, that's never the issue. Just, some shows you have fewer people following your story, and that's fine. But I noted it.

I'll stick to March 14 because you told me you've already talked to a lot of people. You talk to Bella yet? Yeah, Bella and I were a thing for a little while. She's a sweet girl. We were dating when this happened, and the reason I mention that is to brag, because she's a smokin' hot dancer who can put both legs over her head. I also wanted to let you know that I knew about all the drama. That, to put it like Bella put it, "there were people fucking with the show." Which, truthfully, I never experienced. I had bad nights, sure. Nights where people would talk and nights where people would try to stop me from going where I was supposed to go. I was always flanked by actors who had my back and I had theirs, so it was never a problem. Plus, I'm great at not listening to people when they talk. Just ask Bella. She said it was one of the reasons she broke up with me. Whatever. Next up, right?

That night, no one was messing with me. Not a soul, brother. Just the regular stuff where couples who weren't separated yet would whisper to each other. On that night I did the Human Jubilation where the Cleric is murdered—the dude's name was Merrick, and I swear to Christ he only got the job because he was "Merrick the Cleric"—and I moved to the Judas floor and it was only there where I started noticing things weren't going well.

Real quick, man, I have an earpiece in when I'm doing the show. The reason is because as the guy moving through all the special effects, I needed to know if something was going wrong and adjust. I even had my own channel because, hey, I'm the Knight, and usually the biggest group follow the Knight, so if something isn't working I can slow myself down or speed up. Also, if there are VIPs or people with special needs, sometimes they stick them with me, which is cool. But it was all quiet on March 14. What I noticed when I got to the Judas floor was we were already missing some dancers which is usually the sort of thing I would hear about. Bad news. One thing I will say about our dancers is they are on point and where they need to be each and every time. They weren't that night and I clocked it. I did my thing, showed the crowd into the mouth of Satan himself, which is a pretty amazing effect, and moved to the Crypt.

Things were already bad when I got there. Poor fuckin' Penelope had already fallen because, like, the Queen of the Damned is supposed to greet the Knight and if she's going to do that she needs to have already descended. I only learned what had happened to her later so I don't have much to tell you about that but I remember, very distinctly, going up the elevator to Floor Four— the elevator is how the Knight gets from place to place—and opening the lattice elevator door and just seeing Karly, who was one of our dancers, full-on punching a dude in the face.

This, obviously, wasn't a normal part of the show.

I knew Karly, we dated briefly, and she didn't seem to me to be the violent type. I mean, she was . . . energetic, I wouldn't mess with her because she had some power to her, but she wasn't violent. But there she was full-on straddling some dude, just giving him the business over and over. That was the first thing I noticed. My eyes had adjusted by then, and I looked out and saw most of the dancers doing something other than dancing—either punching someone or getting punched by someone else. And I had just a few seconds to figure out what to do.

Why a few seconds? Because if you're following the Knight, you're not allowed on the elevator—that's reserved for actors and those with disabilities. Because of that I get on the elevator, usually in a very dramatic fashion, and everyone else takes the stairs and then finds me once they get on the floor. Or they find something else shiny to follow, but I usually have a pretty core group of people who stick with me, and they were going to be walking through a couple of fistfights to get to the elevator.

I swear to you, man, I knew this was going to happen, and then I saw it happen. I was worried that the fight would spill over into my crowd and, just as I had that thought, someone throws an errant punch and one of my group takes it straight in the face. It was a woman, that much was clear, and a nice-looking one to boot, who caught the fist in her left cheek and immediately went down. I remember thinking it was weird that their mask didn't come off but figured that was probably worse for the poor lady. That's probably some major damage to the face, like, the nose or the cheek, if I had to guess. Either way, whoever was with her immediately punches the person who punched his date, probably, and then everyone was off to the races. Like, the man in the Crypt just let it fuckin' rip and it turned into a Ballroom Blitz, you feel me?

Now, I don't want to sound too puffed up or anything but . . . I'm the Knight. Like *the* Knight. I was in character and I felt like someone had assaulted one of my people and that was not going to stand. So, when it became clear that security was doing something else, I jumped in and started screaming and trying to break up the fights. The "world" was already smashed to pieces, I wasn't worried about that. My bigger concern was we had four or five different fights in a place where it's real bad to have a fight. I only got one fight broken up before what I was worried about happening actually happened.

The Crypt has about a dozen graves peppered around the floor, and each of them are their own little effect. They each have lifts so the actors can "rise" from the grave as the Queen of the Damned descends, and that had already happened so you had this weird-ass scene where a guy made up to look like he was missing half his face and a woman made up to look like she had had her baby ripped out of her stomach were just standing there, not sure how to react to the melee in front of them. Totally natural reaction, but still, kind of funny if you think about it, them being so out of place. But the crypts, themselves, are supposed to close after the actors leave and that wasn't happening. They have these plexiglass partitions that open and close, which is the control room's problem. So, in effect, each crypt was, well, a six-foot drop into hell, more or less. Usually you have the actors standing next to the actual graves to "discourage" people from falling into them as the doors close. We never had anyone fall into a grave and if they did, shit, that would have been a rough ride down to the bottom.

First, you had the small lift that the actors "rise" on and that could smack you in the face or wherever. But the real danger is the fire effects. We have machines that emit flames at a *very* specific height during certain parts of the show from within the graves. The idea is the actors know where to stand to avoid getting turned into a crispy critter, then they can step out, the door closes and the actors can do one-on-ones or follow the Demon Dance or whatever they do. I'd seen it work a million times, and there was no need for anyone to worry as long as everyone was careful.

My dude, people were not being careful.

As I remember it, there were probably forty to fifty people in that room when I got off the elevator. Many, rightfully, had headed for another floor or, even better, the exits, but most of them were sticking around. I don't know if they thought the fight was a part of the show—hell, there is a part of the show where two guys fight for a long time—but I think it was pretty easy to tell things were going bad. People sort of realized it on their own time and started backing away, and I saw one guy who was headed straight for one of the open graves. Because I'm the Knight, I ran to try to stop him, but the poor guy never had a chance. He took a wrong step and ended up full-on falling down one of the graves.

The music is blaring at this point in the show so I didn't hear him scream or hit the floor or anything, but I make my way over there. I'm being careful because, I know, that flames are going to start shooting out of that grave at some point. The dude's date, or whatever, wasn't so lucky. She had seen him fall and ran over to the grave, laid down, but her hand out and tried to help him out. But the flames are on a timer and, yeah. She caught the stream of flame, full onto her body. She started rolling and rolling. I saw her tumble into the grave and then I got smacked in the face so I can't tell you what happened to them after that.

I don't know who smacked me, or why, but I'm one of the few people in this show not wearing a mask so I felt it. Fuckin' hurt, man. I mean, sure, I've been hit in the face before but when you absolutely don't know it's coming, it is a different sort of thing. You aren't braced so your body sort of follows your face and that's what happened with me. When I looked up at who had hit me, this dude takes off his mask and starts, like, fiddling with his fly. Like he's going to whip it out and piss on me, man. I don't know what he was going to do, but I wasn't, in any way, going to let him do anything like that, so I kicked him hard in the junk and he did not find himself on his feet for much longer after that. Honestly, I don't want to seem gross about it, but one of the biggest mysteries of that night, for me, was why that guy was trying to pull his dick out. It's one of those mysteries that will stick in my head forever, right next to Whang-Od and that time Bella put her legs behind her head.

So, I kick the guy, I get on my feet, and that's when it occurs to me my earpiece got knocked out. But that's not much of an issue because no one was talking even though the graves were open and the dancers were fighting the audience and a lady just fucking caught on fire. People should have been screaming into the headset at any one of those happenings but . . . silence. That was when I knew kind of what was up. I didn't bother looking for my earpiece after that. No need. What I was worried about, because I'm the Knight, was getting people out of there.

That's when I got my second big surprise of the night.

So, I start looking around for . . . help, I guess, and what I'm seeing is people are pretty happy about what's going on. Some of the fights were still going on but most had ended and it looked like our dancers had knocked the shit out of whoever it was they were fighting. There were a few other fights but the dancers were teaming up and taking care of business and so I watched for a minute. The Demon Dancers, which were six girls and two guys, and each one of them are incredibly athletic and talented and, like I said, I wouldn't want to get in a fight with any of them. Once they were done kicking ass, a couple of them turned to the audience and bowed. And people started clapping.

That was absolutely crazy. I could not figure out what was happening. Then one of the girl demons, one I didn't know so well, stood up on one of the tables they use for their dance and she did this thing I'll never forget. She had a knife. There are prop knives all over this show, but I knew the one she had, it was real. I can't tell you how I knew, I just knew, right? It gleamed a little different in the low light, catching the reds and the fires coming from the graves. She stands on the table and begins this dance I had never seen her do before. It was slow and it was sexy, lots of muscle control, which is one of the most impressive thing dancers can do, as far as I'm concerned. She gracefully pulled her leg above her head and was doing these spins I had never seen, just amazing shit, and the whole time she is making intense eye contact with this knife she had. Like the knife was the focal point of her dance, like her partner in this whole thing. The crazy part? She was doing this totally improvised thing, as far as I could tell, to the music and the light effects that were still happening.

Dude, I got chills. As it continued, I started to notice she had the eye of everyone on that floor and anyone who came on that floor looked and watched her. All eyes on the girl with the knife. Then, out of nowhere, she did this incredible jump from the table, knocked it over, and plunged the knife into some dude who started screaming.

Everyone jumped and I saw a couple of the dancers sort of flinch. The guy she stabbed, who was just one more audience member wearing a mask as far as I knew, stood up and started running but she ran after him and jumped on the audience member's back, wrapped her big strong dancer's legs around him and just . . . fucking stabbed him over and over and over. The audience member fell, and she rolled the person over and kept stabbing. I was kind of far away, but it was at this point that I heard screaming, and a few people run away because they realized what every cast member already knew—one of our dancers had killed someone. Murdered them during the fucking show, dude! I told you earlier I've got a lot of life left in me, but I had never seen a dead body up until that point, much less someone become a dead body. It was grade-A nutso content, my man, I can tell you.

After she got done stabbing that poor son of a bitch, which took longer than you think it would, the dancer stood up, held the knife over her head, and screamed at the ceiling. It didn't occur to me until later that she was screaming at one of the security cameras, which makes sense to me because, remember, I had figured out that whatever the problem was probably involved the control room either blowing up or getting taken over. But as she started screaming, the other dancers started screaming with her, all of them looking in the same direction. They were all screaming at the same thing and the audience, they started applauding at the screaming. It was . . . a moment. A weird moment. A powerful moment. I'll sure as shit remember it for a while.

Then, one of the Demon Dancers started doing her thing, again, to the music. The others joined her and, before I knew what was going on, they all started the show again as if there weren't a bloody dead guy on the floor, as if we hadn't all witnessed a murder, as if any of this wasn't the worst-case scenario for a show. I mean, what the fuck were they thinking, man? "Oh, I'll commit a murder and then start the show again like nothing happened"?

I'll tell you the truth, I never did learn what any of that was about. I'll be interested to read your book, man, because I don't know if the person the dancer murdered was an ex or a parent or a stranger or what. I don't even know if it was a man or a woman she killed. All I know is I've got a bar story for the ages.

As the Demon Dance kept going, I could tell it was different. The energy was different. There was more urgency to it, definitely, but there was something else. I'm not sure how to describe it other than to say the dance felt like . . . freedom. It felt like these girls and two guys had thrown off the shackles. Like, please don't judge me for this, but it's the best analogy I can come up with, but have you ever danced up on a girl who had just broken up with her boyfriend and then hits the clubs? Those girls are fucking crazy! No-booze-needed crazy. End-of-the-world crazy. Dancing like a curse had finally been lifted. It was the dance of six girls and two guys who had just broken up with their boyfriends. Like I said, freedom.

I did notice one other thing. Before they made their way to the staff stairs to head up to the Desert floor, Floor Five, I saw the stabby girl dance by one of the graves and kick the head of the flame emitter so it was pointed straight up.

I think we all know how that ended.

REDDIT POST ON R/COMEKNOCKING

I Was There on March 14, Ask Me Anything

PolyGoneGirl05
Posted on March 15

I have been a part of this community for the past six weeks, ever since I learned I was going to be attending *Come Knocking* on March 14. I can tell you about some of the events, but not all of them, just my experience. I will tell you I never made it to the sixth floor and can't answer any questions about the people jumping from the windows, or anything. I will say what I can about my experience and then will gladly answer any questions you have.

My experience was incredibly good until it wasn't. I was following the reverse show method and starting on the fifth floor and working my way down with the hope of ending on the sixth floor, like is frequently recommended for "maximum thematic impact" on this sub. When I realized things were wrong I was in the Depot of the Departed and only had one floor to go to get to safety. At no point do I feel like my life was in danger, but I feel terrible for all the people who died last night. I consider myself incredibly lucky.

I understand that I missed a lot of the terrible things that happened but am happy to tell you about what I saw. I am also going to be avoiding speculation. With this many fatalities and this many question marks, I feel it would be reckless. Other than that, please AMA.

What was the moment you realized something was wrong?
It was during the second cycle. I had spent the first cycle on 5 and 4 and was working my way down when I noticed something weird with one of the performers. Something would happen, like a smoke machine going off or some other effect, and they would react with shock or surprise, like they didn't know it was coming. Before I get a follow-up question, you can tell when someone is legitimately surprised, and that's what I was seeing.

That was particularly scary to see. I've always been told "if you're in a plane, don't panic until the flight crew panics." To me, that was the "flight crew" panicking. Then the fire alarms went off and everyone was running for the exits as fast as they could. I smelled smoke just a few seconds after the alarm was pulled but never saw any smoke or fire.

Not to be ghoulish, but what was the worst thing you saw?
The main thing I'd say is a lot of panic, which I didn't realize was so ugly to look at. I had never been in a fire up until last night but I had always hoped that it would be like a fire drill—that people would head toward the exits in an orderly manner. That's not what happened. I saw panic all around me and people pushing other people to get out of the way. I saw one woman get pushed over and her male friend trying to help her and the crowd just carrying him away. The look on his face was some mix of fear and intense effort to try to get back to his friend. It's something I'm never going to forget.

Did you get hurt?
I didn't suffer any serious injuries, but I did sprain my ankle and that was because I got pushed during the run for the exits. While I didn't suffer

any really serious injuries, I saw a lot of ugliness and a lot of selfishness all at once and that's going to stick with me for a while, I'm afraid. The worst, for me, was what I saw outside the building.

Did you see what started the fire?
No, I didn't.

Did you get to talk with any of the cast or backstage crew?
Not really. I will tell you this—when everyone was scared and running for the exits, I got shoved into one of the cast, it may have been the Knight, and I said "sorry." And he told me "It's okay. This happens all the time." I don't know if he was being funny or what. Looking back, he was probably making a joke to lighten the mood.

Did the show break down? Were the actors shaken?
Some were and some weren't, it was sort of a mix from what I saw. Like my above question, when I spoke to the guy who may or may not have been the Knight, he was cool as a cucumber. Others were full-on running for the exits along with the audience, which was weird to see. It was a mix of some people in masks and others who had thrown their masks off and were just trying to get out. Then there were people in full costume using the same exits as everyone else, which is weird. Maybe it was the closest exit, but I'm speculating. But yeah, the show completely broke down and the actors were shaken after the fire alarm went off.

I heard there was chaos outside the show on the street. Was that your experience?
Yes. Outside was a huge mess, almost worse than inside. I was able to avoid much of it because I didn't need medical attention, but there was

a line of people who needed help fighting each other to get it. I only saw it for a few seconds and I could tell it was ugly. It doesn't help that the neighborhood isn't the best, and there were a lot of onlookers who weren't helping the situation at all.

Did you know there was an active shooter at the show?
Not at the time but, thinking back, I definitely heard gunshots. The thing is the show was so loud and there was so much happening at any given time that a gunshot-type noise wouldn't have been out of place. When I heard about it later I put two and two together, but at the time I was only worried about getting out of there.

I'm sorry you went through this. I don't want to trivialize what happened, but this is a sub about *Come Knocking*, so I feel it's appropriate. Do you feel more or less connected to the themes of the show given what you went through?
This is a really deep question, thank you for asking it. I'll try to answer as best I can.

There are debates in this sub about what *Come Knocking* means. I remember reading (but I don't remember what conversation so sorry for the lack of credit) someone saying, "It's a show about life." I don't subscribe to that. I think, truthfully, it's a show about how ugly and terrible life is, and then that it ends, is the entire reason life is beautiful. I'm not saying that very well, but it's all over the show. The train actually says "nothing beautiful stays that way" in Latin. The Crypt has the poem, "Remember me as you walk by/as you are now so once was I/as I am now, soon you will be/so prepare yourself to follow me" in 5 places. I don't think it's about "life." I think it's about life ending and things ending and what that means, with a slight suggestion that maybe you should not take it for granted. That's my reading.

I don't feel that way after last night. I'm sorry, but I don't. I had never seen the show before and some people I had spoken with absolutely feel that way and, bless them for it. But what I felt last night wasn't "YOLO," it was "we're fucked." It was something beautiful being destroyed for me. So, to answer your question specifically, I feel less connected to the theme because what I saw was the opposite. Instead of something beautiful that will not last, I feel like I saw something beautiful being killed.

INTERVIEW 12
RODRIGO GIMENEZ

Come Knocking Cast Member

I do not talk well. Not in English or in Spanish. That is why I fight.

I do not fight, for real. I fake fight, but I use all my energy. I am very tired by the end of each night and I fake fight most nights. Because of all the fake fighting, my body has become very lean, very "buff," like they say. That is why I get many women trying to talk to me and that is why the group, what do you call them, Who's There? That is why they attacked me a few weeks before the bad night. I am lucky I was strong enough to fight them for real before they hurt me. They wanted to hurt me.

I will tell you about my job. Then I will tell you about the bad night.

I worked at *Come Knocking* even though I had never done plays before. The casting lady, she said they didn't want an actor. They wanted a fighter. I did MMA for a while, you know this? Mixed martial arts. I was okay, but I was never going to get rich fighting for real. I may have been hurt doing it, so when the casting lady talked to me, it sounded very good. She told me my job was to come up with a fight that looked real and looked mean and that me and another guy would fight the fight I came up with three times a night. It seemed like easy money to me, and the money was better than I was making where I worked. It was easy to say "yes."

What I did not know then, but I know now, is that theater people are some of the hardest motherfuckers in this country.

The dancers, they work until they bleed and break their bodies all the time. The tech people, they are always working and working fast. The directors, their head is always in the game. Hard work everywhere. When I saw that, I knew they would expect me to work that hard too. I tried very hard because everyone tried very hard.

I met Hao after I had worked out the first fight. He was very small and not very lean. I told him about how hard everyone worked and that he and I had to work very hard, too. He said he would, and he did. We worked very hard to get the fight to look mean and athletic and hard. I remember the day we showed it to the director. He said "full speed," and Hao and I smiled at each other. We did not know how to fight any other way. The director ended up being very happy.

There were others who could do the fight, but no one as good as Hao and me. I do not know why. One of the dancers told us we had "chemistry," but I am unsure. I want to say, so you do not get the wrong idea, that I am straight. I like women. Hao, I don't know, but it doesn't matter. He is a very good fake fighter, and that is all that matters to me.

You heard about the time I was attacked, yes? I do not need to tell you that when my body got as lean as it was, I got much attention from women. And men. But women mainly. Hao also got lean and also got attention for his body which was the first time in his life that he had felt that way. One night, we were fighting very well and sweating very much. Some nights, I am told that we "feel it" more than other nights, and this night, we were both "feeling it." As we fight, Hao begins to take his costume off, because we are very hot. Following him, I did the same. We did the fight very hard, and soon Hao took off all of his clothes. He is a crazy man. If I may say, that was brave of him as his manhood is not very big, but he was showing off his body. I understood that and wanted to do it, too. So I did. And we received very good notices for our naked fight. It was not something we planned and not something that happened every night. But some nights, out clothes came off, and that was okay.

This only made more women come to see us, and Hao and I were both very pleased about that. I was told by some person in the cast that I may have attracted or gone to bed with the wrong woman and that is why I was attacked. I cannot tell you if this is true. I can tell you, with the truth on my side, that I do not know why they attacked me the first time. All I know is after the attack I had a long talk with the director to make sure that my personal life would not be an issue anymore. I told him, "It was never an issue to me. I do not even know why they attacked me," and that's as good enough for him. He asked us to please continue fighting naked if we felt like it, which I agreed to do. Hao and I kept doing the fight and things continued until the bad night.

On the bad night, they came for me again. This time, I believe their goal was revenge for the first attack. During the first attack, it was a night we were "feeling it." They were able to surprise me, very much. When Hao and I are "feeling it," it is very hard to focus on other things. When they grabbed me, I was very confused for the first couple of seconds. Once my mind came back . . . I'm not sure how to say it, but once my mind came back to me, I realized I was being attacked. I attacked them back with anything available to me—my feet, then my fists, then pieces of the set. Hao also helped me with the attackers. At the end of our real fight, they were bloody and we were not.

This is something they did not forget.

The second time, I was not surprised. But I did not need to be. I will say that we had our clothes on this night, which was good because the five men that attacked me were very interested in my penis. I do not know why. But it . . . it is the same as the theory that I may have attracted the wrong woman. The five men, they came up on Hao and I and moved everyone else away. They did not speak, but we knew they were there. They stared at us. Hao stood by me. He did not have to do that, but he did, and I am grateful. He is my brother. Then the five men attacked at once.

I was grateful Hao was there. But Hao was a fake fighter and not a real fighter. I was a real fighter, and that was easy to see when the fight began. They quickly overpowered Hao, and one of the men put . . . plastic on his hands. Plastic so he could not move his hands. Zip ties, yes. Then they tried to do that to me.

I will tell you I am a good fighter, but not a great fighter. If I was a great fighter I would have made money fighting. But even a great fighter cannot take on four other fighters at one time. Once they had Hao on the ground, they were able to tackle me easily. I fought as hard as I could. I even kicked one of them very hard in the chest and he was having trouble breathing. But they tackled me and they put the zip ties on my hands and threw me into the Miller's Manor.

What was the audience doing? Some of them thought it was part of the show. Hao screamed at them, said, "Help us, they are attacking us" but no one believed him. They thought so little of Hao that they left one man outside to keep him on the ground and the other four men pushed me into the Manor.

The "Manor" is a joke. The joke is that "manor" is a fancy word, but where the Miller lives is plain and shabby. There are windows without glass where you can look into the Manor. There are two parts in our fight where Hao and I use the windows to escape each other. When it's my turn, I leap through the window and onto the concrete, which hurts every time I do it but is very impressive. I must be sure no one is in my way when I leap through the window. You do not need to know any of this, but I like telling you about the fight. I miss it. Very much.

The men take me into the Manor and one of them shows me a knife. It is not a small knife and, right away, I think, "How did they get a large knife into this place?" I still do not know. What I do know is they had a large knife and began to threaten me with it. They still did not speak and they still had their masks on which . . . which made me afraid. I do not like to say this. I am strong, but my fighting had failed. Men with masks, whose faces I would never see, were going to make me bleed. I do not like saying this, but I began shaking.

This made the men laugh. They pointed between my legs with the knife and laughed harder and I understood what they wanted to do. This made me panic and I started to fight again, but they were standing and I was on the ground. My fight did not work.

Then two of the men grabbed my legs and began to pull my legs apart. My arms were in zip ties. The man with the knife stayed close to my face. I could feel his breath, even through the mask. He said very simple words to me but words I will remember.

"I want you to watch," he said.

I do not know why he said this. But he took the knife and put the blade at my cheek. My cheek was very sweaty. He made a small cut and traced down my face, cutting the whole time. It was painful but I was more afraid. I very much did not want to lose my penis. The shame of it was terrible, and I began to cry. The man laughed harder. They began to make fun of me. Laughing and calling me names I do not wish to repeat, words about my race, words about the work that I do, words about how I must like men in bed.

While they were laughing, I realized that my zip ties were not on correct. They were loose. I believed that I could pull one hand free. I did not do it. But I noticed.

"We are going to cut your dick off and make you eat it," they said. Their words were terrible. Outside, I could hear Hao screaming and the man outside would hit him. Then he would scream more. Hao is not tall, but Hao is tough. He does not yield easily. Most days, he does not yield at all.

The man with the knife continued to trace the knife down my neck and my chest. Slowly. He drew blood many times but the cuts were never deep. This was to scare me, I think. He traced down my stomach, then raised the knife up and cut off my costume. It was early in the night, so I was wearing a tunic, but underneath the tunic was a pair of underwear that were made to look . . . old. Historic? Is that the right word? Made to look like a costume. It fit me very well. I believe the man thought, in his head, that he would cut the costume off easily. It was not easy. He had to take a little bit of time and I waited. I was scared but I was also acting more scared. I slowly pulled my hand from the zip ties to see if anyone would notice. They did not.

I waited. And waited. I knew when I was going to strike. They finally cut my costume away, and the moment I felt air on my penis, I started punching as hard as I could. For a moment, I thought I was going to win. My first hits knocked two of the men to the ground, and I kicked the man with the knife so hard he dropped his weapon. I am not sure where I kicked him, but I heard the knife on the ground. The men were screaming in pain. It was a beautiful sound. The fourth man was tougher. He tackled me, which Hao had done many times but this hurt much more. I slammed my back into the wall and it hurt, very much. It took me a moment to get back on my feet and by the time I had, three men were on me again. The fourth man came a moment later. He had found his knife.

"Keep your eyes open," he said. "Or I'll cut them out."

I shut my eyes.

I felt a hand on my penis. Pulling it so they could make the cut. I felt the knife, moving slowly. Trying to make me more afraid. I remember tears falling from my eyes.

I do not remember exactly what happened next but I remember hearing screaming. Much screaming. Screaming that was not pain. Screaming like someone makes when they are about to get into a fight.

The screaming was female.

When I opened my eyes the Demon Dancers were fighting the five men. Hao was also fighting as best he could with his hands zip tied together. I remember being impressed by how he used his feet. He kicked the mask off one of the men, and I saw his face. He was young. Young and ugly.

The next thing I do not want to tell you, but I believe the woman who I am speaking of is dead. Because I believe she is dead, I am proud to tell you of what she did for me and what happened after. If she was not dead, I would never tell you about what she did.

The man with the knife—I never learned what he was called—was stabbed. Anna Rodriguez was the one who stabbed him. She is a friend. We have much in common, including our language. I do not remember how she got the knife from him, but she did, and she stabbed him. She did not stab him once. She stabbed him many, many times. I saw her stab him in the back and when the man turned around, she stabbed him in the front. Then she pulled off his mask and stabbed him in the face. The man did not scream when the knife was in his face, but when she pulled it out to try to stab him again, he screamed. Loud.

I never wanted to see something like that, but after I saw it, I felt good. I felt like cheering. Like this woman warrior had saved me and the devil who was going to stab me had tasted justice. And justice tasted like a knife in your fucking face, man.

The man kept screaming and I jumped up and kicked the man, hard. I still had my sandals on, so I did not break anything. I kicked and watched as the man bled on the floor. I remember his face, the look of surprise on his face. His eyes were very big and wide before he began to cough and choke. Good. I will tell you now, I am glad that man suffered and I am glad that man died and I am forever grateful to Anna for being a demon warrior who saved this poor sinner from a life without a penis.

I was so grateful that I joined the Demon Dance. Hao did as well. I don't know why, but he had lost his clothes as well. I think he took them off himself. He is a crazy man. That would not surprise me. I lined up behind a dancer and Hao lined up behind me and we danced and yelled. I screamed and laughed. The dancer in front of me had on a black wig, like the rest of them. She was in a very small outfit. Not much of her was covered. From behind, she was very attractive and I danced closer to her and closer to her. She was happy with my attention. We broke off from the dance, found a dark corner and had the best sex of my life. I never saw her face, but I can tell you that it was as if my penis knew it had almost been lost. It was the most glorious sex anyone ever had. My demon lady screamed and I screamed and we came together. We did not care for the audience. We did not care for the dead man in the Miller's Manor. We cared about the moment, about the flesh.

I do not know why I told you this. You did not need to know.

There are other things that happened that night. Things that were just as bloody as what I told you. I will not tell you these things. I will not tell you because they involved coworkers, people who are alive and who could face . . . problems if I were to tell you about them. You have my story, which is enough. You have more of my story than I wanted you to have. I am told I don't talk but when I do, I talk too much.

I will say one more thing. *Come Knocking* has closed forever. My time of fake fighting is done. I miss it. I felt as if I was hired to do a job that only I could do, a job that needed me. The fight was not in the show when it was in New York. It was new to Los Angeles, new because of me. I take pride in that. There is honor in that. And I wish there were another show that needed a fake fighter. No other theater will take me after *Come Knocking*. I do not get as many women talking to me, either. Those were good days and now they are gone.

    I will say this. If my coworkers tell you stories about a naked man performing violent acts, just know that it was Hao. He is a crazy man.

INTERVIEW 13
ANONYMOUS

Member of Who's There

Author's Note: Due to the possibility of prosecution and negative impact to their life, this interviewee has asked for anonymity. While I am loath to grant anonymity as a matter of course, her testimony speaks to several key motivations and moments during the show that I was unable to find in other aspects of my reporting. I have independently verified her story that she was at the show and several other key facts to the point where I am comfortable sharing her story as part of this text.

If I knew how this was going to turn out I never would have gone along with it.

That's a stupid thing to say. Like, anyone who's ever done anything bad ever would say the same thing or something close to the same thing. It's not like anyone says, "Hey, you know what'd be fun? How about I knock over the first domino that leads to a bloodbath?" I think why people say it all the time is it's true. If I knew what they were going to do, I'd . . . well, I know myself. I would have cheered for them. I just would have done it from my couch instead of almost getting murdered.

I was part of the message board, and I was a part of the first couple meetups. Ever been to an internet meetup? Getting together IRL. It's weird, man. No one ever lives up to your expectations. Everyone's fatter and weirder than you expect, no one is as cool as they are online. Well, almost no one. I've done it a few times with some of the Discord servers I'm a part of, which I'm not going to go into. But I will tell you this—none of them were as fun as Who's There, and none of them were quite as disappointing in real life.

The forum was fun and frothy and full of in-jokes that, once you got the hang of it, were really clever and cool. That's the big part of any online community, I guess. But a weird thing I noticed about this community that made it fun but also kind of spooky was how it was set up. No one knew the admins. They never posted, they rarely explained themselves when there was action to be taken, but everyone had immense respect for them. Their word was law in that forum. Law from up on high. Couple that with a group of people who were really into conspiracies, which isn't really saying anything since most people on the internet are into conspiracies of one kind or another, but it was just a weird mix of people. That was a red flag for me, because I had a friend who was in a cult once, and it sort of reminded me of that. I knew it was weird, but not weird enough to stop posting.

The first meeting was when I realized why the forum was the way it was. That was the day I met Reilly Pegg.

Reilly was a tall guy. Six foot six, maybe. Lean build, like shockingly so. I heard him say, "I'm the same size as Michael Jordan," whenever anyone asked him how tall he was, which was often. You never really think of how many times a tall person has to talk about being tall, but he was tall. And I liked him right away because even though he was skinny, he was strong. Like, have you ever seen any of those videos where the bodybuilder goes up against the person who is actually strong, and the actually strong guy beats them in arm wrestling or whatever? That reminded me of Reilly. You knew there was power inside that guy even if he didn't look like he was powerful. It's hard to put into words.

He locked in on me during the first meeting and we made out that night and had sex the night after that and, before you know it, we were a couple. But Reilly—he was always Reilly, never had a nickname or anything like that—insisted on keeping "us" under wraps. He said he had a plan for the group and if they knew we were sleeping together it would make it harder for the plan to happen. Which was bullshit, because, as I bet you can guess, he was sleeping with between two and four other girls when we were together. Know how I found out? Herpes. That's how I found out. More cultish behavior, but I don't know. This dude broke all my alarm bells—a line I stole from my therapist.

I would ask him about this "plan" of his, because, if there's one thing I know from being on the internet for twenty years, it's that no one has a plan and everyone is just bouncing around trying to waste a few minutes of precious time with something amusing before reality comes back and hits you in the face. So I asked him about the "plan," and he would tease me and give me hints but he never told me. "You'll know it when you see it," he said.

So with that incredible amount of context, when he told me the "plan" was happening, I was like, "let's fucking go!" That's how everyone felt because whatever "the plan" was had been teased for so long. It's hard to describe if you're not on the forum every day, but the forum was so buzzy and so fun that when the admins shined their countenance upon you, you just sort of went with it. Which is how I ended up smuggling knives into *Come Knocking*.

Jesus, that sounds terrible when you say it out loud.

I had three jobs that night. March 14. My first job was to smuggle the knives in, my second job was to mess with the cast on the third floor, and then my third job was to go to the top floor and meet up with the rest of the group. There was a ton of speculation about what Reilly and the admins had planned, but the best guess we all had was that we were going to mess up the show in some way, cause a bunch of chaos, and then all meet on six for a group picture that we could post to the forum. Whenever I asked Reilly about whether this idea or that idea was the right one, he'd always say the same thing: "You have no idea, babe. Just go along for the ride." Every time, same words, same cadence, everything. Not to repeat myself but if I had known . . . Jesus.

For the record, he also didn't tell me about his history with the show, which would have raised a lot more red flags. That came later. I remember being really shocked to learn he had been in the show at one point in New York. That was nothing compared to what came out after.

I don't really want to go into that. I don't know why, but it hurts too much. It hurts because of how stupid I feel. I need to talk about something else.

I'll talk about the knives. The security at *Come Knocking* is just like all security in this country—you can get around it if you think about it for two seconds. In his specific case, they build a show in an existing building with about fourteen entrances from the main floor. You watch the building for a day, you see who goes in and out and when they do it, you mark which doors are unlocked, you put the knives in a backpack, then you put your head down and act like you're supposed to be there. You ever heard of the ladder trick? Basically, you can get into any building you want if you wear a work uniform and carry a ladder. I dressed down, walked with purpose and—boom—open doors. No problem.

Was I curious what they were going to do with the knives? Of course. I even asked Reilly. Know what he said? "You have no idea, babe. Just go along for the ride."

"I get it," I said. "But are you going to stab someone?"

"You have no idea, babe. Just go along for the ride."

I couldn't get anything more out of him than that and, at the time, I was pretty sure he wasn't actually going to kill anybody. At the time. I can imagine the comments now. "How could she not have known?" "Is she an idiot?" "She knew and wanted people to die." I can't convince you of why I did it other than to say my community and my boyfriend wanted me to do something so I did it. Again, I feel so fucking stupid, but it's the truth. I didn't think they were going to kill anyone and I smuggled knives in. Both are true.

I put the knives behind the toilet of the main restroom in the main bar. They were there for anyone to find if they were looking for them.

Second, I was supposed to mess with the cast on the third floor. I was by myself on that one and I was the only "agent" on that floor. We had people on each floor at the start of the night, and we weren't supposed to say what our jobs were, but we all did. Kyle was supposed to ruin the Human Jubilation in the basement by distracting the girl who was supposed to "die" and set the whole show into motion. Jackie was on Floor One messing with the lights on the train. I was curious how it was all going to work but, you know... "You have no idea, babe. Just go along for the ride." So I did.

But, truthfully, when I got down there I didn't really feel like going along for the ride anymore.

I can tell you exactly what happened. I had never been to the show. Not once. How I ended up on that forum is another story for another day but I had never been. After I delivered the knives and started walking through, I was... impressed. Like, when you're posting in the forum and you know all the inside jokes and all that, it's just second nature that these are evil people doing something stupid and they deserve all the trouble they're going to get, especially after they send someone to spy on us and fuck with us. But once I actually *saw* the thing, I couldn't take my eyes off it. I don't want to lie to you and say I "got it" but it was definitely cool.

I wondered around the third floor. What I was supposed to do was mess with this one particular performer. The way Reilly explained it was they were doing this shitty version of Dante's Inferno where the corrupt and the liars were subject to torture. I don't know, I never read the thing. But I was supposed to find the guy hanging upside down on this wheel, find the brake, disable it, and spin him until he puked. Again, I'm aware how all of this sounds now. Just like "smuggling in knives," it makes me sound like I wanted violence, and I want to look you square in the eye and tell you I didn't. I wanted to ruin the show. I wanted these people who thought they were so special taken down a peg. I wanted LOLs in the comments. I wanted something to brag about. I didn't want blood. I got blood, but I didn't want it.

I go to the third floor and there's this just massive screen with the three heads of the devil on it and it's sort of got this 3D projection sort of thing going, like you can tell it's fake, but the lighting made it look really good. And there, suspended probably twenty feet in the air—or it looked like twenty feet but might not have been that high—was a man trapped in a block of ice. You could tell it was a person because their movements were... it's hard to put into words. It was a performance. I stood there and I watched that guy scream and fight and be tortured—he was naked, did I say he was naked? But he was obscured by the ice so you couldn't full on see his cock. Anyway, I watched that tortured naked man and the devil heads and the dancers around me and the fire behind me and I didn't want to do it. I just lost the mojo. Was not in the mood. And I made the decision, right there, that what we were doing was stupid and I didn't want to do it anymore.

Then the block of ice fell from the ceiling and shattered on the ground, and everyone started screaming.

The "block of ice" was fake, obviously, but it looked real from up above. Once it plummeted to the ground, you could tell it was fake, but that there was very real blood inside. The guy . . . poor guy . . . he was either unconscious or dead, I didn't know which, but he landed probably five feet from me, and pieces of that fake ice block went everywhere. You could, um, really see the blood against the blue of the fake ice. I kind of went up and put my hand on it to see if there was anything I could do, but that's when the fire started up. The room is divided, half fire and half ice, and once the ice fell all the fire got turned on full blast on the other side of the room. I hear screaming and look to see people on fire. Not person, people. Multiple—three, maybe four. I don't know who they were or anything, but they were on fire. And when I turned around the guy inside the ice had come to and started to scream. Then the music was playing full blast and the devil quit working and a few security guards ran in with fire extinguishers. It was chaos, and no one really knew what to do or what was going on.

That's when I fully realized that Reilly was right. I had no idea, babe. And whether I liked it or not, I was along for the ride.

I whipped off my mask and tried to figure out how to get the ice open but an actor or someone in some costume shoved me out of the way. I landed on my ass and before I knew it, there were feet all around me, just feet and legs all of them kicking at me just over and over and over. I got my hand stepped on, and that hurt, and I got kicked in the head and that hurt, but I was able to get up. The cast member had managed to get the big block of ice open and just . . . lots of blood. So much. I thought about it later and if there was a spot big enough for him to dance around in while in that ice block, he didn't stand a chance when he dropped. Not a chance. I don't know if that guy lived or not, but they pulled him off somewhere.

Again, I don't know a lot of specifics, like how many people were on that floor or anything. But I do know after the fire flared and the people caught on fire, there were only a handful of people left in there. Some must have thought it was part of the show, I don't know, but there were still a few people lingering around to see all the effects going off at once. It was just fucking insanity. Fire bursts and loud music and stuff falling from the ceiling, all the while the Devil was looking above everything and laughing and laughing. The smell, also. Thick, like a barbecue, but bitter and dense. It was all I could do to not throw up.

Through all of it, I was able to hear someone screaming and, out of curiosity or something else, I followed the sound. And that's when I saw him.

Remember that guy I was supposed to harass? The guy strapped to a wheel that was supposed to represent some sort of torture of the damned? There he was, on the wheel. Apparently, the straps that kept him on the wheel weren't old-fashioned leather or whatever, but were controlled by the control room and, by the look of things, all hell had broken loose in the control room so all hell could break loose on the third floor. I saw the guy on the wheel and he was just spinning and screaming, spinning and screaming. I could see, through flashes of light, that he had already thrown up a bunch and that his color was off. He looked like a ghost on the wheel and by the looks of it, he was trapped and the wheel was not going to stop spinning anytime soon. Also, he was tucked away a little bit, or at least the lighting made it seem that way.

I can't tell you when I made the decision to get involved and try to save him. It wasn't conscious. It was just something that . . . I don't know. Something a decent person would try to help with. Like, I heard this thing once, I forgot where I heard it, that if you are a person and you go to another person and ask for food, ninety-nine times out of a hundred you'll get help, but if you're a group of people asking for food, it's fifty-fifty. I may have butchered the point. Anyway, I decided to help this poor dude who was going to die if I left him on the wheel. When he saw me come up, he immediately started talking to me.

"Oh thank Christ."

"Something is wrong. Please help me."

"You need to hurry."

It was all stuff like that, but there were two problems. The first was he was spinning pretty fast, and I had no idea how to slow him down, and I didn't have any tools to slow him down with. The second I didn't realize right away. In the room there was this track and on the track were a bunch of effects. I honestly don't know what they were supposed to be doing, maybe just creating the feeling of space in the room or something, I don't know, I'm not a theater person. Look, bottom line, there was this flamethrower, and it was on the track and every time it passed my man on the wheel, it got closer and closer to blasting his spinning ass with flames. I can, again, speculate and say that maybe something in the control room would have shut off the flames or moved the spinning wheel or I don't freakin' know. It seems like a really bad idea for the show but, like I've said, I wouldn't put anything past the sick people who ran *Come Knocking*.

I don't even know if he realized the thing about the fire and I'm willing to forgive him a lack of situational awareness. Poor bitch was strapped to a wheel and spinning fully around once every second or two. I'm willing to forgive a lot in that circumstance. But I do think he knew he was in danger and if he didn't, the panic in my face probably clued him in.

Back to problem one. I asked him if there was any way to slow him down and he said something about a "panic button" but he was hard to understand. Plus, the wheel, itself, was very small and the floor was very, very dark and they had taken my phone at the door. No flashlight. My only option was to flail around in the dark trying to find a button that may or may not exist while dodging arms and legs every second or two. Not a great plan. So I got the idea to try to wedge something into the wheel, right? There were plenty of possibilities and I landed on a prop stick that was lying on the floor. I don't know where it came from and, when I picked it up I realized it was made of . . . not wood . . . but time was a factor and I needed to try something.

The problem was the wheel only had hand and ankle straps, so there was nothing to wedge the fake stick against. Still, I wanted to try something so I jammed the stick in between the guy's legs, hoping whatever motor was spinning the wheel wasn't that strong. I thought I got lucky for a second, and I was able to slow him down for a couple of seconds but I hadn't thought what to do after that. I needed both hands to fight against the motor and he was tied up. This was a two-person job so I started to scream for help, but the music was too loud and there were too few people in there. The whole time this poor dude is screaming at me, "Thank you, don't let go!" "Find the button." Stuff like that.

When I let go after a few seconds, he let out a scream that was . . . memorable. Like, I had never heard a scream like that. It was . . . shit, sorry. It was defeat and pain and anger and hopelessness and more. I can still hear that scream. It comes into my brain a lot. I remember it more than the other scream . . .

I tried the stick again but the same thing happened—stop and go, stop and go. The guy kept pleading with me to find the button so the third time I stopped him I asked him where the button was. He told me what side it was on, and I told him, "Okay, I'm going to let go and try to find the button. You're almost out of here," and he asked me my name. I told him. Then I counted to three and let go. I was frantically searching and, sure enough, the button was right where he said it was and it worked just like he said it would. He slowed down and stopped. He, um, he couldn't stop thanking me. Just a constant stream of "oh Jesus, thank you . . . oh God, thank you" and saying my name over and over. I stood up and started to help him out of the straps. I had gotten one arm free and was bending over to grab his foot when the flamethrower went off.

It set my hair on fire. My hair and a little bit of the jacket I was wearing. That was bad. I ran around and beat at my hair with my fists. I . . . I've never felt anything like that before. The pain wasn't just intense, but it was everywhere. I thought for a second that I was completely on fire because the pain was so much, but it was just the top of my head and my hands because I had put my hands up to my head and some of the fuel that the flamethrowers had used had gotten on my hands. I beat at my head over and over and it went out, but not before giving me third degree burns over about 30 percent of my fucking head. I . . . I can't grow hair on most of my head anymore and the scars go down to my forehead and down as far as my eyebrow on my right side.

I was on the ground, gasping for air, when I smelled him.

Poor guy. I . . . I never learned his name. But he knew mine. He had been able to get free of the wheel. That means, to me, he was a tough son of a bitch because even while he was on fire, he was working the strap on his legs or just flailed so hard that he got free. He didn't die on that wheel. I will tell you, I think that counts for something. He was trapped on that wheel but he didn't die on that wheel.

But he did die.

It was worse than I thought anything could be. The worst thing I've ever seen because it wasn't just blackened skin and shit like you see in the movies. His costume had burned into his skin and they had become one . . . thing. One oozy, blackened thing. His hair was gone and parts of him were still on fire and he was alive but he wouldn't be for long. His hands were twitching and curled up, he was shaking and shaking. There was blood, I don't know where from. And he was in so much pain. He couldn't scream but I could tell, he showed me how much pain he was in with his eyes and his hands and the fucking sounds he made. He showed me pain I didn't know was possible, pain that was beyond my ability to understand. Fuck. Just . . . fuck.

I'm going to need a second.

Author's Note: Anonymous took twenty-five minutes to collect herself and returned to the interview.

I'd like to finish this, please. I'm through the worst of it.

After that poor guy lost consciousness, I sort of stumbled my way toward where I thought that bar was. I was wrong, I ended up getting turned around and I got lost for a second. I've never felt more panic in my life. I was lost in the dark with everything going wrong and having just watched a dude burn to death. I was crying, I was hurting, I was scared. And then I found the way to the bar and it was the weirdest damn thing I've ever seen. This was probably . . . fifteen minutes after "the operation" had started, but when I went to the bar, no one was there. Not a single person. No security, no staff, no bartenders, no traumatized audience members, no tech staff, none of my people, no one. It was empty. And while I was in there, I heard a voice. His voice. It was over some speaker system, I don't know where. But I remember what he said.

"I'm disappointed in you."

He used my name. Reilly had watched the whole thing. It's very well known that he was in the control room and all the death and carnage he caused. But at the time, I didn't know that. I don't know what I thought, but hearing him call me out like that made me run to the exit like the devil was chasing me.

Then I hit the street and, for some reason, I started screaming. I don't even know why I was screaming, but I did. There was a guy who had an Uber sticker in his window and I jumped in his car and said, "I need to go to the hospital," and he saw my head and my tears and . . . he drove. I went to the hospital. I got treatment. I spilled my guts to the cops. I got a suspended sentence, and now I wear a wig and go to therapy twice a week.

Like I said, if I knew what was going to happen, I would have never gone along with any of it.

INTERVIEW 14
BELLA EVERS, INTERVIEW 2

Cast Member, *Come Knocking* in Los Angeles

Author's Note: In our first interview, Ms. Evers had firmly drawn a boundary that she would not talk about the events of March 14. She contacted me several months after our initial interview and asked to meet at a bar in SoHo. She gave me consent to record our conversation and later agreed for her interview to be used. As such, I have broken her interview up into two conversations for clarity and to fill in blanks in the timeline.

Look, dude, I was hesitant to do the first interview, but I fuckin' did it. You told me "I just wanted background, you don't need to tell me about your experience that night" because, seriously, my experience that night was fucking terrible, right? TERR-I-BLE! Traumatizing, life defining, a "send-you-to-therapy-forever" type of experience. All that shit.

But then I heard you got hold of some of Punky's voice memos to her boyfriend—I have some really dark suspicions on how you got those, by the way—and the universe was telling me, clearly, I had to defend my friend. So, here I am, but I have a few caveats for our conversation, my dude. Agree to them or pound fuckin' sand.

Condition 1: I am only talking about Punky, because, current situation notwithstanding, I am not a snitch. Anything anyone else did is off-limits. Hard stop.

Condition 2: I am only talking about Punky. I'll add myself and my perspective when I need to but Punky is immune from prosecution, currently, on account of her being a corpse. I am neither a corpse nor immune from prosecution. You're gonna respect that, or I fuckin' walk.

Final condition: You pay the tab so far and keep it open. I am not doing this shit sober.

Agreed? Good. Let me tell you about Punky. She was one of a kind.

Remember our last interview? When I told you us "professional weirdos," or whatever I said, were a messed-up little family. Yeah? Well Punky was . . . Punky. I don't even know what I'm saying. She was one of us, but she was firmly in the middle, right? She wasn't the "mom" and she wasn't the experienced one, and she wasn't the . . . anything. She was a fucked-up girl just like we were all fucked-up girls, and she did her job, and she was damn good at it. Damn good. And I liked her because she was all those things without being, like, pretentious about it. She was real, she was earthy, she came by all her fucked-up-ness honestly. She was a great hang. She was a hugger. She was a hell of a dancer. And she and I shared a lot of late nights and a lot of deep conversations and a lot of substances and she was my friend. She was a good girl.

But we were all fucked up in our own way. And when you're wearing a mask to hide your true self, that mask is going to slip sometimes.

In the weeks before March 14, Punky's mask was slipping.

The whole reason I tell you this is because I'm about to paint the picture of a bloodthirsty total fucking lunatic and I want you to know that's not all she was. She was somebody's lover, she was somebody's daughter. She loved her mother. Her father beat her until she was ten and then left to be a full-time alcoholic, and she overcame that as best she could. She met a guy who was good to her, and she was extremely good to him, except when she wasn't. I loved her and I had a good reason to love her. It wasn't any of this "lost puppy" sort of shit. She was a very real, very full, very flawed, and very awesome person, and if you represent her as anything other than such I'm going to find you and stick something sharp in your eyeball. Clear? Clear.

So, yeah, she went absolutely crazy and killed some people. I'm not going to speculate why other than what I've already told you. Things were bad in the show—we had that group who was trying to fuck with us—but it was that other thing we talked about. That feeling that everything was going downhill and we were all just hanging on until we couldn't anymore. If you ask me why she turned violent and why we all followed her, it was that she finally let go. Like so many of us. I mean, how many times have you thought, *I can't do this anymore. I can't make it another week. I'm gonna lose it.* And then, what happens if you actually do? What happens when you let go? What happens when you lose it? I think Punky is the answer to what happens. She just happened to lose it in a place where other people were actively trying to hurt her. It's the best possible scenario to lose it, I suppose.

    I told you I had been pushed down the stairs and that I had strongly considered quitting, and that much is very true. I even went to the casting director and told her I couldn't do it anymore, and she asked me to give her a couple more weeks to find another dancer, if I was serious. I told her I was serious but don't go looking quite yet which means I wasn't really serious although I was kind of serious . . . shit, man, I didn't know what I wanted. I just wanted to dance and to scream and to do my thing without the constant threat of physical and emotional violence, and I told the casting director this show couldn't offer me that anymore. If they could offer me a safe environment, I'd be happy to stay. She told me to hang tight and she'd have some conversations. A few days later was March 14, so I guess they were more full of shit than a goat colon.

    I worked the night before, too, and don't remember Punky being any different than she normally was. I mean, there were a few incidents and things were tense, but there wasn't any markers that made me think she was about to turn into a blood-soaked warrior queen. Then again, there are never signs, are there? You never get any warning. All you get in this sick country is a body count and then they release the manifesto online. You either never see it coming or you see it coming and you're too wrapped up in your own shit to do anything about it. If I'm going to admit a sin to you, Mr. Reporter, it's that I was way too wrapped up in myself. Way too "woe is me" and not "woe is all of us." If I had reached out a little bit, then yeah, maybe I could have made a difference. As it stands, I cheered Punky on as she lost her mind.

Yeah, another round please. Same thing. He's buying.

You know where the Demon Dance starts, right? A lot of people who follow the show thinks it starts in the basement after the Human Jubilation and goes to the fifth floor and stops because the Demons are not allowed in the Garden. It's all very woo woo and symbolic. What I bet you don't know is only about half of the actual dancers ever see the basement. That's its own thing with its own effects and its own cast who move around, but about half of us start in the bar. Not in the bar but at the offstage area behind the bar, and the dance actually starts there and moves up and up and up. On nights where things are particularly bad or particularly good we will all gather in the bar, do a shot with someone in the audience while writhing all around them, and then kick it. Alcohol is wonderful like that. Good for the good, better for the bad.

The reason I bring it up is because this was one of those nights we all took shots and that's when I noticed something was up with Punky. We had found our "mark," the guy we were going to be all friendly with before the dance actually started, but she hung back and, like, kept drinking. Which is a very Punky thing to do, but not so good if you're about do several hours of really athletic, intricate dance. I go over to her and I ask her what's up as she's holding her third shot in her hand. She says she's getting very bad vibes about tonight and to fuck off, which is our little code for "please leave me alone to be with my thoughts, dear friend." I respect that.

We start our dance and, for the first floor, everything is hunky fuckin' dory. Goes like it always goes, which is to say I'm starting to sweat and my thighs are starting to burn but it's still kind of the "warm-up" phase. Still plenty of show to go.

I started to notice things were off when we got to the third floor, but it wasn't anything major, yet. For context, we spend, like, ten minutes or so per floor, forty minutes total, which gives us ten minutes on either side of each cycle to catch our breath and reset. Sometimes we can address problems that have occurred, right? Just basic theater stuff. Well, I was noting a couple things we were going to have to discuss. On [Floor] Three, usually we'll run into the Knight, who is a total fuckin' douchebag, by the way, and some of us will seduce him and grab on him and all that. But he wasn't where he was supposed to be and if you're not where you're supposed to be, it's usually because something has gone wrong. So, I clocked that.

But I noticed Punky was kind of freaking out. It's not anything an audience would have noticed, truthfully. Not even if you've seen the show a few times. But if you've seen the show hundreds of times, like all of us had, it was pretty clear she was struggling. She was late to her mark a few times. She was breathing harder than usual. And then I noticed why. Some of the parts of the set weren't working. God, I'm sorry to have to keep doing this but there are rotating sets all over this damn show that allows for different elements to appear at different times. When they don't turn, it adds seven or eight steps onto some of our moves, and that makes for blown timing, expending more energy than you're used to, that kind of thing. It sucks, but I'm also noticing other people not on their marks and just other little things going wrong. But we keep dancing. Because we always keep dancing, right?

We dance up to the Crypt, and that's when things start to go really wrong. And really weird.

We bust into our area as a group, because we like to make a big entrance, you know, and immediately someone from offstage is hissing at us. This has never happened before, and we're all trying to hear what the dude is saying without breaking the world. He's hissing the same thing over and over, over and over. So, finally, I dance a little closer to him and am able to hear "Comms are down!" I dance back to my spot and tell all the girls what he said and . . . like, so what? I remember thinking at the time, why do I need to know that?

Then Penelope splattered all over the pavement and it all sort of made sense.

I don't want to speak ill of the Queen of the Damned, but Penelope was a stuck-up bitch, okay? I'm not saying she deserved what happened to her. Not at all, but just because she had some truly next-level makeup skills did not give her the right to be all uppity about it. She never hung out with us and there were always rumors that she bad-mouthed the dancers and said that her effects were some of the best in the show, that kind of shit. If you're pulling in your own direction you're not pulling together, and theater like the kind we were doing, you all needed to pull together to even have a chance. So, I'm sorry that happened to her, that's no way to die, but . . . karma, I guess. I'm sorry if that's a fucked-up thing to say, but consider the source.

When she hit, we all stopped. Not one of the Demon Dancers screamed or cried, we all just stopped. Which is a big deal, don't get me wrong, the show must go on and all that, but there was this beat where we were all just staring at her. Then the pool of blood started forming around her head.

I can't tell you what all the girls were thinking. I can tell you what I was thinking and what I was thinking was "this was going to happen eventually" and I don't mean *Come Knocking*. I meant . . . this is hard to get at, but the type of theater I was doing was risky in a bunch of different ways. There is a razor-thin line between some of the things I had done in the name of "performance" and actual assault, you know? A razor-thin line between pretending and doing. In that moment, I saw and I understood what was on the other side of that line. So "this was going to happen eventually" was what went through my head.

Two dancers away from me, something in Punky's head must have snapped.

Anders, who is this tall, golden-haired Scandinavian god of a man who won't give me the time of day, ran to take care of what was left of Penelope, and I saw Punky say something to him. Then she ran at somebody in the audience and punched him right in the fucking face. A couple of the girls ran over to see what the hell she was doing, myself included, and when we got there, we saw why Punky had punched him. The dude had a knife. Presumably he was trying to stab her. I don't know if she punched him first and then he tried to stab her or he tried to stab her and then she punched him but what mattered, at that point, was a bunch of things clicked into place.

Those people who were fucking with the show had taken it to the next level.

Chances are good they were responsible for what happened to Penelope.

We were no longer in a performance. We were in a fucking fight.

Every single one of the Demon Dancers understood what was happening, I'm pretty sure. I mean, I'm not in their heads but everyone acted as if they understood those things. Every single one of us had been dancing together for a long time and understood certain things without having to talk. I figure every single one of us knew there were more saboteurs and more knives and more danger in the audience then we ever thought possible. And every single one of us followed Punky's lead and started smacking bitches around.

Look, could we have been more discreet? Yeah. Did some people get hit who didn't need to get hit? Maybe, which is bad considering what happened to that lady a few days before. Do I give one good inflation-adjusted fuck? I do not.

Yes. Keep them coming. I'll do your special this time, the Jack and lemonade? Bring two and whatever he wants. Thanks.

I don't have anything dramatic to tell you like "once she showed us the knife, everything changed," because it didn't. It was so strange. We still danced and we still, like, performed parts of the show because of muscle memory, I think. We still hit marks. We were still performers. But whenever anyone got a little too close to us, Punky would punch them or shake a knife at them and they would back off. Except for that one guy.

So Angus, that piece of shit, he had finally showed up about three minutes late, which is an eternity in theater time, and about the time he showed up and brought the gaggle of followers with him, the guy had made himself known. He was in a mask, obviously, but he had a knife as well and was standing in front of Punky. He wasn't like "come on!" or anything like that. He was just standing there, dressed in black, holding a knife and not moving. He blocked the whole Demon Dance, and I don't know how to say it other than to say his intentions were crystal clear, okay? He had seen us take some of the power back and he was here to put a stop to it.

Thing is, poor asshole did not know that they had broken Punky in half and she wasn't going to back down. At this point, she would have run into a gun or a knife or a bull or I don't fucking know, man. She was out of her mind, and this dude was giving her the perfect opportunity to do something I think she'd been thinking about doing for a long time.

That's my long way of saying the dude didn't stand a chance. Even before he took off his mask and made a little "come on" motion with his hands. Stupid motherfucker.

Punky did a full-on leap onto the dude and wrapped her legs around his midsection, like they were in a porno or something. That's really my only frame of reference for what I was seeing, sorry if it's uncouth. Again, consider the source. Anyway, legs around his midsection, knife in his face, as near as I could tell. It was dark and there was a lot of commotion, obviously, but from what I could see she got him considerably better than he got her. Which is to say Punky took a knife to the side but that guy took fifteen or so stabs right to his face and chest area. Even in the low light I could see all sorts of things were going wrong with the guy. Just . . . holes where there should not be holes. I remember when the light hit him at one point I could see his rapidly diminishing heartbeat pumping through the new holes in his face—like, his pulse was visible as he was bleeding out. And he screamed. Jesus, God how he screamed. He screamed because it hurt, but part of me wants to believe he screamed because he knew, true and proper, that he had underestimated Punky. He had underestimated us. That made me feel something.

I am going to tell you something I didn't tell the cops. I cheered her on. Not all of us did. Some of us were silent or gasping or scared, all of which I understand, but I heard myself screaming before I even knew I was doing it. And when Punky finally finished stabbing that dude, she got up, turned toward us and she was just . . . a vision. Covered in gore, knife in her hand, full makeup, she was lovely. I know this is going to get me in some shit to say but I was turned on by her at that moment. Just . . . lovely in a way that no one had ever been lovely before. That was Punky. One of a kind.

Angus, that piece of shit, probably told you all about the dance she did, yeah? He was very impressed by it, right? Sure he was. What I bet he didn't tell you because he's a moron is it was the choreography from Floor Five, when the Demon Dance was ending. The Knight never saw that dance and I'm positive Angus hadn't seen it before. Most of us knew right away she had been stabbed. We saw the tear in her outfit and her dripping blood on the floor. To me, and to us dancers, she wasn't doing some new artistic expression. She was doing something specific.

She was saying goodbye.

My Punky made it a while longer. We all made it up to the fifth floor and helped Rodrigo out. He was in a bad way from what I hear, him and Hao both. For legal purposes, I hung back and didn't do a lot of fighting with the Demon Dancers and, based on what I hear, you can't prove otherwise. I can tell you Punky kicked an insane amount of ass. She was a warrior goddess. She saved lives and ended others. I am not drunk enough to think it's a good idea to tell you any more than that, but I will tell you one more thing.

She died on Five. It was terrible, but it particularly sucked because of where she died. We tried to help her, to give her first aid or whatever, and she wouldn't have it. We kept trying to get her to lie down, and she'd fight us and yell at us and even take a swing at us. I don't know why she wouldn't let us help, but there was no way. Just no way. If you ask me, I think she knew she was going out, and she was desperate to do it her own way. And she did. She danced and she fought and she screamed and when she finally got knocked off her feet, she passed out and didn't get back up. Kind of beautiful on some level. Here's why it's shitty.

The Demon Dancers rarely, if ever, make it to the top floor. It's the most peaceful part of the entire show, an experience that's supposed to make everyone feel serene and slightly creeped out as opposed to the literal devil spitting fire in your face. It's supposed to be heaven, kind of, but we all know heaven is a myth. And that's part of the design of the thing—it's beautiful, but it's fake. But I kind of wanted Punky to make it up there. Just . . . symbolically, I guess. I mean, obviously, my preference would be that she not bleed out doing a stupid show, but if she was going out like she wanted to go out, I wanted her to see the top floor before she succumb. I wanted her somewhere beautiful.

Of course, if we had made it up there, they would have had to identify her body by her fucking teeth.

POST ON THE WHO'S THERE DISCORD

March 12

ADMIN
Volunteers Needed: The admins are looking for a few of you who live in Southern California who can help us out two days from now. This assignment is a big deal and not for the main discussion. Please respond to this post and you will receive a DM. Only people who live in Southern California, please.

USER: VCTOMATO
It's only about 1,100 miles for me. Wish I could help you out!

USER: ILOVEBEANS
For the record, the last time the admins spoke to us lowly users was 7 months ago to update some of the terms of service. This is kind of a big deal and if I were ANYWHERE near LA, I would be all over this. You would have to drag me away with meat hooks.

USER: PARADISESHITTY
I live in LA. Please DM me.

USER: TELSTARBRONSON

Things are about to get interesting. I will be paying close attention over the next few days. To those about to rock, we salute you.

USER: BUDDYBRENT

God, I hope whatever is going on really sticks it to them. All us sickos have known for a long time what a messed-up cult that show is. Who knows what the hell they're doing in there. I cannot wait for our GAs to strip away all the bullshit and finally expose Dumb Willie for the global criminals they really are.

> **Response by User: DeepCorner**
> You couldn't be more right. Justice for Joanna!

USER: DEALIN'SCREAM

Oh my God, it's happening! It's going to be glorious when the storm clears and everyone gets what they deserve. It's coming!

USER: PRETTYSCARE

I live in LA and would be happy to help.

USER: ENDEDBYCHANCE

I've been on this server a lot longer than most of you so I'd like to give you a little perspective, you little fuckheads. When this started, it was just what it seemed—a place for people to make fun of a really stupid piece of art. But since then, it's grown into something a lot more important. We aren't just a family right now. We're a motherfucking movement. We are going to stand up for everyone who has ever been shit on by the establishment. We are going to show the fancy artists in their high tower what it means to fuck with us. I hope it's ugly. I hope they take pictures of the gore, I hope the cops slip in pools of blood and fall onto their face into piles of bodies. I also cannot tell everyone how proud I am to be part of this. Go get 'em, admins.

> **Response by Anonymous User:** I don't think anyone wants to see anyone hurt, right?

USER: CARMONAVERONA

The more I hear about the people who run that show, the more confused I get. Why would they send someone to spy on their haters? It just doesn't make any sense. I've seen the texts and I've followed the threads, so don't yell at me please. It just seems like such a petty, stupid thing to do. I guess that's the point.

USER: CAPTAINWOW

I want to point something out for everyone on this thread. If you'd boost this comment, that would be smart. I'm as excited as the next person that our little "operation" is finally happening. But I want to please remind everyone, including the admins, that this is a pseudo-public forum. While you need to be accepted into the group, we're well over 400 members right now which means not everyone can be trusted. Whatever happens next and whenever it happens, you've got to be careful. If something serious happens or if something goes wrong, this is the first place the authorities are going to come. If the Dumb Willies know about us they'll tell the cops. Be excited, party down my dudes, but don't post anything incriminating. There are eyes upon us.

USER: KNOCKTHISBITCH

Yeah! Fuck those guys! They've had this coming for a long time and now they're going to pay! I want pictures of the blood!! Admins, please please please make sure to document what happens and let us have a look. Let's fucking gooooo!

USER: BOOKSMARTLOVEDUMB

Since the admins are back, does anyone want to speculate on whether the rumors are true? Whether RP used to work for them? Because if he did and if he knows enough he could shut the whole thing down.

    Response by User WeederofthePack: I thought that had been confirmed.

    Response by User CaptainWow: It's not been confirmed. Please stop speculating.

USER VINCENTPRICEISRIGHT: I read a thing the other day (I can't find the link) that the Show-That-Must-Not-Be-Named is going to close anyway. I wish I remembered why, exactly, but their ticket sales are already suffering and soon they're going to be out of business entirely. Not a minute too soon, if you ask me. There are so many better ways to spend your money.

USER SPIRALCITY: I told all of you! I fucking told you! I told you that the admins last message was 58 words long. This one was just 51 words long. 58-51 is 7 which is how many months was between messages. They're telling you everything you need to know. Some of you think this is a game, and to you it probably is, but some of us see through the curtain to the life-or-death situation this really is. If they can come for Joanna they can come for any of us and the admins are the only ones standing in the way. I will be on my hands and knees praying for the brave people who go into that den of sin and I will be refreshing my computer every couple of minutes. I cannot miss anything in this, our most important battle. I hope that building and everyone in it burns for what they're really doing in there. I want a barbecue! I want to see the blood. Come on, admins. Do what God put you here to do.

USER WOLFETHAN: I live in Glendale. Please DM me. It's important.

INTERVIEW 15
TALIA HILLS

Audience Member on March 14

My therapist told me that I shouldn't do this. And I don't want to do this. I don't want everyone to know that every time I close my eyes I see Brent staring up at me, pleading with me to save him. I didn't ask for this pain, but it's mine now, and I have to live with it. So I decided I'm going to give it to you. Every last drop of my misery. Or, if you need a nicer term, I'm going to give you some "radical honesty." If you can take it. None of my friends have been able to.

Brent was my husband. We'd been married for twelve years. We had come to the show to celebrate our anniversary. It wasn't our anniversary, that was a week before, but this was when we could make it work. I work in insurance, he worked at a car dealership, John Blume Ford out near the Valley. He was very good at his job, and between the two of us we made a comfortable living. We have one son, Charlie, who is starting middle school this year.

I was cheating on Brent. I had been cheating on him for six months with a coworker. I tell you this not so you'll judge me, though based on your look something about your opinion of me has changed. I'm beyond caring at this point. I no longer feel much of anything unless it involves Charlie. If it weren't for him, I would probably have ended my life a while ago.

I told you, radical honesty. The whole story. Every last drop.

Brent had to have known. Had to have. One night when I was on my way to see my coworker, Scott, I spent the evening getting ready. I put on a nice dress over a pair of fancy underwear. I did my hair and my makeup. Then I told him I was going to Target. I came back three hours later, and he was asleep. He never asked where I was. I never volunteered the information, though I like to think I would have had he asked, or had the roles been reversed. In my darkest moments, I think someone that . . . weak deserved it. But in most of my waking hours I deeply regret it.

The reason I say this, other than as an act of radical honesty, is so you know this "date night" was an obligation for me and likely for both of us. But I did want to see this show.

Scott had told me it was something special. He told me I would love it and that it might change my life. He was right, it certainly changed my life. He told me a lot of things. I was intrigued and Brent, well, Brent was not. He was not a fan of the arts, much less a patron. He used to be. He used to love music. When we started dating, if you put him in front of a great jazz saxophonist, he'd be transfixed for hours. His job changed him. The atmosphere was very macho, very condescending toward anyone who wasn't a white man. His coworkers hated women. I imagine if he told them he had once liked jazz saxophone, his manager may have called him a "fag" or something like that. It was that sort of place.

Brent understood, though, that if he suffered through an arts performance there was very likely sex in it for him later, and sex, well . . . radical honesty. He was not an attractive man, or rather, not a man I am attracted to any longer. I have always been considered attractive. I work out, I don't eat much, and I've always been small. Brent went from a trim, fit, and vibrant man to someone much uglier. Inside and out, if I'm being radically honest, which I am. Sex was a chore, just like going out that night. If he didn't know I was cheating on him, and I took no pains to hide it, he must have at least understood how little I enjoyed fucking him. He must have. I made it so incredibly obvious.

The fact the show started off at a bar was a mark in the positive column for Brent. He quickly ordered three drinks for two of us and downed the first one quickly. He drank a lot when I was around him. My therapist suggested the two are related. I can see why she said that.

The doors opened very soon after we got there. This meant that Brent had to drink quickly, even though I told him he didn't have to. He had no problem drinking quickly, but it annoyed him. He was also frequently annoyed when he was around me. I'm not saying . . . shit, it sneaks up on me. The grief. The regret. My therapist says it's something that will be my companion for a while until we "grow accustomed to each other." Right now it's like a ninja. It just . . . jumps in there and messes with my day. It's not just Brent, it's my hair and my face and everything that came after. And the guilt. Always the fucking guilt.

Brent didn't know he had to put on a mask even though I had told him, at least three times and twice that day, that masks were part of the whole deal. When they handed him the mask he looked at me like it was a completely foreign concept, like someone had handed him a sheet of graph paper and asked him to do geometry. I put mine on, and he sighed that stupid sigh he did whenever anything was the slightest inconvenience for him. And off we went.

Can I tell you something? When he put on his mask and his face was covered, I was forced to confront what his body had become and it was not fun for me. Brent was probably six foot, two inches, and pushing 280 or so. I'm not an expert. I just know the mask made me less attracted to him, which was something I wasn't sure was possible just a few seconds before. The guilt is telling me "enough of that."

I don't know how other people like the show or how they even . . . interact with it, I guess. But when we first started I was lost. I was expecting a tour. Or maybe some sort of guide, but I didn't get it. With no one to guide me I just sort of started walking around and Brent just started following me, wherever I went. We weren't supposed to talk, but I motioned to him that we should go up or down the stairs, and he followed me. When we got to the stairwell, I whispered to him, "I'm not sure what we're doing," and he whispered back, "This is your thing."

I don't know what it was about his tone or the way he said it, but that really made me hate him at that moment. It's like . . . yeah, I wanted to come to this but it's not like you don't have a mask on your fat face and it's not like you couldn't help me figure out what was going on, right? I get that this wasn't his thing, but I could just . . . I could just hear him laughing about this on Monday morning with his stupid salespeople and them calling me all sorts of names for having the temerity to suggest we go to something that's not a fucking movie. It'd have been the same if I said "let's go to a play," but this was a more extreme version of that, and I know I was never going to hear the end of it. I just felt that this was going to be a sore spot, that he wouldn't let this go for months.

I decided I didn't want that and because of that, one of two things had to happen. This either needed to be an amazing night that even he couldn't deny, or I needed to file for divorce the next week. I know that sounds melodramatic, but it was just one of those moments, those life defining moments that come at the strangest times.

I didn't know how defining it was going to be at the time.

All this happened in just a second or two. So, while we were still in the stairwell, I put my face close to his ear and whispered, "Having trouble with the stairs?" I'm not sure what came over me and I can't tell you what his face did. But he shut up and followed me to the third floor.

Once we opened that door and were hit with the lighting and the music and the signs and the smells, I think I finally "got it." I was on board for whatever this was, anyway. I grabbed Brent's hand and pulled him through the frozen part of the show toward the fiery part, and while we were moving, some cast member, this scantily clad woman in body paint, grabbed Brent and pulled him in another direction. I let him go and before I knew what was going on, I couldn't see him. Again, I had a flood of different emotions but the bottom line is I started exploring on my own . . . radical truth? I was smiling because I knew the story had just changed. Instead of "the stupid wife took me to a stupid show" it became "the wife dragged me to the show but this crazy dancer grabbed me and pulled me into the dark and it was kind of fun." I considered that a victory.

As I explored, whatever the show was trying to do worked on me. I was taken in. I was engaged. And I had time to reflect on what was happening. My therapist tells me that really good art is the sort of thing that engages you, wherever you are and whatever you're going through.

I think he's right because when I got to the part with giant Satan with Judas in ice above him, the fact that I was cheating on Brent came into stark relief. I realized instead of telling Brent what I was feeling, who I was becoming, I had chosen to let something else happen. I don't want to be cheesy and say, "I saw Satan and I felt my sin," but that's more or less what happened. I saw my son, Charlie, as the kid trapped in the ice and Satan as the sin that was destroying my home. I cried. I cried more than a little. I hadn't cried in years. Maybe a decade. But I cried and I was left alone to cry, under that stupid mask. I felt my feelings and then had a deep desire to find Brent, so I set out to look for my husband.

I looked all around the third floor and didn't see him. Then I had a decision to make. Do I go up and continue to explore, possibly on my own, or do I go back to the bar where he likely went? I was sure I didn't want Brent to see that I had been crying. What would that conversation have looked like? So I went up.

The fourth floor had the exact same effect on me when I opened the door. All the elements of the show almost felt like they were reaching out for me, waiting for me to get sucked in. It was glorious. Again, I "got it." But something was a little strange about it. When I was on the fourth floor, things seemed a little more . . . chaotic. Something was just off, and then I saw the woman in the middle of the floor.

Almost the second I saw her, Brent runs up to me and starts talking faster than he's talked to me in a long time.

"I saw her fall."

"That wasn't supposed to happen."

"I think she's really hurt!"

First off, I was impressed, so very impressed, that Brent had taken the chance and gone up instead of back to the bar. I remember thinking "what a surprise." And then "I want to surprise him, too," so I tell him, let's get closer to the woman who fell. I hadn't seen her fall so maybe it was part of the show, I didn't know. We both started moving toward the woman, you could tell where she was because there was a big crowd of people around her, and suddenly Brent gets socked in the face. Time for some radical honestly. Brent is a gun guy who owns a big truck and likes to go shooting on the weekends. I always thought, though I never told him, that he did these stereotypically manly things because he knew his marriage was in trouble and his wife was cheating on him with another accountant with three inches on him. I always thought he was a "weekend warrior" and about as tough as a bowl of pudding.

Turns out, my husband could take a punch. And throw one.

He turned to the masked person who hit him and just hauled off. He put his whole weight into the swing and connected. I saw the person who hit him just fly backward and land, hard, on their ass about ten feet away. Before the person—I wasn't sure of their gender, truthfully—could even get up, Brent had started to run over to punch them again, moving faster than I'd seen him move in ten years, easy. It had been a long time since I had seen him run, and it took him a few steps to get up to speed.

Then he just . . . disappeared.

I don't even remember him falling. I don't remember flailing or a scream as he fell. I just remember watching him through that mask, watching him run, and then he was gone in the blink of an eye. I ran toward where he disappeared. I'd tell you my state of mind but I honestly don't remember it, I don't remember what I was thinking. I was just moving and as I moved, I stopped just short of falling into the same grave Brent had fallen into.

I hadn't even clocked them when I first entered the room because there was so much going on, but they were deep. I ran right up to the edge and just barely stopped before falling in. Just barely, and that's when I heard him. Over the blaring music and the effects and other people getting into fights, I heard Brent at the bottom of the grave, screaming. I laid down at the lip and yelled down to him. Honestly, I don't remember what I yelled. My brain was off, and I was in survival mode, or so I thought. I saw him down there and the only thing I noticed was that he was moving strangely. Very strangely. And as I started to realize what had happened and how bad the situation actually was, that was when I got hit with the flamethrower.

I remember what I was thinking during that part.

First, I remember thinking that I had never known pain like this, not at this level and not in so many places. I work out, I push myself, and I like to think I'm tough, more or less, but the pain stripped away anything resembling toughness that I might have had inside me. It was so much, I don't know if I screamed, but my body was screaming for me. It . . . as I was on fire, my brain was also on fire. It was on fire with the pain and then on fire with the overwhelming idea that I needed the pain to stop. I would have done anything in the world to get the pain to stop. The pain was so sharp and so . . . high and all consuming. I can't do it justice with words, not even close.

Second, I remember looking at my arms and seeing terrible things, everything going wrong. I remember the hair on my arm curling and blackening, the skin starting to melt, but not like candle wax. It melted differently than anything I'd ever seen melt. The closest I can come up with is cheese on a pizza and even that isn't even close. But everything was wrong. I remember the smell. Burning hair, mostly, which is not a smell you forget once you've smelled it. And I remember the sound, the "whoosh" sound that the flamethrower made.

All this was in the span of maybe a second or two. Not long, but eternally too long.

Did I make the conscious decision to roll into the grave? That's a good question. I think the answer is "yes," but I don't remember a moment when I said "maybe rolling into the grave will help" so it's even odds, really. I just wanted the pain to stop, so I rolled. Then I remember my stomach flip-flopping as I fell, and I hit really hard. The pain didn't completely stop, but it was different. It wasn't the pain that comes with fire anymore, it was the pain you felt when you fall four feet onto your side. I don't know how I avoided hitting my head. I could speculate, but the radical truth is I have no idea. I should have hit my head during the fall and I didn't. Maybe the universe wanted me to suffer. It sure feels that way now.

Brent, he hit his head. His face, if you want to get specific.

The screaming that I heard after he fell, before I caught on fire, it was definitely Brent, because when I gathered back my higher brain functions and realized I wasn't on fire anymore, the first thing I remember is Brent screaming. Screaming and moaning, sort of going back and forth in his pitch. The grave we had fallen in was bigger than it looked from up above, but it still wasn't big. I couldn't stand up. I remember that because I kept trying to get up but my legs were not wanting to work for a variety of reasons, and then realizing there was no point as the space was maybe four feet tall, if that. It was a little alcove for the actor to hang out. Then there was a little ladder, but neither Brent nor I were in any shape to climb up it.

I crawled over to Brent, which was hard because there were parts of my arm where the skin was basically gone, and . . . it's just too painful to think about. I noticed later that parts of my burnt skin had stuck to the floor. When I made it to Brent, he was laying on his stomach, holding his head and moaning and screaming. I don't remember what I said. To be honest, I was trying to both stay conscious and not vomit. I was very nauseous at this point and, strangely, cold. Very cold. But, even still, I managed to help him roll over.

When I woke up that morning, if you had asked me to rate being set on fire and rolling into a seven-foot pit on a scale of one to ten, one being a normal occurrence and ten being the worst thing you'd ever lived through, I would have ranked it a ten. When I rolled Brent over and saw his head was split open and his brains were literally visible on one side of his head, it realigned my scale. I think that's how I'll put it.

Being radically honest, the first thing I felt was disgust. Disgust at his body leaking out. The blood mixing with the white goo, the strings of spit coming out of his mouth as he screamed, it was more than my already queasy stomach could handle. The second thing I felt was complete helplessness, helplessness that I didn't know it was possible to feel. However I felt about Brent going into the evening, the father of my child was injured in a way I could not begin to deal with. I needed help. And help was seven feet away covered with fire and music and people screaming and punching each other. Help might as well have been on the other side of the moon.

How did Brent hit his head so hard? I don't know. And again, I don't know why he hit his head and I didn't. I wish it had been the other way around.

I threw up. I wish I had been able to hold it in, but I couldn't. I puked and I tried to turn my head, but I know some of my vomit got on him. We had eaten a lot before the show, and there was a lot in my stomach. On top of that, when you vomit in a small space, it's almost as if nothing else exists except the vomit, the smell is so overpowering. The smell triggered something in Brent's . . . let me say this a different way. The smell made Brent scream more. I don't blame him. By now I was crying and I would love to be able to tell you that I cried for help, loudly and clearly and consistently. I did not. I cried and then would call for help, and then I would break down and cry for help and the whole time Brent was screaming and I was choking on the smell of vomit and trying not . . . not to focus on the brains that I could see leaking from his head, and I screamed, and fire was shooting somewhere above me. I'm sorry. It's just . . . It was like that for a long time. Long time. I don't know how long, but part of me is still there.

I cried and I screamed and my skin started to leak and hurt and Brent's screams got softer and softer. Soon he was just moaning. Moaning like he does in his sleep after a big meal. Moaning like he did when I use to touch him between his legs in the morning. Moaning like . . . like he was a child and he was hurting. And he was and so was I.

You know what, fuck it. I told him. In that pit, I told him everything. I told him how I hated him and how I had cheated on him. I told him what I loved about Scott, about how what we were was beautiful and what we had become was ugly. How much pain I was in, emotionally. How much pain I was in physically. I told him my hair was gone, or mostly gone, and I screamed at him for making me stop loving him. I screamed at him for voting for Trump. I screamed at him for hating my mother. But mostly I held his hand because I wasn't going to risk moving his head and I talked and cried and screamed, and his breathing got worse and worse until he started going into convulsions. When he started convulsing, more of his brains spilled out, and I cried and leaked and bled and no one came to help me. He died and I was there, holding his hand. I watched it happen, step by step by step by step until his body was an empty fucking shell.

At some point I passed out. I don't remember when or how. Truthfully, radically truthfully, I might not have ever seen Brent die. Maybe I imagined it. There's no way to ever know. All I know is I woke up in the hospital and Scott never came to visit me, and afterward he only called me once to talk about what happened and to say that he never wanted to see me again. The scars all the way across my head and face probably had something to do with it. I was never with him for a long-term commitment, but it still hurt. I wear a wig now. I am on Lexapro. I live for Charlie, who I've told this story to. I don't know how much he cares or respects me, but I will be there for him no matter what.

I spent a lot of time hating everyone involved. I still hate them, but it's not as active now. It's a passive hate, it's just something that is.

I hope you've gotten some insight. I hope you've gotten what you wanted. I hope you understand more. But I didn't tell you this for you or your project. I did it for me. And for Charlie. He needs a record. He needs to know.

There's nothing like being on fire to help you clarify your priorities.

INTERVIEW 16
NAPOLEON GUTIERREZ

Security for *Come Knocking* on March 14

Man, it is not fun to talk about getting your ass kicked. Please pardon me if I seem in a bad mood.

But I got my ass kicked that night.

I had been working security for several months, and it was cool. The best part, for me, was working under our head of security, Shawn. Since you can't talk to him, it would be good for me to tell you what he was like. Then I can tell you what happened. Trust me, man, it makes a lot more sense if you know who Shawn was and what he was all about.

This was my third job working security and the first time working under someone who treated me with any kind of respect whatsoever. In my other jobs I was treated like a cog in a wheel, I guess you could say. The "expectations" of the job was the only thing my bosses cared about. If I couldn't stop shoplifters and the company I worked for saw a slight dip in profits, I was of no value and was treated that way. They just pointed me at a store and said, "do the job." That's a long way of saying it sucked ass. At *Come Knocking* it was different. I was part of a team, and that team's job was to keep everyone safe. That was new and that was cool and that felt good, man.

As you can probably tell from my name and the way I look and the way I talk, my parents had some interesting ideas about things, and I grew up a weirdo. My Dad is Guatemalan, and my mom is white trash via Kentucky, which is how she would describe herself. I grew up weird and a little trashy, too. I got my first tattoo when I was thirteen, and my uncle gave it to me, if that gives you any idea of where I come from. I won't go into it too much, but one of the first things I noticed when I started working for *Come Knocking* was Shawn didn't make me feel like a weirdo. Everyone there was a weirdo. What he did do, though, was make me feel important. Vital. Part of a team with an important part to play that no one else could do. Because he did that, I showed up and did the best work I could every chance I got.

I miss that feeling, man. I miss that dude.

How'd I get hired? You're gonna get me on a tangent, man, and I got material for you. Okay, it's kind of a funny story. Since I got all the tats and the look, I tend to attract some pretty interesting girls, which is the way I like it. I ain't talking shit about "interesting" girls, man. Definitely not. You'd get yourself stabbed doing that. But I hooked up with this girl, Maddie, who was way out of my league, and she worked at *Come Knocking*. She hooked me up with the job because she saw how much I hated what I was doing but, I wasn't qualified to do much else. But she knew that I seemed like a tough dude and that I didn't run away from violence if it came to it. You wanna know my trick for working security jobs in general and *Come Knocking* in particular? It sounds like bullshit from *Road House*, but I swear to God, it works. I'll tell it to ya because it's easy to describe but hard to do. Shawn believed in this too. Okay, here's what I do.

Step one. Respect. It doesn't cost a damn thing to call someone "sir" or "miss" or to just be polite. "I'd like to help you solve your problem, sir." "I'm here to help, ma'am." That sort of language.

Step two. Outline, clearly, what's about to happen. "Sir, you're disturbing the audience. I will hear everything you have to say but we're going to do it in a different location." "Ma'am, if you continue to attempt to grab the actor's dick, you will be expelled and no refund will be given." I've said both those things, verbatim.

Step three. Give them one more chance, but be very, very clear that force is the next step. Some people love to argue, so I tell them, "If you continue speaking I will zip-tie your hands behind your back until the police get here." Very specific. That usually calms them down.

Step four, kick ass. Step five, fill out all necessary paperwork.

I always knew the steps, like, intuitively, but Shawn, he helped me put it into words and had me memorize them, first thing. He said "this needs to be muscle memory for you." And I got there, man. Got there pretty easy, and the dude was right. A very big number of cases we dealt with would de-escalate if you followed the steps. Shawn led a good team. We were the people who protected everybody. We had issues, sure, but we were reasonable and could work through them. We were a good team, and Shawn was very much our leader.

I'll skip over all the escalation other than to say things were getting worse and worse. I will tell you, we definitely noticed, and we noticed what our "friends" were doing. Shawn insisted we call them "friends" because . . . well, if we weren't polite about it, we'd call them greasy motherfuckin' bitch boys, if you follow me. Step one, respect, right? So, we noticed right away that our "friends" were organized and were testing us to see where we were weakest and what we would do when we were confronted. I hate to give them any credit at all, man, but they weren't dumb. So much of what I saw from night to night was just people acting foolish, but not these guys. When we saw them messing with the dancers on Four, we stood watch, so they moved to Five. When we split our team between Four and Five, they started fucking with the train on One. Always bobbing, always weaving. And they knew how many of us there were, man. They knew. And they knew where we were likely to go, so it was frustrating. And it kept getting worse and worse, which you know.

Real quick, before March 14, I asked Shawn if this sort of thing happened in the theater on the regular. I didn't know any theater before I started, man, none, and I thought maybe this is how it worked. Shawn kind of got this look like I had asked him something really stupid and just said, "No, man. This is different." That was all he ever said about that, just in case you think he was a moron or something. He knew. We all knew. We knew this was weird and it was getting more and more threatening as it went and that . . . well, that it would probably come to a head and something major would have to change. There was a night coming where something really bad would happen and management would have to make some very tough decisions. But that was above our pay grade, right? Right.

So, the night of the fourteenth. The show had barely started when I got a sense that this was going to be the night everything went to shit. Like, small things were going wrong in bulk. Lighting was off, effects were off, some stuff didn't happen that was supposed to, other things happened that weren't supposed to. I was on Four when I got the news about the control room from one of the bartenders who was running around like a maniac. They told me Anders was trying to get in but they had barred the door and that Anders was freaking out. That Anders, man, I don't know where they found that dude, but his dedication to his job and the things he could do were just next level. Just the most solid dude in the world. And he was panicking, which basically confirmed my instincts. Shit was about to go down.

I can tell you, honestly, the damage that could be done if someone with bad ideas got into the control room didn't occur to me right away. It seemed bad, but not "dozens of people are about to die" bad. Because of that, when I got to the bar on Three and no one was there, it still didn't sink in. If this were important, someone would be there trying to break down the door, right? Then Shawn showed up and set my ass straight.

"Penelope just fell and is probably dead."

"We can't shut the graves on Five."

"They could turn the fire on full blast and burn this place down."

I had a moment of total, like, shut-down shock—Penelope is dead, what are you even talking about?—but it didn't take long for my brain to kick in and for me to get with the program. If I'm telling you the truth, man, even if he hadn't said those things, his tone and the way he was acting and the way his eyes were bugging out of his head would have done the trick. I "got it" and we got past the shock pretty quick and started trying to figure what to do. We tried the door and it wasn't budging. Like, did anyone ever "penny lock" your door in a dorm or an apartment? Where they stack pennies under your door until it gets stuck? Someone did that to me once, and I thought we were going to have to hack the door down with a fuckin' axe because it was so stuck I didn't think we'd ever get it open. This was the same deal. Whatever they did to get the door stuck, it wasn't even giving a little no matter how much shoulder we put into it, man. And I don't know if anyone told you this or not, but there is only one way in or out of the control room for a very good reason—you don't want anyone wandering into the place, so you do your best to limit access. What I'm telling you is that door needed to come down and that sucker was made of thick wood and didn't look like it was giving up easy.

We didn't have an axe handy, plus we didn't know how they were jamming the door up, so I remember Shawn and I spending just a couple of seconds kind of looking around trying to figure out what to do. No real solution presented itself and, for some reason, we both sort of found it funny. Like, do you bust up a chair and use that? Do you stab at it with a broken bottle? At one point, Shawn said, "Why don't I pick you up and use your head like a battering ram?" and for some reason the combination of the situation being real bad and there being no good way to deal with it struck us as funny. We were laughing and the laugh sort of started soft and then got going until we were laughing pretty hard. It's stupid to say "you had to be there" but, man, you've been there.

That's when that huge blond dude came in the door and started shooting.

Man, I grew up around guns, I went hunting dozens and dozens of times, and I can tell the difference between caliber of bullets just by listening to the shot, so when I tell you I didn't know what the fuck was happening, I mean I next level didn't know what the fuck was happening. I just heard something that scared me and then saw Shawn crumple to the floor like someone flipped a light switch to the "off" position. I remember it, remember it being so weird, right? Like, my brain thought, *why did Shawn do that?* Then I took a bullet in the shoulder from this blond dude who looked like he was seven feet tall and a gun that looked just as big, man. And, while I know a lot about guns, I didn't know what it felt like to be shot. Man, let me be the hundredth person to tell you, it's both weirder and worse than you think it's gonna be, but the immediate sensation feels like you've been punched pretty good. The force of the thing threw me to the ground and the dude kept shooting.

Luckily, I was behind the bar and toward the end closest to the doors everyone used to go to the show, so I had pretty good cover, as it stood. I had never been shot at before and, man, I'll tell you . . . it ain't fun. How's that for a fantastic piece of wisdom. "Being shot at is no fun"—Napoleon Gutierrez. Put it on my fuckin' tombstone, I guess. What I'm getting at is there are about six ways I could have reacted that I can think of that would have been smarter than what I ended up doing, which was not a lot. I kind of sat there as the guy walked over and shot Shawn a couple more times. I don't know that for sure but I heard a few steps and a few more shots, so I've got a pretty good chance of me being right.

I wasn't . . . I don't think I was terrified into staying still. I don't think that was it. I didn't freeze out of fear. What it was . . . I was trying to come to grips with what was happening, I think. I mean, part of me knew what was up and was screaming to run or fight or whatever, but another part of me just, like, vapor locked. Just a full-on screeching halt at the worst possible time. And you know what finally shook me out of it? The noises coming from the other side of the door to the control room.

There was a loud banging on one side of the door and then Mr. Huge Blond Gunman banged on the door with his fist a couple times. Could have been a code or a message, I don't know. What I do know is that it shook me out of whatever stupor I was in and got my ass thinking about what was going to happen next. Chances are good the guy knew I was there but since I wasn't making noise, he didn't seem too concerned about me. Or maybe he thought I was down for the count. That's what I was hoping, anyway, because I'd have a chance to maybe do some damage. Who the hell knows, if I got real lucky maybe I could David that Goliath motherfucker, which is what my brain started thinking about. What could I do to slow the man with the gun down? What could I do to stop him? So, I started looking around and my eyes landed on the sign.

Nothing Beautiful Stays That Way

You ever hear someone say something like, "If something that stupid were in a movie, everyone would roll their eyes." Yeah, this was one of those situations. The sign people pass under to get into the show says those wise words in bright pink and blue neon above the door. What I knew that Tall, Blond, and Heavily Armed didn't know was there were smoke machines on either side of that door that could be set off by a button behind the bar. It's a chance for the bartenders to give folks a little jolt right before they go into the Netherworld. There was no rhyme or reason to when the bartenders decided to push it, as near as I could tell, but it was one of the perks of being a bartender. Every now and then you got to give someone a little smoke up their ass. It also made that loud hissing sound just to make sure people came as close as possible to shitting their pants.

My point is I knew the sign and the smoke were there and Blond Kong didn't. And that was the only advantage I had since I was losing more blood than I was comfortable with losing.

The big problem was the button to make the sign go all happy was a couple feet away from where I fell, and I would have to shuffle on the ground to get there. And shuffling draws attention, and with attention come more bullets. To make matters worse, the door to the control room was on the inside part of the bar where I fell, so three things would have to happen, in sequence, to stop me from getting a bullet to the head.

First, that gargantuan towhead would have to go on the outside of the bar to get into the show.

Second, he would have to not notice me shuffling toward the button.

Last, he would have to be headed straight into the Netherworld. Then I'd have to time pushing the button for maximum impact and then I'd do my best to close the distance and tackle him with a bullet hole in my shoulder before he got his gun up. So . . . I was completely fucked. Or I was gonna get lucky. No in between.

So, seeing no better option, I shuffled. And big-ass Blondie, he took the long road and walked on the outside of the bar. I have no idea why he did it. It was out of his way, but he did it. I don't know why he didn't hunt me down and finish the job. I don't know if he forgot about me. All I know is I moved as quietly as I could, which was aided by the rubber honeycomb thing the bartenders stood on, and I got to the button. And I held my breath.

I heard his big-ass boots stepping. Stepping. Stepping. With each step, I pictured him poking his gun over the bar and then things going dark. It was scary, man. I don't mind telling you I was freaking the fuck out, but I did my level best to keep my breathing quiet and my heart rate as low as I could get it. My hand reached under the bar and found the button. I sort of caressed it like it was the button that would make all this shit disappear and I'd wake up in my shitty apartment. And, sure enough, Biggie Blondie did exactly what I hoped he would do, walking straight to the entrance to the Netherworld. I waited . . . and I waited . . . and, when he got to where I wanted him, I pushed the button.

Sure as shit, the smoke machine triggered and the noise machine hissed and the big dude freaked out, spinning around and losing his bearings. I took a big breath, I pushed myself onto my feet, and I started running toward the dude with the gun as fast as I could, my legs shaking the whole way.

I closed the distance pretty quick, or at least it seemed pretty quick, and right away I realized the first flaw with my brilliant plan—I was running into a bunch of smoke. If the big dude was in there, I couldn't be a hundred percent sure where he was, man. And I had no time to stop running if I was going to make a decent hit on the guy. It was "all gas, no brakes, and make an educated guess" or "turn around and run like hell." I made a guess and threw my good shoulder.

Luck be a lady, man.

I hit giant Debbie Harry pretty hard in the chest. I was "aiming" for the stomach, but I certainly wasn't going to complain at this point. What happened, from what I can tell, is the dude's gun went flying as he didn't see me coming. My hit took the dude off his feet, and I landed not too far away. So, to recap, after being shot in the shoulder, which hurt like a bitch, I was able to wait out the shooter, trigger a trap, and hit him, disarming him. Pretty good for a day's work. That's enough to get me a free beer at most bars in this city.

But remember what sort of story this is. This is a story where I get my ass kicked. And, man, did I get my ass kicked.

In my defense, the dude had a foot and a half and probably fifty pounds on me. It felt like more. Felt like a lot more if I'm being honest, because after my heroics in the smoke, we were both on the ground. The gun was out of reach, but Big Blondie didn't worry about it like I had hoped he would've. I was hoping he would go on a mad dash for that big-ass gun of his, and I could maybe give him a knee to the back or . . . something. Again, the fact I made it this far is pretty dope. But he didn't go for the gun. He came after me.

I remember the elbow first. That elbow was pretty memorable. Cracked a rib, or so the doctors said. The first of a few. I don't know if that dude rolled and got up a head of steam or full-on gave me the People's Elbow, but it knocked the wind square out of me, and I could sort of feel any "fight" I had left leaking out of my ear. I mean, I put my hands up and curled into a fetal position like you do in any fight and I screamed a lot, like that was going to make a difference, but after that elbow, it wasn't a fight, man. It was me getting my ass kicked.

You wanna know the crazy thing? Some people are like "what can you tell me about it" and I tell them "I can tell you everything." I remember everything, and I wish I didn't because it's fucking terrible to think about. I remember after the elbow he pulled me by my feet a little closer and caught me with a punch under my face. That was where I bit into my tongue. That was where the taste of blood started and didn't stop for, like, a month. I remember seeing stars after that punch and then trying to put my hands near my face when I saw him coming. He threw my arms away and got one more, really good shot in my face. I remember throwing up shortly after that, just spewing all over the floor and some of it must have gotten in the guy's pants or something because he hit me harder than he did before I puked. I remember trying to throw him off me but it was really no use. I remember thinking "he's gonna shoot me" over and over and over and that's the only thing that kept me conscious, I think. The fear kept me awake. He had at least three shots that should have knocked me out but he didn't. If there's anything I can take "pride" in, it's that I didn't pass out.

But I wanted to. It hurt, man. Hurt lots. Hurt more than anything had ever hurt before. It still hurts. It was a beating that changed my shape, man. Physically and otherwise.

He beat the shit out of me and when there was no more shit to beat out, he left. At that point my brain wasn't working. I don't remember thinking "he's gonna shoot me" anymore. But he didn't. Didn't say anything either. Just left me. That's the theme, right? I don't know why the Blond Bomber did anything the way he did it. Or why. I just laid there and bled. I'm still not sure, to this day, how I got out of there, but I woke up in a hospital bed and stayed there for just about three weeks.

I had a few people try to tell me I was a "hero," and I was like "get outta here with that shit." A hero wouldn't have gotten his ass kicked like I did. I even had one cop tell me "heroes get their ass kicked all the time," and I don't know, man. That doesn't sound right to me. A hero would have helped more people. A hero would have made it so that Shawn was still alive. Heroes find a way.

I'm just some bum who got his ass kicked.

INTERVIEW 17
EVELYN SWEET-BACHMAN

Stagehand at *Come Knocking* on March 14

I started smoking again. You can smell it, can't ya? Yeah. That's me. I smell like a fuckin' ashtray again. It sucks, man.

You don't know how significant that is, the smoking thing. I mean, of course you don't know, you just met me, so let me lay it out for you. I saw my grandfather, a smoker all his life, wither and die from cancer because of cigarettes. I watched that man die in a sterile hospital bed. I was in the room, even, and he did the whole thing—coughing and gagging and falling into a coma, and I saw the yellow fluid from his lungs and all that shit. My mother made me swear I would quit smoking. She pointed at my grandfather in that bed and said, "This is going to be you if you don't quit." We both cried and hugged, and I promised my dear sweet mother, for whom I am the light of her life, that I would quit smoking and then . . . I did it. I followed through. Hardest fucking thing I've ever done, but I did it. And after that night, that bad fucking night where I saw all that bad shit go down, I went right back. It wasn't even a thought. Just right back like the cigarettes had never left my hand. It wasn't even a conscious decision.

That's what that night did to me. Manifested a cigarette in my hand. Poof. There it was. And here I am, smelling like a fucking ashtray. But what are ya gonna do?

You told me that you'd interviewed a bunch of people so you know about the Human Jubilation and all that, yeah? I figured. That's where

I worked, down on the first floor. You know, not to go off on a tangent, but other people have told me that shit was really wild on the upper floors—folks on fire and stabbing and dancing that absolute shit show on Five, but I didn't get any of that. They got the weird shit. I got the guy with the gun. Regular, run-of-the-mill American stuff, that's what I got. I go into some bars in this city and ask, "Anyone in here dealt with an active shooter?" and I bet in half the bars at least one hand goes up. Check for yourself, but it's an educated guess, and I'm pretty educated on educated guesses.

I'm gonna give you another quick fact you may not know. All that shit with the online trolls, they dealt with that a lot on other floors, but not so much on One, at least not that I saw. Maybe it was because a big-ass party with lots of loud yelling ain't an easy thing to fuck with, you follow? After the Human Jubilation wraps up there's other stuff, yeah, but it's easy to, like, overlook. But the Jube, that's the thing. If you're whooping and hollering and dancing and groping and flailing around like everyone did, how do you break that up? How do you interrupt a conga line, man? You don't. The conga line is its own thing just like the Jube is its own thing. *Was* its own thing. And that was basically all that happened on One that was most worth noting. Don't get me wrong, there were some acrobatics and some great dancing and an effect or two later on in each sequence, but the whole point of the entire floor was nearly twenty almost naked sweaty bodies blowing the place up, and, brother, these actors blew the place up three times a night. Until the appointed moment when someone died in the context of the show, then the energy went way down, obviously. But that staging area was pretty easy to control because it moved around every night, which is why I don't think we felt like we were getting fucked with at the same level as everyone else.

Oh, oh, I take it back. Let me go back for a second. You know what messes with a conga line? You know what really puts a damper on twenty nearly naked sweaty dancers, grinding and dancing and lifting their legs over their heads. Bullets do that. Bullets do that quite effectively. It slipped my mind, I should have said.

The first floor is kind of a pit, if I'm being honest—brick walls and no carpet so there was nothing to dampen the sound of that first shot. I gotta tell ya, it was a weird thing because during the Human Jubilation there's a moment where a woman screams and dies and it's all supposed to symbolize the suddenness of death and yada yada, symbolism is someone else's department. The point I'm making is it's a lot of noise leading up to one terrible moment where the mood changes. So, when there was a loud bang, and one of the dancers started screaming before the music and the lights said they should, it was easy to figure what was happening. Plus, if you're a six-foot-seven blond motherfucker with a gun screaming about the devil, you might also be drawing attention to yourself.

God, do you hear that? My voice, you can tell I'm smoking too much. I know we just met, but I can hear it. That scratchiness. God, I'm a hot mess right now.

The Jube, it only takes about ten minutes and happens first thing in each cycle, so my friend with the ArmaLite or whatever it was, I don't fuckin' know guns, waited until the second time through. Which I get. He waited until all the Demon Dancers had already left—they leave about halfway through to get to their marks on the upper floors—but the Jube is still a hell of a thing, even without the Demon Dancers gracing our presence. The fun thing about the show is that word kind of spreads even though no one is supposed to talk. I wish I didn't sound woo-woo about this, but some people, they just catch a vibe and go to the basement. When you get there, brother, it's just sex. I'm sorry, I'm not supposed to say that but that's what it is—hot people just being hot with their bodies. I went home some nights so fucking turned on, I don't mind telling ya. I am cursed to like men, and I mean cursed because men are the worst thing on the planet and I have not infrequently let the worst thing on the planet fuck me behind the bushes at the dog park—I told you, I'm a hot mess—so all this is to say . . . let me tell you about Attila.

Beautiful boy. Just beauty and sex appeal dripping off the kid. And, look, I am a professional and I know my job and I do my job, but I'm being as straight with you as I can be when I tell you, I went out of my way to watch Attila dance. I was always a busy chick, but I always made time, even when I didn't have it. That kid. I never made a move on him because I've got ten years and probably forty pounds on him, plus I was seeing someone at the time, but I would've done amazing things on that body of his. I'm not even sure I could tell you what his voice sounded like 'cause he was a quiet kid, but I would get in a horny trance when he danced, not just because his body was perfect, which it was, but because he was free when he moved. Almost like physics didn't have the balls to make a move on him either. Just beautiful and graceful and free. I always watched him while I was waiting to do my job, he never failed to take my breath away.

So I found it quite distressing, as you might imagine, when a good part of his face exploded.

Pal, I remember it clear as hell and I wish to Christ I didn't. So, I was looking at him, right? I'm in my little horny trance, and then I heard the noise and looked back, and I saw the end of his fall from the table he was dancing on. I ran up to him, out of instinct or whatever, I don't fuckin' know, and I saw he had landed face up and half of that face was in pieces on the ground. I saw it had been blown apart all the way to the skull, parts of which I could see. The bullet must have hit him from behind because the big exit wound was on his face. His eye was open, and there was nothing behind it. I remember that. I remember there were these . . . chunks. Bloody chunks. Just, fuckin' pieces of his face that had clung on, but the hole stretched about from the top of his cheek to around his temple. I knew by the look in his eye he was dead, but his beautiful body was still twitching and kicking when I got to him. I hated that the most. Like his body, his muscles weren't ready to go yet even though his head was fucking gone.

Physics finally made its move, I guess.

From there, I saw the crowd running and other people dropping. Some people I knew, some audience members I didn't know. No one I knew well got shot, I tend to not form lasting relationships with coworkers for good reason, but they were people I had created a show with. They were just dropping and screaming and bleeding. Lots of blood. Lots of it. I remember one dancer had been shot but she was crawling toward another dancer. She was bleeding bad, a big bullet wound in her leg and another one in her stomach area and she just kept saying "I'll help you, I'll help you" to another dancer who was already dead. I've, um, told my therapist about that one. Yeah. The way she was both whispering and screaming "I'll help you, I'll help you" as she bled to death, that shit is never leaving me. I'd give anything if it would.

And, don't ask me why, but with all the terror and pain and sorrow I was feeling, I felt one emotion above all others. I was really pissed the fuck off.

Again, as you can see, I'm nothing special. A hot mess. I do my job, I go home, I got cats and the occasional fella who is the worst thing on the planet living with me, but on that night the right launch sequence got entered into this fucking messed-up head of mine, and I turned into something else. I got mad. No, I got righteously mad. Mad at that fucking gun-toting Nazi slug motherfucker for ruining Attila's face. Mad at that sick, disgusting, no-dick, puke waste of skin for making me watch what I was watching. I got mad. Then I did something.

I swear to you, pal, it was almost like a trance. Among the many set decorations in the basement are a set of swords, one of which had been loose for a little while. A week, maybe? Maybe more, I don't remember, but what I do remember is getting yelled at by Anders because he saw it and painted me this very specific scenario where an audience member grabs the sword off the wall and stabs a dancer with it. And, I mean, he was right, what can I tell you? I just hadn't gotten around to it yet. But, in that moment, among all the blood and the screaming and the dead Adonis twitching in the corner, I remembered the sword on the south side of the set was loose as fuck, and I grabbed it. It came right off like I was the new leader of the Round fuckin' Table.

Sword in hand, I looked at my man with the gun. People were hiding at this point, so he was taking his time, not just firing randomly like at the start. He was in it, feeling all fuckin' proud of himself while I hid in the dark and watched him for a second or two. He was a tall guy, but when he came into the light, I could see he was a mook. A dork. A loser. Pal, I can't tell you exactly how I knew that, but I was able to take in the way he carried himself and the way he was dressed and his oily fuckin' face and the activity he was involved in and it all just screamed "MOOK!" The kind of kid who justifiably got his ass kicked all through middle and high school because he smelled like bad sausage and talked about anime all the time. The kind of guy who stalked you after one bad date and then called you a whore online. That sort of fuckin' mook.

Don't ask me why but the second I saw him in the light and recognized the sort of dude I was dealing with, I knew I had him.

I had the sword in my hand and the lights were spinning all around, but I could see him clearly, and I knew he wasn't looking in my direction. The lights were flashing blues and greens and reds, and my brain was screaming for me to do something, but I held for a second or two. Longest seconds of my life, man. But I waited. And then he turned and shot his little gun three or four times at someone opposite me, so he couldn't even hear my ass coming. With all the music and the screaming I could have been shouting like a Viking and he wouldn't have heard me. Not that it mattered because I hit him dead center in the back of his mook head and the sword came out the front of his mook throat.

Strange thing . . . I don't even remember, like, having to push. I was running at him, sure, but you'd think you'd have to actively "stab" a guy to stab a guy, yeah? Or, like, when you're cutting meat and you really gotta put some effort into it? Well, this wasn't like that. I didn't have to push. The sword was just . . . doin' that thing it was designed to do. Easy as pie, man.

Strangest thing, after you stab someone. My brain hadn't figured out what came next and what came next was a lot of spitting and gagging and blood. Lots of blood, but there was already lots of blood all around the place. But Mr. Mook, I hear him gag and spit blood and he tries to turn around, but I've still got the sword sticking straight though his neck so he wasn't doin' shit without me directing him which way to go. It took me too long to realize what was happening. He was trying to turn around so he could shoot me, but, in his rapidly deteriorating state, it didn't occur to him that he couldn't turn around. So, he would buck one way and buck another way, and the sword in his neck still held by yours truly kept him from turning around. It was a little funny until he started pulling the trigger out of desperation. Then it got real not funny.

See, I'll tell ya what was going on in my head because I remember it really clearly. Once I got the sword in his big stupid neck—which was weird given the angle because of how fucking tall he was, but you didn't ask about that—my brain didn't relax, exactly, but more like I was silently patting myself on the back. And I know that sounds terrible given I was killing someone, but let's be honest with ourselves. That guy deserved worse than he got, and he got pretty bad. Fuck him, I don't feel bad about it, and if he's got a mother somewhere who wants to write me a letter about how her little guy was a saint and I shouldn't be saying what I'm saying, my address is [REDACTED], Los Angeles, California, 904fuckyou. Because your little guy got what was coming to him. Shit, I've lost my place, what was I saying?

Yeah, my mental state. I was relieved that I had stabbed the guy, but then when he started firing his gun again, well, that brought back all the anger I had before. The sound of the shot was like a switch in my brain. "Patting myself on the back." *Bang!* "Pissed off all over again." It was that fast. So . . . I started twisting the sword. Because fuck that guy.

As is the theme of this little spiel of mine, I didn't have anything resembling a grand plan. I just sort of did it, but when I did, he stopped firing the gun and actually dropped it. His hands went up to his neck—at this point maybe ten seconds had gone by since I stabbed his mook ass—and he started clawing at the sword. I imagine that much time without air had something to do with it, but my point is he dropped the gun. And I made a calculation. He dropped the gun, and so I let go of the sword.

This might seem like a mistake, but I'm here and I'm in one piece and I'm talking to you, so it's cool. Don't get all nervous on me, pal.

The second I let go, he starts reaching behind him and actually gets a grip on the sword. I see this happen and I know that I had to act fast. I run around him, but you know what that little fucker did? He tripped me. Sword in his neck, oxygen leaving his body, heading toward the great anime convention in the sky, and he has the wherewithal to trip me. I'm not going to say anything nice about that asshole but if I was, it would be that tripping me under those circumstances was a pretty boss move. I couldn't have done it. Anyway.

I crawl toward the gun. It wasn't far, probably a couple of feet and I get there, grab this heavy-ass thing, and spin on my ass to face him and am surprised. Again.

He got the sword out.

Okay, I lied. I'm going to say something nice. He never left his feet. All dripping blood, losing air, giant stab wound in his neck—any two of those things would be enough to knock me down for a while. Tough motherfucker for a fuckin' mook. But he never left his feet.

Until I pulled the trigger a bunch of times. That did the trick.

I ain't gonna go into it with you, but I'm an SA survivor. Sexual assault. Not bad, but bad. And without going into it with a stranger such as yourself, I will say one of the top three things I remember about the whole experience was the look on that fucker's face after he did it. Scared, like a little boy. That look? Same as the mook with a big hole in his neck. Everything about him screamed "danger." But his eyes were all "scared little boy." Good. I hope he died scared, wondering where it all went wrong, wanting his mommy. Again, you've got my address, send me all the letters you want.

After he fell, I stood up, stood over my guy, and pumped probably fifteen shots into him. I lost count after the first few, but I remember what they did to him. I remember his stomach convulsing and his head jerking around really violently as I shot him in the cheek and then in the eyeball. Right one. His right, my left. I remember not wanting to stop. I shot him in the shoulder, I shot him in the chest, I shot him again in the stomach, I shot him in the dick twice, I shot him in the legs. I've told the cops this and they tell me it's not the most common thing in the world, but they've heard of it happening. I don't give a shit if I was a trailblazer in dealing with an active shooter or not. I shot him until I didn't want to shoot him anymore. Then, the music stopped for some reason, and the lights came up, and I all I heard was screaming.

He killed twelve people. That's four actors, another stagehand named Billy Pavuk, who was a badass at his job, and seven audience members. The rest were running up to the bar and . . . you know how that turned out. The screaming I heard was from some of the people he shot but didn't kill. There were five of those. I . . . I didn't help. I could have. I know first aid, it's a requirement of the gig. But after the lights came up and I saw all the blood, that's when I shut down. That's when my brain was like "enough." I dropped the gun and sort of stumbled to the stairs.

I should have helped but I didn't, and I really am sorry about that and now regret giving out my address. Redact that, please.

Ever since then, what can I say? That night lives in me. I can't get rid of it any more than I could get rid of my grandma's funeral or my first kiss or that one time some fuckin' mook fingered me in a nightclub on Staten Island. Can't get rid of it. I really want to.

Shit, man. I need a cigarette now.

You wanna hear something funny? I mean something really funny? I didn't have that first cigarette until I got out of there, but I sure did smell some smoke before then. Too dark? Yeah. Probably, but what are you gonna do?

AN EXCERPT FROM THE MANIFESTO OF ETHAN APPLETON

Author's Note: It is not an exaggeration to say the decision to include a portion of the Appleton Manifesto in this book kept me up at night. I deeply understand arguments for and against the inclusion of such a noxious, extremely meandering, and potentially dangerous piece of writing. My decision finally came down the fact that I felt I understood the events of March 14th better after reading this excerpt from his twenty-two-page angry, violent, piece of self-aggrandizement. Specifically, there is some crucial context about the inner workings of Who's There that I was not able to represent in other parts of this book. I understand the pain this causes Appleton's victims but, after reading, I hope you understand my decision and, if you disagree, I hope you find it in your heart to forgive me.

Fuck everything.

How do you come to a different conclusion? If you have even an eighth of your brain working, you HAVE TO know everything is fucked. The environment, the economy, fertility rates plummeting, new diseases inside us and we don't even know it. Everyone knows everything is fucked, just some people are pretty enough or rich enough or popular enough or successful enough to ignore that fact. But you know it's true.

You fucking know or you're in denial. Everything is fucked and the only way to unfuck it is blood. Lots and lots and lots and lots of blood.

Blood will wake people up. Blood will make people afraid which is going to sharpen their senses. Blood is going to make everyone pay attention to everyone they've thrown away. Blood will lead to more blood, but at the end of it, blood is going to be the great "unfucker." Let there be blood in the streets and let it begin with me.

Thank GOD people online understand that. Especially the folks who post in the Who's There Discord. They get it. And they gave me the courage to finally stop being such a worthless, empty, nothing piece of shit and start the blood flowing. I know what you're going to say. You're going to say "they were kidding" "it's just online" and shit like that. But that's not what the people there are about. They're about starting something. They're about "the great unfucking." (I made that up, by the way. They didn't say that on the Discord at all) You can tell. When people are trolling, they don't answer every post right away. When people are trolling they don't put THOUGHT INTO IT! They fuck around. These people don't fuck around and the admins don't fuck around.

God, I want to be like the admins.

They're smart and they know when to show up and when to leave it all alone. They give us enough direction to be a community while letting ANYTHING happen. I've had conversations about rape and incest and stalking and Hitler. You don't have to say shit like "un-alived" in that forum. You can just be yourself whoever you are. Do you know how hard it is to find a place that isn't scared and pussified about language? I mean, just LET US FUCKING BE! If you don't like what someone says, quit talking to them. It's so fucking stupid. Just one more thing to "unfuck."

As for me, I was nothing. I have atopic dermatitis and have for a long time. That means I look like a fucking loser and everyone called me a fucking loser and I believed I was a fucking loser. No girl would look at me. I had one that was a friend once and she told me, straight, that she was never going to fuck me. That made me SO PISSED! Some of the people in Who's There got it. They agreed with me about what a bitch Josie was. I couldn't even say that shit anywhere other than Who's There and if I did, they'd have called me a cuck or an incel or a bitch boy or a beta or like that. And I was those things until someone told me I wasn't. Then I was something else.

I was the Angel of the "unfucking."

Author's Note: From here Appleton spends long pages detailing the mythology of the "Angel of the Unfucking." For everyone's sake, I will skip ahead to a final, relevant section. If you are interested in reading the manifesto in full, which I do not recommend, it is widely available online.

And there I will be. The Angel in his full glory. Finally born, finally whole, finally ready to do what the Gods demand. The Unfucking will start in the Gummar Bar. The admin has told me to watch out for the bartender as he is "expecting something." I told him, "He should watch out for me." I will shoot his face off his dumb fuck body, I will watch his skull scream, I will wash the floor with his blood and the blood of anyone else in that bar. Then it's time to rescue the children.

The children in the basement are real. I know it. I know it and I feel it and I feel them and I will rescue them. The admin warned me the children were a rumor and he didn't believe it. I'm sorry, but as the Angel in its final form I can say it. Fuck the admins. They don't know what they're talking about. The Angel knows and the Angel will rescue them. Into the basement I will go, into the lower levels, into hell, and I will find them if I must spill gallons of blood, oceans of blood to do it.

The Gods have given me size. I am tall. I am capable. I am strong. The Gods will protect me. The Gods will allow the Great Unfucking to begin in the basement of that abomination. And, when the bullets stop and the screaming stops and the police await the Angel as he emerges, he will do so with rescued children holding his blood-soaked hands. And they will know. Everyone will know. The Great Unfucking will begin.

What happens to me is insignificant. Finally, FINALLY FINALLY FINALLY I AM PART OF SOMETHING BIGGER! I am needed. I am the conduit from which justice will flow, from which understanding will come.

The Angel is almost here. And you all are not ready. Let it begin with me. Let it begin now. Let it begin with my hands and my gun and my strength and my anger and my power.

Let it begin.

INTERVIEW 18
FRANKLIN HAWLEY

Actor in *Come Knocking* on March 14

When I was auditioning for this role, they told me they wanted a poet to play Death.

There were specifications. I had to be a certain height, a certain weight. I had to be able to move very slowly, which was difficult for some actors, but something I am trained to do. But mostly, the director wanted someone who understood what it meant to be Death in this show and in this setting. To do it poorly was to scare the audience or to seem terribly hokey. To do it correctly took a poet.

I have written poetry, yes. But I do not wish to speak about that now, though I appreciate you asking. To promote my work would be ghoulish under the circumstances. What I need to do is tell you about Lydia.

Lydia was my counterpart in the production. She was beauty and nature, life and resurrection. I, by contrast, was the black hole of nothingness that comes after it all ends for each and every living thing. The sixth floor was its own environment with a different color palette, a different sound, and even a different smell than the rest of the dank and slightly frightening production. There were only two actors on our floor, in the Planetarium Garden. Lydia, who was Life. And myself, who was Death.

I will say, of three hundred audience members on any given night, roughly half would ever make it to the sixth floor, and there are many uninteresting reasons as to why that is. As a man who is getting up there in years, though I do take very careful care of myself, I can understand the reticence of many to ascend so many godforsaken stairs. When they got here, Lydia and I would do our best to make a solid connection with them, even though I was clad in heavy robes and heavier makeup, and Lydia's face was completely covered. As an aside, I will praise our director to the moon for the decision to make the only masked character in the production the physical embodiment of life. It's quite lovely. As was Lydia.

And, again, before I come off as a lecherous old man pining after a younger, often nearly naked woman, please do not ascribe that to me. She was an artist. An amazing artist. And I got to enjoy one more production in the sky with her as the sun. Please chalk it up to sincere artistic admiration. She was clever and beautiful, kind and daring, and even though she wore a mask, I would dare to venture the audience members who ascended the stairs and had an experience with her will keep that experience in their hearts as long as they live.

She died terribly that night.

As Julie Andrews so beautifully put it, let us start at the beginning.

Much of the troubles the cast had experienced throughout this troubled production were not troubles we experienced in our corner of the show. To the contrary, our situation was quite lovely. If I may, I believe this was by design. *Come Knocking* is a chaotic experience, meant to throw an audience off their bearings, to confuse them and then have them find the meaning and the art where they may. It was quite daring, if I may say so. Some will look for a plot, yes, but to be thrown, without warning, into the whirlwind of the show is part of the appeal. Then, if you ascend all the stairs and are, presumably, exhausted by the physical exertion and the dancing and the lights and the fire and the set design and all the rest of it, when you arrive in the Planetarium Garden, your experience is markedly different. There is a peace. There is an obvious beauty. You are not harassed and overstimulated. I could go on as to the psychology of the floor and how, after being subjected to horrors below, the peace above only drives the point of the production home further, but I will abstain. There is a story I believe you want to hear.

One more bit of context, and I apologize for prattling on. Lydia and I had no direction. Our instruction was "appear to the audience and make them feel it" which I took to mean, be in the shadows, be a mystery and then appear when you feel it has the most impact. Lydia had the same instruction, but it was her idea to appear topless, which, if I may, was quite the stroke of genius. Nature is beautiful but also vulnerable. Nature can shock you if you're not paying attention and I think it was, conceptually, a brilliant call. It certainly stopped everyone in their tracks as the metaphor was potent, and Lydia was very beautiful.

So, with that out of the way and with all my context now expended, I unfortunately must turn to the events of March 14.

As Lydia and I had no instruction, we weren't tied to the cycles as were the actors below. On the fourteenth, I started, as I often do, in the shadows. There are always one or two groups who start with us and, when Lydia is feeling it, she shows herself and creates a unique experience for them. On that night, I witnessed her take a couple who had started on Six to the large telescope in the middle of the room, and the woman left with tears in her eyes, something that was not uncommon.

What was uncommon was the man who appeared, found me in the shadows, and stood, staring at me.

Don't get me wrong, plenty of people see me and approach me but when they realize I'm not going to respond to them—Death is on its own schedule, after all—they move on. This man did not. He stared at me. I stared at him. This is a perfectly acceptable interaction in the context of the show, but there was something uncomfortable about it for me. Something sinister. And, sure enough, when he approached me and whispered in my ear, it was nothing good.

"You're going to be very busy tonight," was all he said.

Very spooky. Very uncomfortable. I briefly considered using my radio, which I had stashed offstage, to report this incident, but in the end I did not. I have countless stories of inappropriate behavior that drove my decision not to report, but this particular incident set the tone for the strangest and most violent night of my professional career, which spans almost thirty years.

After he whispered in my ear, the man walked in the middle of the garden, which was composed of real flowers, by the way. The reason the producers employed a gardener for one effect was for the aesthetics and the scent. It smelled amazing on Six, and, if you made it up that far, you could not ignore that fact. It was undeniable. But this man, after his sinister words, clomped right into the middle of the flowers and simply stood, crushing the beautiful white petunias and lilies underneath his boots. Barbaric, if you ask me. He didn't break eye contact with me for around five minutes, I'd say, which is a very long time to stare at a person. Part of me thought I was creating an experience for the man, but the longer it went on the more I thought this was something else. Still, we stared at each other. Eventually, he moved on, out of my line of sight, and I was glad when he did.

Whether or not the Demon Dance comes to the sixth floor depends on how fast they get through their routine and whether they have to reset. As a result, they tend to make their appearance during the last round of the night and not so much during the first. On March 14, the Demon Dance didn't make it to Six after the first cycle. Very normal. The first sign that something was amiss that night was when was when I started to smell smoke around the time I expected the Demon Dance during the second round. It wasn't strong, it wasn't overpowering, but when you're used to the scent of flowers, smoke tends to cut through the palate sharply, like an unwelcome guest who won't close his mouth. I remember trying to steal a glance at Lydia, but she was nowhere to be seen. At that point we had, probably, a dozen or so people on the floor. Again, not atypical. But the smell persisted.

As actors, we knew the protocol for when something was wrong. In case of a fire, there were alarms, flashing lights and multiple exits on every floor. This was very clearly outlined when we were onboarded by the company—HR training and all of that. There was no reason to be concerned until the alarms went off, as far as I knew. So I kept in character as best I could as the smell grew stronger and stronger.

I do remember, at one point, seeing a small woman who was also in the flowers. There was no explicit rule about not being in the flowers, though in a civilized society it seems to make sense not to stand on living things, but I digress. I noticed her, as is part of my role in the show, and I saw the smell of smoke hit her. It was the oddest thing as, even from behind the mask, I could see her reaction clearly and explicitly. She smelled the smoke and began looking around for an exit, as any rational person would. When none presented itself, she began looking around to see if anyone else was smelling the smoke or taking action. I took it upon myself to approach her with the intent of reassuring her that there were exits and that everything would be fine. I did not mind breaking character in this instance but, when I started moving toward her, it made her panic and retreat. It got her off the flowers, at least.

It was at that point I started to notice more and more people coming to our floor and some of them were quite flustered. Several had removed their masks which, of course, is against the rules, but allowed me to see their faces. There was panic in their eyes, as if they had come to my floor and my garden not to see the show but to escape something. Of course, now I realize what they were fleeing, and they looked quite appropriate given their experience, but at the time I did not understand. And, after seeing the room go from six people to twelve people to closer to twenty people, I was finally able to locate Lydia.

There were two men who had her in a corner.

Now, I have expressed to you my advanced age, but what I have not expressed to you is I am tall, I am fit, and I was dressed as the literal incarnation of Death. To put it indelicately, I am an imposing presence. And, while in the general run of things I am a mild-mannered sort, seeing an assault take place in front of me of someone of whom I was very fond triggered an anger response that I had not felt in quite some time. And I acted. It took me less than five seconds to cover the distance between me and the men who had Lydia cornered and in that time each step seemed to bring about new horrors.

One step, the smell of smoke increased sharply.

Two steps, I noticed the men had their hands on Lydia.

Three steps, I noticed where they had their hands.

Four steps, I saw others notice what was happening and reacting.

Five steps, I saw Lydia's eyes through her mask, and she was terrified.

Now, as you might imagine, Death is not unarmed. He carries with him a scythe. My scythe, as to fit the aesthetics of the show, was not traditional. I heard it once described as "steampunk" though that phrase means nothing to me. It is taller than I am and fitted with pipes and knobs creating the effect of a modern workman's instrument instead of a much older harvesting device, which, I suppose, was also a modern workman's instrument at one time, but I digress again. Also, it should be noted, the blade is not real, but a very realistic-looking polyurethane. But it was solid, or at least solid enough for my purpose, which was to strike one of the offending men across the back and bring him to his knees.

Once the first man was on the ground, the second man spun to his friend and then looked up at me. While I don't know if he actually filled his pants, it would not have surprised me had he done so, given the look on his face.

Needless to say, he ran.

The man whom I had struck immediately takes his mask off and begins to cry foul. "You hit me." "Everyone saw you hit me." "I'm calling my lawyer."

It was at this point, to Lydia's great credit, that she punched the man in his face, and he fell backward, grabbed his bleeding nose, and ran off. Good riddance to bad rubbish.

Of course our little incident had gathered a crowd, and I noticed masks were coming off and revealing high levels of panic underneath. At this point, the "world was broken," as we are fond of saying in the show, so I held up my hands and spoke, not as Death, but as an employee of the production.

Yes, I remember exactly what I said.

"Ladies and gentlemen, it seems as if this evening's performance is going to be cut short. I would point you toward the exits located behind you, in the stairways, and a third exit that Lydia is going to show you right now." I nodded at Lydia who agreed. I will note that she was bare chested at his moment, which is probably what drew her attackers. I told her "grab a shirt and show our guests to the exit," and she nodded.

By now, the smoke was visible in the air, which was terrifying. Simply terrifying. I grabbed my radio and quickly turned it on, but the damnable thing wouldn't work. I played with it for a moment to make sure I had it turned on correctly, but still, no sound. This was not a positive development, but not nearly as bad as what happened next.

The doors to the exits were locked.

All of them. The door to the stairway had locked. The employee entrance had locked. The mandated emergency exit was locked. And the room was filling up with smoke. I saw people trying to work the doors and pushing, kicking, and utterly failing. People were beginning to cough. Now, I cannot describe to you what that panic did to me, because, inside, I was a torrent of emotions. But I can tell you that I immediately took my scythe and started banging out windows.

The building purchased for this production had utilized the light that came from surrounding areas into the aesthetic of the garden, which is a long-winded way of saying the beautiful views of Los Angeles were worked into how the room looked. It was the only part of the production with visible windows. One whole wall looked out onto other buildings and the city beneath. It was not floor to ceiling, but it was the first time in the show where natural light was permitted, which, again, was part of what the production designers were trying to do. The windows went easily, and when the audience saw what I was doing, some of them ran over and began breathing fresh air out of the newly smashed windows I had made.

I then grabbed a few men who were, understandably, shocked when a large man dressed as Death puts his hands on them.

"Come help me with the doors," I said, and each and every one of them did, without question. Such is the power of Death, I suppose.

However, the doors to the stairway didn't require more force. They were simply inoperable. I don't know how to describe it other than to say the locking mechanisms had been engaged and whatever happens when you push the big metal bar on the door suddenly did not work. So, we went to the emergency exit and tried the same thing with exactly the same result. The staff door, however, was a simple lock-and-key affair, meaning by force or by expertise, we could likely get it open. So, that was the door we focused on.

I remember, quite vividly, three men following me from door to door. Between the useless emergency exit and the employee door, I snuck a look at the seventeen other people in the crowd. Panic had gripped them. There was a fight near the smashed windows, and I saw a woman scream as others pushed her into the broken glass, cutting her face and arms as everyone jockeyed for fresh air. I saw the man Lydia had punched on the ground, idly being stepped upon by the crowd. And I saw the attacker I had knocked down on the ground, hitting someone with his fists.

I wish I had disengaged. I wish I had gone to see what the attacker was doing. But the three men who had come with me were "gung-ho" to get the door open. And I, as the employee, was their de facto leader. So we took turns kicking at the doorknob, loosening it with each kick. It had only taken us a minute or so to bust the lock and open the door, but in that time, terrible things had happened.

Smoke was completely filling the room, making it hard to see across to the smashed windows, and I noticed people were leaning out the windows, as if they were considering the six-story fall. Finally, I realized what the attacker was doing. He had Lydia on the ground, and he was beating her unrelentingly.

I screamed *"Get the door open!"* and ran to Lydia's aid. The man had simply overpowered her, straddled her and was raining fists. I don't know why. At that point, I did not care. Using the momentum I had built, I lowered my shoulder and plowed into him, effectively knocking him off her.

Let me . . . let me tell you a story. A fictional story that definitely did not happen. Once, Death was very angry at a young man. Very angry. More angry than he had been in his entire existence. And Death, being Death, was not merciful. On the contrary, Death saw a terrible solution in front of him because Death had encountered this man on the side of a mountain. So, using his surroundings, Death simply threw the man off the mountain and the man screamed as he fell, his head and torso hit a car before the rest of his body hit the ground, the impact effectively folding him in half. Death smiled thinking the man suffered immensely before his heart stopped beating. The end. But that is fiction. Now, let me return to recount my very real experience to you.

Lydia was a terrible mess when I returned to her. I would prefer not to describe her injuries out of respect for her memory. I will say she was having trouble breathing, likely from both the beating and the smoke. I saw her condition, saw she did not have long for the world, and then I heard the second . . . I mean first person fall out the window. I looked and the three men had taken the doorknob off the exit but hadn't opened the door.

Being overcome with rage and grief, I ran at the door, full force. I hit it with my shoulder. I broke several bones in that part of my body and damaged a good bit of my neck while knocking the door open. The moment I did so, more smoke poured in, turning the room into soup. Audience members began flooding into the exit and I got trampled, as I tried, and failed, to get up off the ground. My injuries were severe. I broke my nose, lost several teeth, punctured a lung, and had more bruises than I could count. But after the room had cleared, I still tried to go after Lydia.

My friend, I could not find her. I'm sure I was feet from her. Maybe inches. I reached out my hands, but I couldn't find her. I tried, but I was injured. I was hurt. I have had dreams where I explain this to her and she screams in my face and she starts to drown in a sea of blood. The guilt I feel not finding her is immeasurable.

What I did see, as I searched, were flowers in the smoke. I saw them, unaffected. Still beautiful. Then I saw one on fire. I don't know to this day if my brain was playing tricks or if I saw a flower burn. But my brain interpreted it as a sign. A sign that I was not going to save Lydia. A sign that this show was dead. A sign that something beautiful had died. Because nothing beautiful stays that way.

I almost didn't find my way back to the exit, but I did. I went down the stairs, I made my way to the bar, but that's a whole different kettle of fish.

I will close by saying I . . . I think about Lydia every day. I have reached out to her family and shared as many details as they felt appropriate, but it has done little to abate my substantial guilt. I told them I wish I were stronger. I wish I could have saved her. She deserved to live, she deserved to thrive, and she deserved someone better than me who could have found her in the smoke and gotten her the hell out of there.

Typical last words, I know. Not eloquent. Not enough.

I never said I was a good poet.

INTERVIEW 19
BRIE TRULOVE
Audience Member on March 14

I had been having these dreams. God, is there a more boring sentence in the English language, but about a year ago I started having these dreams. They, um, they were rough. In it, something was chasing me, always chasing. The locations were different. Sometimes it was my childhood bedroom, sometimes it was some forest somewhere, sometimes it was the swimming pool I worked at in high school, but most often it was through the apartment Mike and I lived in. Those were the worst because. . . . You know there's that moment when you wake up where everything about *you* hasn't loaded yet in your brain? Where, for a moment after you wake up, you're just a person? Whenever I had one of those dreams, that moment was more terrifying than anything. I would feel like I'd lost my grip on myself, on reality, and that whatever was chasing me had taken everything. Yes, my heart rate was always up and sometimes I screamed, but it was that feeling that was the worst. That feeling of . . . nothingness. Whatever was chasing me wanted me to be nothing.

I work in a high-stress job, so that's what I thought it was, you know? It wasn't until I saw *Come Knocking* where the really obvious metaphor played out. I saw it one time with a girlfriend and left in tears of joy. Tears that someone else understood that feeling. I told Mike about it, but he didn't . . . he was supportive but it didn't really register. I pushed him to come see for himself. And, of course, he eventually agreed because he would have done anything for me. Anything except not get a stupid tattoo. He loved tattoos and got this one of a skeleton that the band Social Distortion uses. Ever seen that? It's a skeleton dancing and smoking and drinking. I told him I didn't like that one but he got it anyway because he was a doofus like that. A really, really lovable doofus.

So, in a way, whatever was chasing me in my dreams missed me. And got him.

Come Knocking wasn't really up Mike's alley, which I get. But I've got a lot of fight in me for a girl that's barely five feet tall, and he knew it. I drug him along and, like the dutiful boyfriend he was, he put on that mask. Then we got split up on the second floor, and that was the last time I saw him until the police asked me to help identify the body.

When I saw *Come Knocking* with my girlfriend we had been separated early on, which is part of the show, and I warned Mike about that. On March 14th, dinner had taken longer than we wanted, so the show had already started when we got there, which is okay. The only weird thing I remember is after someone scanned our tickets and put our cell phones in the little pouches, the bar was dead. Not a lot of people there but there were two guys behind the bar who clearly weren't supposed to be there. I didn't know what to make of that, so we just went on in. No problem.

Everything was fine and we started our show and went down to the Depot of the Departed. I remember it was broken. The lights were flashing and the horn was blaring and I turned around to Mike to sort of get a sense of what he was thinking, but he was gone. I hadn't seen him leave. He hadn't tapped me on the shoulder. I knew he was behind me when we first got on the floor but then he just wasn't.

With my girlfriend, it hadn't been like that. I had heard people had either been "taken off" by an actor or they had wanted to linger somewhere longer than the rest of us wanted to linger, everyone would meet up at the bar later and debrief, which is how it's supposed to work. Your boyfriend isn't supposed to vanish when the show is clearly having technical issues. We had put our cell phones in the little bags . . . it was such a strange sensation. I had no idea where Mike had gone and had no way of getting hold of him. That was when the "feeling" started.

Look, I don't want to get into this too much because I've already said the phrase "I had this dream" out loud to a stranger, but I have this thing. I know when I'm in a bad situation. It's not clairvoyance or any sort of mystical thing. I don't believe in that. Nothing like that. There's no astrology involved. But I know when something doesn't feel right. At times in my life, my body and my brain have told me to get out of a situation and it's been the right call, each and every time. Without adding too much drama to my story, the second I turned around and Mike was gone, my brain started telling me I was in a bad situation, and I wanted so badly just to get out of there. I knew something was wrong and I was very, very right.

In a low-grade panic at that point, I started looking for Mike on the second floor. I was moving fast. I remembered what he was wearing—he had wanted to wear something that would look good with the mask so he had this dark shirt on and a pair of jeans that looked really good on him—so I was looking for that. But I couldn't find him. The floor wasn't even that crowded. If he was on that floor, I would have found him, but I couldn't.

After I realized I had to try to find him on another floor, I had to decide to go up or down. I chose up, only because it was closer to the main exit, and I was listening to my body and I was listening to my brain. Stay close to the main floor. Don't get trapped at the bottom or the top, right? That was my instinct. My instinct was to get the hell out of there, but it was also not to get trapped. So I went up.

I started high in the Crypt and started looking. I didn't want him to get past me. The last couple times I had gone, the Crypt had been my favorite. I'm a little bit of a closeted spooky girl and just the whole thing felt very fun to me, but not that night. I was scared and not in a fun way. I looked and I looked and Mike wasn't up there and then—I don't care if you believe it or not—I felt this intense urge to look up. Maybe it was the show's lighting or whatever but I remember looking up just as someone fell onto the concrete. I remember watching her all the way down, and as she picked up speed, I knew that this was the start of the bad stuff, that my instincts were right, and when she hit the ground, I saw it and I heard it and I remember the sound of bones breaking, like little snaps amid all the rest of the noise. I remember feeling sick but not throwing up. That would come later.

It seemed that everything escalated from there, started going haywire. I just remember that things were on fire. And the fires were spreading, obviously, to the set, and I saw at least one cast member break character, trying to put the fire out. There were also dancers who were fighting people and there were people laughing at it and taking off their masks. It was chaos.

What did I do? I ran. I ran down a floor to the Judas pit. I'm going to admit something to you that it took me a long time to realize. When confronted with danger, real life-threatening danger, I forgot all about Mike, and I ran. Briefly, I had thought of myself as a hero going to find her poor lost boyfriend, but I can promise you, when the chips were down, I ran. I've gotten to the point where I'm giving myself credit for stopping on Floor Three, but honestly, I wish I hadn't.

It wasn't any better down there in the Judas pit. There were more fights and screaming. Around that time I also heard what sounded like gunshots but far away. I thought they could be from somewhere else in the city but I learned later what was going on. I didn't have any contact with the shooter but . . . I'll get there. I just . . . I need to work up to it, please. This isn't easy for me.

Okay. I open the door for the third floor, and, like I said, a lot is happening. I see this group of four guys by where the Miller fight was supposed to be happening, and they are just fighting everyone they can get their hands on. I saw one poor woman, um, just get grabbed by her shirt by this guy and thrown, as hard as he could throw her, into the dark. She flew into some area I couldn't see, and then she vanished. The guy then turned and started walking toward me, and, at that moment, I didn't run. I had run from the danger above, but this guy coming toward me, clearly wanting to hurt me, it just froze me in my tracks. I couldn't move. And he grabbed me by the shoulders and something about him actually touching me shook me loose, got me moving, so I kneed him in the balls as hard as I could.

He fell backward, away from me, and as I tried to collect myself for a moment, the giant Judas ice cube fell from the sky and shattered with the poor actor inside. Everything was happening so fast at this point, but I took it all in for a second, the guy dead on the floor, and then I ran into the Judas Pit.

People were screaming and freaking out, as was appropriate. Another woman was just standing there, looking at the dead actor in the block of fake ice. I ran by her. Whatever cowardly impulse had taken over me disappeared for a moment and I ran, from person to person, looking for that black shirt and jeans, black shirt and jeans. I was panicking, and the panic was fueling my legs and my arms. Keep moving, keep moving. Black shirt and jeans. I started screaming his name, looking up and screaming "MIKE!" thinking putting my head up would amplify my voice somehow. And, all around me, things continued to go haywire.

That's when I got stabbed the first time.

The guy who I had kicked in the balls, he had found a knife somewhere and had stabbed me in the shoulder. I remember feeling a vicious, shooting pain, looking over, and seeing his stupid face in a grimace, trying to pull the knife out. I remember he looked young. I don't know how to describe it but the frustration of him not being able to get his knife back and the rage on his face made him look like a little boy. Like a child. And, for some reason I can't begin to unpack with you or anyone else, that made me so mad. So unbelievably angry. It wasn't the pain. There was already so much adrenaline running through my body that I hardly felt the knife. But his face, trying to pull the knife out of my shoulder . . . I lost it.

The second he got the knife out, my knee and his balls got familiar again, only this time I wasn't hesitant about it. I used everything I had, and he dropped. Then I grabbed the knife and stabbed him in the ear. I didn't plan it. I didn't mean to do it. But I stabbed him in the skull behind his ear and, unlike him, I didn't have any trouble pulling it out. I stood up and stood back, holding the bloody knife, breathing hard, and that's when he came after me for a third time. He ran, screaming, right at me and I move forward, screaming back at him. I don't know what had gotten into me, but I was able to stab him, once more, in the neck. But he was able to fully lift me off my feet, and he threw me onto the concrete floor where I banged my head.

I don't think I lost consciousness, at least not completely, because the next thing I remember was the guy straddling me, pulling the knife out of his neck and screaming. So much noise, it was so loud all around us. The second he pulled the knife out I just got coated with his blood, it spurted out of his neck and when he saw it hit me, he stood up and started running. I don't know where he ran or where he ended up, but I bet you someone identified his body. When he got off me, the giant Satan character was already burning, part of him falling off. I wiped the blood off my face and made my way to the door.

Just before I got there was when I got stabbed the second time. That time wasn't nearly as bad as the shoulder, but it hurt more. I was on my way to the stairs when I heard a huge noise behind me, just impossibly loud, and I was knocked off my feet. I was able to shield my head, but when I had a chance to look around, there was something sticking out of my leg. I looked a little farther and there was the face of Satan, not twenty feet away from me. The fire had spread and the statue had collapsed, and a piece of fiberglass had broken off when it landed, embedding itself in my leg. That one hurt. I screamed and grabbed at the shard and noticed it had gone all the way through my calf and out my shin. It had gotten the meat but missed the bone, which was the only positive I can think of because if it had hit the bone, I wouldn't have been able to limp out of there.

I tried, just a little, to pull the fiberglass out. It looks so easy in the movies, right? But the second I got near it, all the adrenaline in the world couldn't have gotten me through pulling it out. I remember trying just a bit and looking past my leg and there was half of Satan's face, glaring at me. Then the head, Satan's head, began to roll toward me.

To this day I don't know if I imagined it or if the flaming head of Satan actually almost crushed me to death. What I can tell you is I felt the same way as I did in that moment when I first woke up from one of my nightmares. I felt hopeless. I felt lost. I felt . . . God, it's not grief but it's, like, the grieving of all the emptiness to come, all the nothing that lies ahead. I felt the loneliness of death. It was coming for me. So I started to crawl.

I crawled toward the door. I didn't look behind me. I didn't need to, I knew what was back there, what was coming toward me. That feeling of hopelessness had a vise grip on my lungs and my heart, and I felt like I was going to pass out, but I crawled using my arms, then I crawled on my knees, and then . . . goddammit . . . I got to my feet and hobbled the last little bit to the door. I threw it open and went down those stairs on one leg. I did it. That floor tried its best to kill me, to end me, to make me dead, but I fought, and I stabbed, and I finally crawled out of there. And nothing is ever going to take that away. I beat it. I'm alive. There's nothing more to it.

Going through the lobby was an adventure. People were streaming out of there and there were bodies. I saw them and I didn't feel one way or the other about them. Some people were getting trampled, but I stuck to the walls and was able to avoid the worst of it. I hit my leg twice and the pain was something else. I screamed, but there was so much noise no one heard me. Something was happening at that show that didn't have anything to do with me but, in some way, it had everything to do with me. It had been coming for me. I don't know. That sounds dumb but it's how I felt. I have never been so happy, before or since, to see flashing police lights on street level. When the police and fire and EMTs showed up, I was one of the first out the door. The EMTs were very nice, although they were dealing with a lot. I don't know about that. I was in an ambulance with the door closed. I know they numbed me up, and I didn't watch when they pulled the fiberglass out. Once I was able, I told them I'd like to talk to an officer, who hopped into the back of the ambulance.

He wanted to know where all the blood had come from and anything else I could tell him. I told the dude what I had done. I told them I had stabbed someone after they had stabbed me. I could tell he was overwhelmed, and he just ran back into the building. I never heard anything else about it. I'm only telling you because I feel like someone needs to know. I don't know why, but my instincts are telling me it's a good thing to tell you, tell everyone. I don't dare go against my instincts anymore. If the police want to know more, please tell them where to find me. I'll tell them everything I remember.

Someone eventually took my name down, and I spent a night in the hospital. I got a call from the police on my way home to see if I could come to their precinct or whatever they call it and identify a body. I don't want to tell you about that though. I've already said too much about myself. Way too much. But Mike was burned, badly. He had died of smoke inhalation and they said he didn't suffer. They didn't show me how badly he had gotten burned, but they did show me his arm and that stupid Social Distortion tattoo. It made it through the fire. It was about the only part of him that did.

I think Mike would have liked that, or at least smiled at it if he were alive. But he's not.

I miss him. He was beautiful. And now I am alone.

So it goes.

INTERVIEW 20
MALCOLM RICE, INTERVIEW 2

Bartender at *Come Knocking* in Los Angeles

Author's Note: What follows is a continuation of my interview with Malcolm Rice. I split his story into two parts for the clarity of the story and for the insight he brought to what took place at the Gummar Bar on the night of March 14.

I told you I was gonna get to March 14 eventually, so here it goes. Buckle up, my man.

I was there when they took the control room. Right there, man. I was there with a new hire named Nikko who might have been Ukrainian, maybe? I don't know because he was new, and we hadn't chatted yet and he left to go smoke after we let the first group through to the Netherworld. No problem, right? I could hold down the fort. Well, Nikko had hardly stepped outside when a dude jumped behind the bar, held a knife to my throat—that was a new experience I did not dig—and started screaming at the camera above the control room and said, "open the door." It wasn't the same guy who showed me the knife before and left me that very considerate tip. This was a different guy who was there to do something bad. I didn't even have a chance to try to charm the dude, just "over the bar" "knife to throat." Didn't even buy me dinner first.

Truthfully, I didn't even see dude with the knife except out of the corner of my eye. Couldn't tell you exactly what he looked like. One minute he wasn't there, then he was there, knife to my throat and screaming and words I'd prefer not to repeat. Racial stuff. Ugly stuff. The worst stuff.

Anyway, without going too much into it, they opened the door without me having to be under the blade for too terrible long, which was nice. Then the dude holding the knife and his friends pushed me down and kicked me a few times, which was not nice. At that point, there were at least three, possibly four, people, and they had the jump on me. I ain't proud of it, but the proper strategy in that situation is to cover up and try not to die, which is what I did. And hey, success! I'm here talking to you.

They kicked me for what felt like a while, and I was covering up okay, until I heard something happening. I looked down and there was a gun pointed in my face. Nine millimeter. I know that because I have one myself because, I mean, I live in the neighborhood. A gun is a tool in that scenario, you follow me? Anyways, I knew what it was, and I saw the barrel pointed at my head. I am fully aware it's clichéd to say "my life flashed before my eyes," but, friend, my life flashed before my eyes, and, unfortunately, it ended with me on a filthy rubber mat.

Like so many other things in this world, I can't tell you why I did what I did next. Can't tell you, man. But as he pulled the trigger, I moved my head to the right as fast as I could and shut my eyes, hard. I heard the bang which was loud the way God is loud, and I felt some of the most intense pain I'd ever felt in my life. Strange thing, I can tell you I felt that pain and I thought, *it's good you're feeling pain. It means your brains aren't on the floor*, and I held onto that with everything I had as I kept my eyes shut on the floor.

Up above, which might as well be on the moon as far away as it seemed at the time, the shooter and the other kickers are fighting. "Why'd you do that?" "Someone's gonna call the cops too early." "They're never gonna open the door now." And in the meantime, I'm just trying to stay as still as possible, dealing with some of the worst pain I've ever felt in my life, trying not to panic at the amount of liquid I feel by my face. It was blood. I knew it was blood. But I stayed put because I knew my life depended on it.

Just then, Phil, the director, saved my ass.

Even though the last minute and a half or so had involved me having a knife held to my throat and getting kicked a few dozen times and then getting shot in the head, I was able to figure out that these people wanted in the control room. And Phil, rest his soul, opened the door and they streamed in like it was the rope drop at Disneyland, man. Rushed in there. Phil, he's usually in there with two support staff, an assistant director and someone who could solve problems as they came in. This night it was Yeti and TB, nicknames, obviously, and I hear them shouting. At that point I try opening my eyes just in time for Yeti—her real name is Yvonne, but she goes by Yeti because, as she'll tell you, she's six-foot-five and likes a sandwich—and TB to almost trip over me. Yeti sees me and starts screaming and I sit up and hold my hands up like "it's okay," but it's not okay.

When I sit up, I get dizzy and puke, right? The only thing worse than puke in those gross rubber mats behind a bar is puke down your nice white shirt. That was just the first wave of things that went wrong on the SS *Malcolm Rice*, because Yeti started screaming, and I reached up to feel my head, right? I could feel with my fingers the path the bullet took. That twitch had saved me, but the bullet hadn't missed. It had traveled basically the circumference of my skull without ever, like, getting through. Kind of a miracle in retrospect, but at the time I was losing a lot of blood out of my head, and I mean a *lot* of blood. TB, thank Christ, was a little more composed than Yeti and grabs a bar rag and holds it to my head. Then he spends a few minutes with the first aid kit wrapping my head up. I think he may have yelled at Yeti to call 911, but Yeti was not doing great. Hyperventilating, her breath coming in these huge gulps. But TB was calm enough for both of them and he got me in pretty good shape.

At that point, TB was like "we're outta here to get some help" but the second he says that, Anders, who is tech director for the show and a damn good one, comes flying around the corner and starts ordering us around. He screams, "*Get that door open!*" and, like, I'm not in a place where I can fully comprehend what's going on but he just sort of keeps screaming at us. I don't remember exactly what he said but I do remember he called us "do-nothings," which I thought was the most Anders thing Anders had ever said.

I'll tell you what's weird, even with the blood and the puke and the dizziness and the bandage on my head, it all happened so fast I never really, like, panicked, you know? It never got down into my guts, it was just a series of things that were happening that I didn't like. But when Anders, the most analytical man I may have ever met in my life, started losing his mind and running around like a madman, that was the first time it sunk in. Like, I remember thinking, "this must be bad because Anders is losing it" and then, even with less blood than normal, the penny dropped. They were in the control room, and if they were in the control room they could fuck shit up in a way I hadn't even imagined.

So, I fought my way up to a standing position, I took a deep breath, and I told Yeti and TB, "You heard the man. Let's get that fucking door open."

Now, I'm sorry to derail the story, man, but when we get there you'll thank me. I gotta tell you just a bit about Yeti and TB.

TB's real name is Tane, and he's got a Polynesian last name that I can't start to pronounce, but he was being groomed to be another director of the show. Big D. Smart as a whip, always solving problems, exactly the kind of guy you could look at and say, "He's who I want on my team," because he was a grinder but also had the big vision in his head. And then you've got Yvonne, who is almost the exact opposite. She's emotional and she stands out and she is gregarious and would make a great bartender. That sort of vibe. And, because you don't judge books by their covers, TB was not a physical guy at all, and Yeti could do the splits and flip you over her shoulder, because she knew some kind of martial art. I saw her do it once at a cast party and everyone cheered when she did it. Great lady.

What I'm telling you is we've got brains and we've got brawn.

TB immediately goes for the keypad, but Yeti stops him and says, "They're armed. We've got to have a plan." TB gets it immediately and says, "I'm going to go for the phones so someone can call 911. You figure it out and I'll be back." Like I said, smart guy, that TB. Yeti, she starts going over a few ways this could go. "We could kick the door really hard." "We could put something in front of the door to draw their fire." "We could throw the door open and tell them the cops were here." But then we heard something fall over, and Yeti and I ran over to where TB was and found him out on the floor, bleeding.

The phones are kept in this cage off the bar and are opened by this electronic thing that was its own independent program, not tied in with the control room at all. They're all stored in their own little cubbies, including the employee phones, so it shouldn't have been a problem at all for TB to go into the room, find his phone, use one of the devices to open it and then, boom! Cops are on the way. What we didn't realize was there was already someone back there, one of the group that had taken the control room, and by the time we got back there, they were kicking poor TB about the head and shoulders, and he was bleeding all over the place.

Yeti sees this and just rushes the lady doing the kicking. It was a lady, about five foot, seven inches, only about a buck forty maybe. I only mention it because I want you to picture 280 pounds of six-foot-five fury running at someone who's five-foot-seven and who wasn't paying attention all that well because she was busy kicking someone else's ass, and, well, I'll just say it's an image I'm gonna remember for a long-ass time. When Yeti made contact, both of them crashed back into the cubbies and the woman let out the sort of scream you let out when all the air is suddenly forced from your lungs. Now, I'm still a little unsteady on my feet, but it looks like Yeti has it all in hand, so I turn my attention to TB and the poor dude . . . he's been stabbed in the side. I can tell because there's blood pouring out of there and, man, I got first aid training but it was a while ago, so I kind of ask "you okay?" and he shakes his head "no." Doesn't say anything, which was really worrying to me at the time.

Just as I'm pondering what to do, the smaller lady who stabbed TB bolts from the room with Yeti right behind her. I think Yeti yelled "*Get her!*" or something like that because, next thing I know, she and I are running into the Netherworld, leaving poor TB to fend for himself. I feel bad about that because I could have been more caring or more considerate, but given I had a huge head wound and wasn't doing my best thinking at the time, I followed Yeti. I mean, I could have helped TB, I could have gotten the hell out of there, I could have tried to figure out how to get the door open, but I didn't do any of those things. I just ran into the show right behind Yeti as we tried to catch the woman. The woman with the knife.

Of course it's dark in there when you first start out in there. Of course the woman had enough of a jump to disappear on us. And, of course, with all the adrenaline pumping as fast as it was, Yeti did not want to stop until she found the woman who had attacked her. I catch up to Yeti and am like, "Where'd she go?" And it's then I realize the lights in this part of the show aren't working the way they're supposed to. There's supposed to be this flash of light that us bartenders can trigger sometimes . . . I'm going to resist going on a big tangent about how that was one of the best parts of the job but, seriously, it was one of the best parts of the job. But then, after you get past that part there's supposed to be lights leading you through this little mysterious path where you are then presented with your choice of going up or down into the belly of the show. And those lights weren't working. Of course, later on, I put together that the control room was fucking with us, but at the time I can honestly tell you it didn't occur to me. I blame the head wound, and you should cut me some slack.

So, to recap, bleeding a bunch from the head, locked out of the control room, me and a coworker chasing a crazy lady with a knife into the dark. The fact that I'm here to tell you this is a minor miracle.

Once we get in the dark, I can still, like, sense that Yeti is a few feet in front of me and I thought about whispering to her but I just didn't know if that was smart or not, you feel me? Crazy Knife Lady could have been twenty feet away or breathing on my neck and I wouldn't know, so all I was doing was trying to keep where Yeti was clear in my mind. Now, when I say "dark" I mean pitch dark because it was an effect of the show. You were supposed to be in the dark and the lights were supposed to guide you to the sign guiding you to different floors. Without the lights on, I literally couldn't see anything but I could hear things. I could hear Yeti breathing really hard. I could hear shuffling sounds that might have been Crazy Knife Lady or could have been someone else coming back to the bar from the show, though that was unlikely because they *just* got in there.

Then I saw it. A door opened, and the emergency lights we were required to have on cut through the dark. The sound of the door opening was loud, too, and I heard Yeti turn and start making for the door. Again, like a lot of that night I don't know why but I reached out and I grabbed her arm and I whispered "don't." It seemed to me like a bad idea, and if Crazy Knife Lady really had opened the door and run to another floor, than that was another floor's problem, you follow me? I had enough problems of my own at the moment.

But Yeti didn't listen. She just ran at the door.

Look, I get it, man. She's hyped, she's mad. I don't blame her for it. I blame that sick bitch who stabbed her in the dark.

I heard it. Shit . . . I don't want to get too deep with you, but I think hearing it was worse than seeing it. When you see it, you have actual proof of what's going on, right? I don't know if I phrased that well, but when you hear your coworker getting stabbed you gotta imagine where the blade went into her and when you hear sounds of a struggle you gotta imagine what's happening and when your coworker screams "help" and later "it hurts," that's a hard thing. Very hard.

You know what's harder than that? Living with yourself for running away.

That's what I did, man. I heard Yeti . . . I heard Yvonne get stabbed in the dark and I didn't help her. I'm telling you the truth and the truth is hard, because that's not how I see myself, but I turned around. I ran toward the pinprick of light that was my bar, and I ran to the little side room where TB was bleeding, and I opened someone's phone and I called the fuckin' cops, or tried to. The first dozen phones I tried had a passcode until TB comes to and asks me, "Where's your phone?" And, of course, I don't know, they all got knocked over. So we spent probably ten minutes until one of us remembers there is a way to make an emergency call on most cell phones . . . what can I say? We weren't thinking so straight on account of the significant blood loss.

Then I held TB's head up and grabbed a first aid kit off the wall and tried to wrap his wound as best I could, but the wrap wouldn't work so

I just kept pressure on it. It was a big wound, man. Like, he had been stabbed and then fell and ripped out open more. I looked, and the hole was probably three to four inches wide and looked like a mouth without teeth. Just huge and gushing blood. We stayed in that room for what felt like a year, but it probably wasn't more than fifteen minutes or so before the gunshots and the stampede and all the rest of it. We stayed in that room, and I tried to tell him it would all be okay.

Truthfully, I didn't hear the shooter come in. Just heard the shots, and that was its own "let's just keep our head down and hope the cops are here soon" sort of thing.

TB made it. I made it. Yeti didn't. I know you know that, but it . . . it makes sense to me to say out loud. I turned and I ran and didn't help my friend, but I helped my other friend, and I don't know. It was a bad situation. The worst situation. But you better believe every time I have a good meal or every time I get laid or every time something just takes my breath away, I think of how I almost didn't get to be here to see it. Then I think of Yeti who's not here to see it, who bled to death in the dark.

I think about it almost all the time.

EXCERPTS OF 911 CALLS TO THE LAPD ON THE EVENING OF MARCH 14

8:56 P.M.
911, please state the nature of your emergency.
I work for *Come Knocking* at the Darnold Center just off of MacArthur Park. Somebody came and took over our control room and shot me.
Someone shot you?
Yeah, shot me and stabbed my friend and there are like, a bunch of them. Like, I don't know.
Sir, you're slurring your words. Are you sure of what you're telling us?
No. I mean, yes! You gotta send someone, man. I've been shot and my friend's been stabbed. Please send an ambulance right now. Right now.
Yes, sir. Please stay on the line.
I can't. I gotta go. Please send someone. Please.

9:19 P.M.
911, please state the nature of your emergency.
I just saw a man with a gun go into that building where they're doing that big play.
I'm sorry, where?
That building. You know, that one building with the line every night. It's on . . . what is that? I think it's between MacArthur and Lafayette Park, shit, I don't know the street . . .
And a man with a gun went into the building.

Yeah, man, big tall guy with a big-ass gun. I don't know, but I bet you it's not part of the play.
Sir, what is your location?
I mean, maybe it's part of the show. I don't know. Is this Beverly Glenn? Maybe I don't know what the hell I'm talkin' about.
Sir, please stay on the line.

9:20 P.M.

911, please state the nature of your emergency.
Yeah, hey, there's smoke coming out of one of the windows of the building where they're doing that show. It's, like, a block away from the Lafayette Community Center.
Is it just one window?
Yeah, just one window but it smells like . . . smoke, I guess. Like it's not supposed to be happening. I think you should send fire trucks.
Is anyone fleeing the building?
I don't see anyone. Should I talk to them if someone comes out?
Yes, sir. We are sending a unit now. Please stay on the line. Are you still there?
Yes someone's coming out . . . oh my God.
Please hand the phone to the person coming out of the building, sir. Hello?
I need help.
Ma'am, what's wrong.
I can't breathe. I need help. Stepped on . . .

9:23 P.M.

911, please state the nature of your emergency.
You need to send cops and medical people to the building where they're doing *Come Knocking*. I was supposed to pick up my kid . . . oh Jesus.
Sir, please . . .
People are coming out and they're covered in blood . . .
Sir, please tell me your situation.
My kid is in there! My . . . fuck, my kid is in there. There's, um, there's smoke up high and there's people, people stepping on each other to get out. They're getting trampled, oh God.
Police and fire are on the way. Please tell me what else you see.

I see . . . people have stopped coming out. There are, maybe, twenty-five people on the sidewalk, and half of them are hurt. Okay, more people are coming out. They look okay. They look scared. *Sandra! Sandra!* Where's Riley? Sandra, where's Riley? Why isn't she with you? Where is she? Oh, shit. More people are coming out. Why are they like that?
Sir, police are almost there. Please stay with me.

9:29 P.M.
911, please state the nature of your emergency.
I hear the sirens.
Sir, what is your emergency?
I hear you coming. But you're late. It's been going on for too long now. The damage is done.
Please state the nature of your emergency.
People are going to remember this night. Remember what we did. Remember the evil we destroyed.
Sir . . .
Don't forget the basement. That's where they hide the bodies of the children they've killed. Just remember . . . the basement.

9:33 P.M.
911, please state the nature of your emergency.
Hello. I work at the play *Come Knocking*, and things are really bad in here.
Okay, ma'am. Please tell me your location.
I'm on the fourth floor. People are dead, and shit is on fire.
Police and rescue are on the way. Until they arrive can you get to a safe place?
I've been trying but I don't know. Everything is wrong. The show is wrong and everyone is wearing a mask. I don't know who . . . I don't know.
Ma'am, please take a breath. Where's the safest place you can go?
There's fire here. I heard shots lower. I could go up but the smoke is probably worse. There are people in here but they might want to hurt me. There's no safe place to go.
Is there someplace you can hide?

I don't want to burn. If I hide I might burn. I need to keep moving but I don't know where to go.
Ma'am, you're doing great. Please keep talking to me. Police and rescue will be there soon, just be as safe as you can.
I . . . I don't know if . . . someone's watching me.
Go to a safe place if you can.
Someone's following me. They see I have a phone. They see my phone and they're following me, oh fuck, they're following me.
Ma'am . . .
They're chasing me! They're chasing me! They're . . .
[*sounds of a struggle for fifteen seconds*]
Ma'am
Hello.
Sir, who was on the line just now? Can you put them back on, please?
No. I can't.
Sir . . .
She's not in any condition. Come find me. I'm the one in the mask.

9:39 P.M.

911, please state the nature of your emergency.
Hello. My name is Reginald, and I am the executive assistant for Clark Cardigan. My employer is the producer of *Come Knocking* here in Los Angeles, and we've just heard that the building my show is housed in might be on fire. I don't know who else to call so I called the emergency number.
Yes, sir. We've had reports in that area but I cannot tell you anything definitively.
Right. If we drive there, which is what I am doing this very moment, might we be granted some special access to assess the situation? My employer has a very large financial stake in the show and needs to assess any damage as soon as is possible.
Sir, we don't know the situation right now. Please speak with officers on the scene, they will be able to direct you.
No special access, then? I see. I will endeavor to speak to law enforcement upon my arrival. You've been less than helpful.

9:42 P.M.

911, please state the nature of your emergency.

Hello. My name is Anders Petersen, and I am the technical director for *Come Knocking*. Officers are on the scene, but I have vital information that is going to save lives.

Go ahead, sir.

A group has taken our control room and barricaded themselves inside. They have access to everything from safety lights to flamethrowers used in the show. They have shown direct intent to cause harm to as many people as possible. Your officers and rescue personnel must not go into the show until the control room is retaken. This must be conveyed or people will be hurt.

Mr. Peterson, please tell us where the control room is located. We will give this information to our officers.

The control room is directly behind the bar on the main floor. They are barricaded inside. If your officers go in before they retake the control room people will die. I realize I am repeating myself but this must be known and must be clear. Retake the control room or your people will die.

Understood. Please stay on the line.

It is very difficult. I may not be able to do so.

Please do your best.

I will.

9:46 P.M.

911, please state the nature of your emergency.

Hello, I'm Kyle Simmons with Orange County Action News 10. We are calling to get information on the *Come Knocking* fire. We're hearing some pretty insane reports and no one is answering questions at the scene.

Mr. Clark, you know we can't help you with that.

I'm aware. Can you confirm that someone with an axe started killing people in the theater?

Mr. Clark, get off the line.

Can you confirm that three people have burned alive? That there are dead children in the basement?
We are ending this call.

9:51 P.M.
911, please state the nature of your emergency.
Yeah, my girlfriend is a dancer at *Come Knocking* and she left me a bunch of really disturbing voicemails earlier today. She's not answering her phone which makes sense, she's at work, but then I heard that something happened there. I don't know. I'm worried she's involved.
What's your name, sir?
Daniel Corona.
Mr. Corona, there has been an incident at that location. We are gathering names and numbers of family members and will be contacting them later on when there's more information. Is this a good number to contact you?
What? Oh, yeah. You're 911, right. I would have answered her sooner, you know? But I was at work, and my boss is riding my ass.
Yes, sir. We will contact you when there's more information.
She needed me and I wasn't there.
Yes, sir. We need to keep this line clear.
Oh yeah. Sorry.

INTERVIEW 21

DANA TELLER

EMT/First Responder to *Come Knocking* on March 14

If there's one thing I remember about that night, it's that the bodies came at us in waves. I'd never seen that before. I've never seen it since. I've wanted to be an EMT since I was a little girl. I knew it would be hard. But that night . . . it was almost enough to make me give up.

I still might give up. But I haven't yet.

I was one of two EMTs in our vehicle that night. I'd been an EMT for just about nine months. Um, there was this bad joke that some other EMTs had that if you don't have a really bad night in the first six months, then you were basically cursed for the rest of your career. That's what they said. I hadn't had a bad night yet, not a really bad one, so they all started teasing me about it. It doesn't help that I have a high voice and even when I wear my uniform I look like I'm wearing a Halloween costume. On top of that I started after COVID, so the real EMTs, the tough ones, they had no time for a "little girl playing dress-up." That hurt every time they said it. Every time I went out, someone at my station would ask, "Is this your night?" and I always played it off, like, "Ha ha, very funny, boys." But I wanted them to stop saying it because they were putting it out in the universe. It felt like something bad was building, and every time they said it, I felt like my "bad night" was getting a little worse.

I was right.

The second we pulled up to that building in that scary neighborhood we were just . . . mobbed. There were twelve or fifteen people, all yelling at us that they needed help or their friend needed help or that people inside needed help. It's terrible to say but the second those back doors swung open I actually thought, *this must be what it's like when the zombies eat you.* It was my only frame of reference that made sense. In the zombie movies, you always see the person get grabbed and drug into the mob but you never see that person's point of view right before the teeth start tearing into them, do you? If you did, I bet it looked like a lot like what I saw that night.

The other EMT in there with me, in the back, was Carlos. Carlos and I didn't work together a lot, but he became the best friend I ever had that night. I think I became his best friend, too, but you'd have to ask him.

When we pulled up and the door opened, Carlos saw me freeze up in the face of the zombie horde. I'm not proud that it happened but he saw it, recognized it, and jumped in front of me. He actually pushed me back into the bus a bit and he took charge, telling everyone more help was on the way. Carlos was taking charge and I'm very glad he did. It took me a minute, but I eventually shook off the shock of what I was seeing and got to work.

But the zombie thing, that feeling, it came back. Actually it never left. Every time I got someone alone enough to start treating them, two other people would come up, desperate for some sort of attention, pushing and screaming. One woman, I remember, had this loud cough and she kept coughing in my ear and screaming when she wasn't coughing. "Am I dying?" *Cough cough!* "I feel like I'm dying." *Hack hack.* I told her "You're not my priority right now," and she told me she was going to talk to my manager for being rude.

What sort of injuries did I see? I'm going to have to say "lots." I saw lots of them. There were burns, there were cuts, there were people who had been stepped on, I saw at least one collapsed lung, a few stab wounds which I have no idea about, head injuries, broken legs, broken arms, contusions. But that was all secondary to the gunshot wounds.

Gunshot wounds are the worst. I take that back, some gunshot wounds are the worst. If there's a hole in your arm and another hole where the bullet went out, I can treat that. Even if the hole is pretty big, I can get you to the hospital which is where you need to be. But when you have one hole in you and no hole where the bullet came out, that means the bullet could be anywhere, which is bad. When you're looking at some gunshot wounds, you might be dealing with a person who needs help immediately or you might be dealing with someone who's basically dead but doesn't know it yet. And almost everyone in that first wave, except for the Karen coughing in my ear, had a gunshot wound. Almost all of them. Before I knew it, I had blood all over my uniform, and I wasn't even sure where it was coming from.

Can I tell you something else? The smell. The other EMTs, they always would talk about this particular smell when you're having a really bad night. It's sweat and adrenaline and blood and other chemicals and it all becomes this one smell. Like all garbage eventually smells the same, right? All "mass trauma events" have a smell. I know what that smell is now. I can't tell you what it's like. You have to smell it for yourself.

Carlos, God love him, had set up a triage by the time the other units rolled up, and thank God he did, because there were some people in bad shape. The second they showed up, he loaded up the ones who needed immediate transport and sent them on the way while I was doing what I could for the others.

Then the second wave hit us.

The second wave came all at once. I mean, that's sort of the definition of a wave but . . . never mind. I'm not sure what was going on in the building and after I'm done talking maybe you can tell me if you know. I mean, you might know or you might not know, but I'd like to know why another twenty people or so all came out at once, falling all over each other, screaming that there were more people inside who needed help. There was no way in hell that I was going to go inside there with what I was dealing with outside. When the second wave hit, one guy grabbed Carlos and said, "You've got to help him. He's in there and he's really hurt." And Carlos, God love him, ran inside even though there were already police officers and firefighters and all sorts of other people starting to pull up who were much better trained to deal with whatever was happening in there. I heard one firefighter got stabbed in there, is that true? Can you tell me later if it is, because if I worked the scene where a firefighter was stabbed, I think that would be a cool story.

My point is the second wave just overwhelmed us, and we were on the edge of "overwhelmed" as it was. And with Carlos running in the building like a hero, the zombies came back. I had people pulling on me one way and people pulling on me another way and I had to fight them as much as I could just to breathe, it felt like. Other units weren't getting there fast enough, and people were desperate. Looking back on it, I don't blame them. I understand they needed help but they had to see that I was just one person and I was working with what I had and that I was completely overwhelmed by the situation. I will say this for myself, I didn't freeze up like when we started. But with all the police inside and the firefighters running inside and Carlos inside, no one was doing crowd control, which meant any time I started working on someone, another person would grab me and tell me they were hurt worse. And, of course, I didn't know if they were really hurt worse or if they just felt like they were hurt worse.

Everyone was grabbing at me like I was their ticket out of hell. But I wasn't. I was their ticket to LA General, which is its own, different sort of hell. Anyways.

I'm going to tell you something I'm not proud of. I grew up religious . . . that's not the part I'm not proud of. That sounded bad, please don't take that out of context. Okay, the thing I'm not proud of is I had to start yelling at people to get them to back up. I'm ashamed about that because they always say of EMTs, "You meet people on the worst day of their lives," and I always used that as my guiding light. Be kind to people who are having the worst time and try not to make it worse, right? I made a few people's night worse by what I did.

The woman with the cough, she kept trying to get my attention. Every time I turned around, there she was, *cough cough!* "I'm calling your manager." "*Hack hack.*" "You are very rude." And, I lost it. Around me were people bleeding to death and other people trying to help people who were bleeding to death. One man was large and bald and was holding what looked like his boyfriend . . . I don't know if they were gay or not but he was caring with for this man very tenderly. I locked eyes with this big, bald man and I just said, "Get this woman out of my face!" I said it with a voice that actually surprised me with how angry it sounded. I sounded vicious! My voice is high and I seem very small sometimes, but at that moment, I sounded quite large.

The large bald man, perhaps looking for some place to put all the panic and energy, hauled off and hit the woman in the face. Hard. I clearly remember seeing his body move and realizing what he was about to do, and then turning my head to see it happen. The woman was completely unprepared. She didn't brace herself, she didn't put her hands up, she didn't even see it coming. The man flattened her face and she fell backward. She didn't scream so the best I can theorize is that he knocked her the fuck out.

The reaction to the man's violence didn't take long.

Everyone saw the punch as an invitation to throw punches themselves, and that was very much a party some people were eager to attend. There were friends of the woman throwing punches, the large bald man throwing more punches, people who were helping people just a moment before all of a sudden attacking others. Because of all the punching, more people required medical attention and . . . those who already needed medical attention needed it worse. I saw a man try to jump over a gurney with someone on it. The jumper's foot didn't clear the man on the gurney, and, I hope I'm remembering this wrong, but the jumper's heel caught on the man's chest where a bullet wound was. He tipped over, and the gurney tipped over, and the man on the gurney tipped over, and I remember seeing some blood, but I'm not sure where. If I were telling this story at a bar or whatever, I would have said "I saw a guy stomp another guy's bullet wound," but that's not how it went, and I might be exaggerating a little bit. I sure hope so. I never got to that guy.

Whether I'm remembering it correctly or not, the result was a melee. A donnybrook. A mosh pit with no music, a riot, a destructive dance. The zombies stopped lumbering at me and started slamming into me.

At that point providing any sort of help was off the table completely. People were slamming into me, pushing me to the ground, and a few seconds after the big bald man punched that woman coughing in my ear, I was on the ground being stepped on. When people start fighting like that, I'm pretty sure any higher brain function is also off the table completely, so any "help" I could give them wasn't nearly as important as punching the person in front of them. Because of that, I quickly found myself fighting for my life and . . . losing. It started when someone stepped on the outside of hand and broke several of my fingers. The heel of the foot that smashed my fingers did a quick turn, meaning a painful break for one finger became a compound fracture for two. To put it another way, a big freakin' boot stepped on my fingers and tore them up so badly I could see my own bones. I remember when I picked up my hand, part of my skin clung to the concrete and I remember . . . wanting it back. I was angry that, in the blink of an eye, part of me was gone forever. I don't know if I'm making any sense, but I felt that more than any pain that I remember.

I'd lose a lot more before the night was over.

I was able to pull myself up into a sitting position and cradle my destroyed hand. I had just found my balance when I was kicked in the ribs and went down, and the moment I went down, the pressure on my head was too much to take. Just too much. Someone was pushing, or falling, I suppose, directly onto my head, forcing my face into the concrete. I had just seen my hand turned into hamburger and as the concrete got closer, I had images of losing parts of my cheek or my eye or my jaw, so I panicked and pushed back, hard. Even with everything I had, the pressure, wherever it was coming from, was too much so, just before I started to scrape my skin on street, I leaned forward and tried to turn over, tried to take the pressure off my head. It worked. All the pressure, which turned out to be two people being pushed by another two people, transferred from my head to my chest, and I landed flat on my back.

The two people, balled together, and the two people on top of them, continued to kick and scream and curse and fight, and I started getting crushed to death.

It started with pain. The pressure immediately hurt and then continued to hurt and then, and this is hard to describe, but it didn't stop hurting and got worse. I still . . . I still feel panic, physically, in my body, talking about this because when you're in pain, most of the time you can make it stop or it doesn't just ramp up. But this kept intensifying and kept intensifying until I screamed both out of pain and panic. I couldn't breathe, but I remember the panic, the panic that I was going to die like this. It was the worst experience of my life, like everything that made me "me" disappeared in that scream and I was a wild animal, screaming and kicking and . . . not breathing enough.

My hand was still clutched to my chest, which was allowing me to breathe enough to not pass out which would have killed me, I'm sure. It was a mistake. A fluke. But I had accidentally done the one thing you are supposed to do when being crushed, and that is to give yourself breathing room with your body, if you can. My fingers were spurting blood onto my face and into my mouth, but at that moment it was worth it to be able to breathe, even a little bit. That's when, using the same voice I used that kicked off this whole mess, I screamed *"Get the fuck off of me!"* as loud as I could. And it worked! The men rolled off and their attackers followed them and I grabbed breath as much as I could until someone stepped on the back of my head and basically curb stomped me into the street, knocking out four of my teeth.

I screamed again, swallowed a tooth, swallowed much more of my blood and thought, seriously, again, that I was going to die. I thought, again, that if I passed out, that was it. I pictured my mom crying and my cat starving to death and grief . . . the grief of my own death, I guess, hit me. I had a lot of things I wanted to live for and I'll tell you the truth. It was is if God heard me because I shut my eyes and cried a bit, and when I opened them I saw the most amazing sight. The sight that, for the first time, gave me hope on this "bad night."

I saw my ambulance.

I rode in a Type 1 ambulance, which is built on one of those big, large, glorious truck chassis. There was more than enough room for me to crawl under, breathe, spit blood, cry, spit more blood, and wait a few minutes until I heard the glorious sounds of more ambulances and police pulling up. I waited until I was sure the fight was being broken up, and it broke up pretty quickly, and then I crawled out. Another unit from my station was there and the EMT, an old-timer named Bruce, looked at me, and I saw him tear up. I must have looked terrible. He loaded me up and I was able to croak out to him, "I guess it was my night, huh?" He just shut the door, and I was on my way.

Carlos? I don't know when he came out or what he saw. I liked medical leave so much I decided to find another job. I now do something a lot safer that I'm not going to tell you about. But Carlos? No. I haven't spoken to him since.

I bet he's got a great story.

REILLY PEGG

Administrator/Founder of Who's There

Author's Note: I spent two months speaking with family members, friends, attorneys, and correction professionals at the California State Prison where Reilly Pegg was housed in an attempt to secure an interview with the infamous founder of Who's There. I was met with consistent resistance and was ultimately unsuccessful. After exhausting my options, my last-ditch effort was to write Mr. Pegg a letter, asking him his side of the story. Reilly Pegg was murdered by another inmate at the California State Prison on November 29 of last year. Four days after his death was announced, I received this handwritten letter.

I have confirmed details of this account and believe it to be accurate. To the best of my understanding, this is the closest we have to an explanation of Reilly Pegg's actions on March 14. I have cleaned up the spelling and grammar, and you are welcome to read the letter for yourself on my website.

To: Adam Jakes
From: Devin Scoville, Inmate #735567
California State Prison
44750 60th Street West, Lancaster, CA

Mr. Jakes,

    I was roommates with Reilly Pegg. We were friends. He asked me if he died to send you this information. I took notes in case it happened. Here's what he wanted to tell you.

    Before I start, I want you to know that Reilly was always honest with me. He lied sometimes, but he always had a good reason. Also, when he talked to me, he had a lot of detail I can't include here or that I've forgotten. Please know I don't think I'm feeding you a line of bullshit. Please get Reilly's story out, if you can.

    When Reilly was very young, he was in a relationship with Clark Cardigan, the man who ran the company that did *Come Knocking*. He said he was "of age" but I don't know about that. Either way, he said Clark hurt him. That he would "pass him around," if you know what I'm talking about. He said his early life was like that Elton John song, but I don't remember the one he's talking about and I didn't write it down. Reilly said Clark Cardigan promised him big things if he'd do things like have sex with a lot of men at a party while Clark Cardigan watched. He said he was young and didn't know he was being taken advantage of. Somewhere during that period he became HIV positive, but he didn't like to talk about that. There were other "party boys" but Reilly was Clark Cardigan's favorite, he said. That's why he made him the Knight when *Come Knocking* opened in New York City.

    Reilly said he loved playing the Knight. He said for almost a year playing the Knight made all the sex parties and drugs that he did with Clark Cardigan worth it. He said his favorite part was watching someone "get it" and I think he meant "understand the show." I don't know much about theater so I'm sorry if I've got some of the terms wrong. I'm just telling you what Reilly told me.

    While he was the Knight he was too busy to see Clark Cardigan very much or go to any of his sex parties. I always thought Reilly made hints that there were underage boys there, but he never said that was the truth. Because he was busy, Clark Cardigan had to call him, which made Clark very angry. "You call Clark Cardigan, Clark Cardigan does not call you!" Reilly said. Because Clark had to call Reilly, he was immediately very angry with him and they had a big fight over the phone. Reilly told me other people heard the fight, and, after that, he was worried that he would lose his job. He loved his job and did not want to lose it.

Two weeks after the fight, Reilly was told by the director of the play that they were replacing him as the Knight with a new actor no one had ever heard of. Reilly said that it was Clark Cardigan's latest "party boy" and that he didn't even know anything about the play. Reilly was very angry about this and asked the director how they could do that? The director said it was his job to make the producers happy. After that, Reilly got very angry.

He said he broke things in the show. I asked, "What do you mean?" and he just said he "broke things." But, one time, when we were able to get our hands on alcohol (I will not tell you more), he told me he threw a big fit and security threw him in the control room to stop him from bothering the audience. That was when, he said, he came up with his plan. "If you control the room, you can burn the show down," he said. I asked him if that's what he wanted to do . . . burn down the show. He said "yes," and I believed him.

One of the things Reilly missed the most in prison was the internet. We have access to the internet for certain things in here, but it's not like it is on the outside. Reilly said, after he was fired, he was online all the time reading about the show and posting about the show. He said he made up a bunch of people and got the show's rating on some website dropped by a star. He said he was very proud of that. I told him it didn't seem like a very big accomplishment to me and he didn't talk to me for a day or two. What I mean is Reilly was on the internet all the time. A bunch of times I saw him reach in his pocket for his phone that wasn't there. He said it felt like a "phantom limb." I don't know what that is like, but I've gotten off drugs, and the people on TV say it's the same thing.

I asked him once why he loved being on the internet. He said he was "good at it." He explained to me what he meant, but I'm afraid I didn't understand. I know Facebook and Instagram but past that, I don't know very much. But Reilly said if you were "good" at the internet, you could do anything. You could make people believe you were a different sex or a different race, you could pretend to be whoever you want. I asked him what he pretended to be and he said, "a genius." He said people thought he had a grand plan and that he was leading a revolution. I didn't understand that and he tried to explain it to me. It seemed like if you turned off the computer, all the problems they invented would go away but that's my idea, not Reilly's.

I asked Reilly (he always liked to be called Reilly) if he meant to kill all those people and he'd always say the same thing—"I wanted to burn it down and it's sad people weren't smart enough to find the fire exit." Everyone in here would ask him that and he said the same thing so many times I could move my mouth along with his. He didn't think that was funny. He didn't have much of a sense of humor. But, one night, after we had gotten some alcohol (I won't say how often that happened) he told me more. He said he didn't want to hurt people at the start. He said he wanted to hurt the show and really hurt Clark. He said, "the show is the way to hurt him." I don't know what he meant, but he said it several times. But that night we were drinking his story changed. He said that something happened the night before that changed his mind. Someone "called him out," he said, and that day the place burned up he said he "woke up angry and just got more and more furious as they day went on." By the time he got there, he said, he could "smell the blood."

I asked him a few times what it was that made him mad or who "called him out," but I was drunk and forgot. Sorry.

What I do remember, and will never forget, is what Reilly said next. He told me once he got in the control room, the things he could do were "worse than he realized." He said he knew he could control the flamethrowers, but he didn't know he could disable the smoke detectors. He didn't know he could lock certain doors from the control room. He didn't know how many cameras were there. At one point he got a faraway look in his eye and said, "I could see everyone in the monitors. I could see them all and I would pick one and make something bad happen. I would burn one person who was trapped and then I'd drop a prop on someone who was running to help them." Then he said, "it was the most power I've ever had. I felt like God."

I don't think God goes around dropping things on people, but I'm in prison for the next ten years, so what do I know? I remember what he said because he said it slow, like he was chewing a steak. His eyes weren't focused. And he was smiling.

I have written too much. The stuff above is what I remember, which Reilly told me to include. I will also say that Reilly was a good roommate and never hurt me. That's pretty good in here. That's all from me but I need to tell you the three things Reilly wanted you to know. He wrote them down, told me to write them down "word for word" and then flush the paper he wrote them on down the toilet. He did that because at least two of the guards had already sold photos and descriptions of him to magazines and websites that wanted information on him. I hope this is good for you to read. If you were to write me back, that would be great. I don't have a lot of people who write me letters in here and have never met a real reporter before. Thank you for considering it. Here's Reilly:

To Adam Jakes:

If this reaches you, I've been killed in this place. Thank you for giving me this witness. There are three things I'd like the public to know.

1) *To the media, I am not a monster even though I did monstrous things. I am a broken, angry guy who had a very bad day. I wish it were more complex than that, I wish all those shows that write me wanting an interview would tell that side of the story, but that's not what gets clicks and that's not what they want. They want the monster, and I can't give it to them. When I think back on that night, I remember some things I did very clearly, but not all the things. What I remember most is the feeling. I had never been so angry and never had the ability to hurt people before. It was a bad combination. I'm not explaining myself very well but it's the best I can do. Plus, I'm dead. I don't care if you don't get it.*

2) *To everyone on Who's There, I underestimated you. I had no idea there were legit psychos in our midst. I didn't know that your Warrior Queen would end up so bloodthirsty. I didn't know this fight wasn't just mine but ours and I will forever be grateful for the camaraderie and love we gave each other. And while I underestimated you, I'm afraid you all overestimated me. I'm not a genius. But I did get it done, didn't I? Keep the faith.*

3) *To Clark Cardigan, I remember the more I did things for you, the more you became abusive. It started off as domination and turned into abuse. I remember, you prick. I remember you binding me up and spitting on me as guy after guy after guy took their turn. I remember you getting very, very close to my face and saying "you're nothing. You're spit. You're shit. You're nothing." Over and over and when I started crying, when you finally broke me, you started laughing and laughing. Doubled over. You almost spilled your scotch, you were laughing so hard. Who's laughing now, motherfucker?*

—Reilly

INTERVIEW 22

CLARK CARDIGAN

Producer of *Come Knocking*, co-owner of Dumb Willie Productions

Author's Note: After receiving Reilly Pegg's letter, I contacted Dumb Willie's attorneys with the chapter you just read. Three hours after I hit "send" on the email, I was asked to get on a plane and meet with the publicity-shy Clark Cardigan in the British countryside, overlooking his estate.

All right, then. Let's get his over with.

You're a writer, yeah? Writers are fuckin' scum. I hate 'em. Never have any vision, just yap yap yap all the fuckin' time talking about what geniuses they are. Reporters are even worse. The only time writers and reporters are worth anything is when they're drunk, which is why you're having a drink with me. I don't care what time it is, I ain't drinking by myself. I don't fuckin' care 'bout much of anything, if I'm being honest.

All right. I can see you're a bit of a pussy, so I'm gonna have to ease you into this with a story. I'm gonna tell you a story about a soprano. It was one of my first shows, yeah? Third one, *Absolute Filth*, the one that started making money enabling all the decadence you see around you. This soprano, whose name I'm gonna leave out because it'd be rude to say, "This story is about a soprano named Linnea Beckett who never amounted to anything" out loud to a reporter, this soprano was perfect for the role. Sang just right. Like, just right. It's a rare thing to find a fuckin' soprano who sings just the way you want her to. Sexy, if you're into that sort of thing. Which I ain't. I think you may have heard that. Anyways.

Perfect soprano. But she comes with a boyfriend, and this boyfriend thinks he's the fuckin' man, the cock of the walk, yeah? He comes into my office, doesn't make an appointment or nothin', and says, "Here's how it's gonna be. My soprano girlfriend is gonna have her name in lights. My soprano girlfriend is gonna get her own private dressing room. And my soprano girlfriend is getting a big fat fuckin' raise, and if you want to work with her, you're gonna have to go through me." Thought he was her manager. Thought a lot of things, mostly about himself.

Now let me ask you, writer fella, how do you handle that situation?

Before I tell you what I did, let me tell you about being a producer. It's nothin' but a big long list of bullshit every single second of every single day and those who survive, those who make it, are able to check things off their fuckin' list. Check them off. Not worry about them. The good ones build a machine with the right cogs in the right places so the thing runs itself. That's the goal.

I wanted to throw this manager out of my office, yeah? Bust his fuckin' head on the floor and take a piss on him. But that only creates more things on the list. Maybe he sues me. Maybe I get a bad reputation. Maybe he punches me, and I have to show him to make an example. Remember, fewer things on the list. Not more. Always.

So I tell this fuckin' big shot, "Sure, mate. We'll write down everything you say and me and my partner are going to have a conversation. Let's talk next week on Tuesday," or whatever the fuck. Then, the second he's out of my office, I call Dan, I run the plan by him, and then I destroy this woman's career. I fire her. I call other directors and tell them what this soprano's fella did. I call the casting director and tell her, "All hands on deck. You did great work, but she's too dicey. Get me another soprano, please and thank you." Always be nice to casting directors. Then I tell security to lock her ass out of the show that night. The boyfriend, he huffs and he puffs and he's got no leverage. Not a fuckin' bit. Scream all you want, mate. The body's been buried and you dug the hole.

Then I get another soprano who's not as perfect but pretty fuckin' good, and I plug her in and she does the show for three years. I checked that off the list. Don't get in my way of checking something of my list.

Come Knocking was a hard show to build. Fuckin' brutal. Everything was an issue, but Dan, he was so hard for that fuckin' show, man. Just on fire for it and we work well together, so yeah. Let's build it. Took a long time to find the right people. I had to fly some folks over from the UK, one guy from Holland. Those Scandinavian guys, they have attention to detail like you wouldn't believe, in work and in play, if you follow. Took twice as long as I thought it would, which is four times as long as I told everyone it would take. But we got it built and I have to agree with Dan. When we opened in New York, which is a city I fuckin' hate by the way, it was a thing of absolute beauty. That's why I work with Mr. Darnold. He's the flamboyant one, yeah, but he's the one with vision. He's the guy who can see what no one else can see in terms of what a show's going to be. I'm the poor bastard who has to make it fuckin' happen.

Have a drink. I wasn't kidding. I ain't drinking alone.

So. So, so, so. I imagine you wanna talk to me about the accusations Mr. Pegg made. That right? You'd like me to "give my comment." Well, here's my comment.

Yeah, I am a homosexual. Have been since I could remember fancying anything. Yeah, I knew Mr. Pegg, had a sexual relationship with Mr. Pegg and, probably, did everything he's saying I did. Probably worse. But my comment is this—everyone was of age, everyone had given consent, and that's that. I ain't ashamed about none of it. You want further comment I'll tell you those little parties of mine, they fell off completely after everything happened. But I never messed with anyone who was not of age, and I never did anything illegal. I did some things most folks would find objectionable, but over the years I've done more than a few objectionable things to more than a few sexual partners, and none of 'em broke into one of my plays and murdered a bunch of people, so I would say that puts him in a special class, don't it? A psycho class. A fuckin' loser class. We've all been hurt. Get over yourself.

But that's not what Mr. Pegg did, was it? He decided to hold a grudge, to pretend like I was some boogeyman keeping him from his happy place. No matter what he did, how he lived his life, he built me up into such a big deal that he could never check me off his list. You wanna know somethin', mate?

I get off on that.

I know how that sounds. I know it ain't PC or woke or whatever the fuckin' word is, but the truth of the matter is this—I like my boys, I've got predilections, and I'm rich enough to where the party never had to end. So fuck it. Yeah, the fact I lived in that fuckboy's head right up until the moment someone put a shank through it, yeah. I'm half hard right now just thinkin' about it.

Not accustomed to this level of honesty, I take it. I guess this is a good time to mention the cancer diagnosis. Remember when I said the party never had to end? Well, the party's comin' to an end, isn't it? Truthfully, part of me thinks I'm getting out at just about the right time. Danny Boy and I ain't never gonna get another show made, not after Mr. Pegg went all murdershow on us. I'm fat, I'm old, and I don't like it. My throat hurts all the time, even when I'm pissed, and they tell me if I don't do nothin', I've got a year, maybe. But hey, if I fight it I might get skinny again. Who knows?

So yeah, I'm on my way out, I fucked all those boys and spit in their faces 'cause I liked doing it. What else are we talking about? I don't have all day.

How'd I hear about the show burning down? All right, I'll talk about that but I want you to know, mate, that is dangerously close to a "how did you feel when" question, and there ain't no lower form of question on this earth than "How did you feel?" I've got six tattoos on my body and a judge can only see one of 'em, and it's this one on my forearm that says "Death Before Small Talk." 'Cause I believe it. You can talk about the weather or you can talk about how temperatures are higher because of man-made climate change and start a fight. You can ask "how are you" or you can tell someone about the shit you took earlier that day and gauge their fuckin' reaction. And, you can ask "how did you feel?" or you can ask "what did you do?" I know which question yields the most interesting answer, not to tell ya how to do your job.

Drink your drink. I ain't asking again. Atta boy.

To your question, I was in London at the time. I hate New York, but I love LA, which you might not think, but . . . the boys. They all end up there, don't they? I'm a man with vices, I never represented myself otherwise. So, if something went really wrong, like really wrong, I could expect to hear that info from my director. He's the only one with my contact info and he has strict instructions that if he dials that number . . . ha. Shit, mate, you caught me in something. This is the first time I've ever said this out loud, but my instructions were, "If you're dialing my number, it means the building is burning down." That building didn't burn down, but it burned up and the joke stands as pretty funny. Dark but funny. What he fuck was I talking about?

Yeah, how I heard. So, it wasn't the director who called me. It was a fuckin' presenter from some LA station. I don't know how that fucking knob got my number . . . actually that's not true. I know how he got my number and it's because he graduated from the Clark Cardigan school of cocksucking once upon a time and I'm too lazy to change my number. Anyways, that news guy calls me and is like, "Your show is on fire." Now, I'm a man of vices, and that time of night I've got my sheets firmly in the wind so it took me more than a minute to figure out what the fuck that old queer was talking about. Once I got there and realized I was "on the record," I hung up the call but it was too late, some of what I said made it on the air and made it sound like I didn't know what I was talking about. Which I didn't, but you never want to seem that way. Anyways, that's how I heard and my next call was to Danny Boy, who was in LA.

He and I, we share one brain but different sides of it. I love him enough to have never fucked him, and that's a special kind of love for me. He's the reason I am who I am, and I'm the reason he is who he is, and we tell each other that at least once every time we see each other in person, so when he answered the phone and I heard his voice, I knew I had to get on a plane as soon as possible and I started making some drunken, slurring calls trying to get on the red-eye. What did he say? He didn't say much. It was how he said it and, if you'll excuse me, what I mean by that is "it's private" so quit fucking asking.

By the time I had touched down the police had that stupid "manifesto" from the shooter and were working on the rest of it. As soon as I saw the name Reilly Pegg, I knew. I fuckin' knew, and I volunteered to go with my lawyer to the cops and spill my guts. Tell them he was a former "friend" of mine, tell them we had left things on bad terms, tell them the lot of it. They appreciated it and my very, very expensive counsel told me that when the civil suits came, and they sure as hell have tumbled down the fuckin' mountain with all speed, that it would look good that I volunteered information.

Tell you what, I'll answer that question when you finish that drink. That's right. Go on, down the hatch like a big boy. There ya go.

Do I feel responsible? Fuck no, I don't feel responsible. I was 5,400 miles away and if I had been there, then what? Seriously, you answer me, mate, what would constitute accountability in your eyes? Maybe if I took a bullet? Maybe if I had caught on fire. Any of that work for ya? No, I'm not fuckin' responsible. I built a show, a great show, a show I was proud of, and a bunch of losers on the internet led by a twink who cried all the fuckin' time decided it was part of some grand conspiracy and shot and burned and trampled a bunch of people. If someone dropped a bomb in a football stadium, do you blame the coach? If a hurricane hits an amusement park, do you blame the owner? Dumb question, mate.

Oh, maybe I could have made the show safer? Tell you what, you go through the records of over two thousand shows in New York and tell me the security concerns. We had been running for . . . shit, I don't know how long in LA and had a spotless record. Maybe you go and you ask any of Reilly's internet misfits which fuckin' safety protocols they thought I should implement. Maybe you go ask the guy with the gun what sort of things would have slowed him down. You do that. You do that and get the fuck off my terrace. I'm about done with you.

After leaving the terrace I was met by Dan Darnold, who requested a chance to talk with his business partner. Twenty minutes later, I was ushered back onto the terrace.

Yeah, all right. I've got one last thing to say.

I might be a right prick, but I'm not a monster. Never was, I don't care what Reilly will tell ya. I have achieved a lot of success by being hard with people because, as I told you, I've got a big long list of things to check off. As I've gotten on and as I face this illness I'm facing, I find the list of things I need to check off is getting shorter and shorter. It's going to drop and drop until there's just a few things. Then just one thing. I can see that from where I'm standing and I fuckin' hate it.

So here's what I want you to take away. *Come Knocking* was a great show. Just a great fuckin' show. It challenged people, it pushed actors, it definitely pushed the technical staff, and it was something you never, ever forget. The fact that it got wrapped up in something that I had a part in . . . no. No, I'm sorry, I ain't fuckin' saying that. I treat people how I treat people and they can take me or leave me and over the years, more people have taken me than have left me, and I've been handsomely rewarded with money and fame, so fuck it. Fuck. It. I am who I am and I ain't changing that for you. I'm not sorry for how Reilly feels. That's his fuckin' business. To me, I got what I needed from him and if he didn't like that, then he could have been a big boy and figured it out. He didn't and that is not my problem.

You know . . . the view out here, it's really great. I grew up with almost nothing. The view I had? It was a fuckin' smokestack and a field full of dead, poisoned fuckin' grass. I built myself into someone of power and fame, someone who can afford a view like this. I accomplished things. Big things. Assholes like you can pretend I'm some sort of sad sack, but that ain't the truth. I came, I saw, I conquered, and I fuckin' know it.

You can leave now.

EPILOGUE

As a journalist, one of the last things you want to do is sound trite or reductive. Stories like the events of March 14 at *Come Knocking* are complex and layered, there are unclear motivations, histories that come into play, and decisions made long ago that come to bear on the future. This situation was complex, and I hope I have presented it as such.

With that being said, I am taking a simple, one might say trite, truth away from my time spent reporting this story. Before I get there, a little "behind the scenes."

I was tempted to finish this investigation with a treatise on the symbolism of masks. I have a draft of this introduction where I wax philosophically about how wearing a mask at *Come Knocking* and looking at depictions of hell was actually the wrong way around. That hell was underneath the mask. But I scrapped it because, as it turns out, if I have to summarize this investigation in four words, the words I would choose are not "Hell is other people." The words I would choose are "the masks are off."

It might sound reductive. But it is my honest personal and professional takeaway.

Let me tell you what I mean. Months and months ago, I started this investigation with a hunch after researching the initial facts—that selfishness and fear brought about the events at *Come Knocking* on March 14. Reading through this material one more time and spending some time thinking about my time with Malcolm and Talia, with Anders and Brie, with Clark, and even with the words and sentiments of Reilly Pegg, I have come the conclusion that "fear and selfishness" might be a bit reductive.

As with *Come Knocking* itself, there were so many moving parts, so many ingredients in the brew of toxicity that led to March 14, that it's hard to identify any single cause as the primary culprit. Where do we lay the blame? Guns or the internet? A fraying society or sins of the past? Maybe the violent and "satanic" imagery of the show caused God in Heaven to turn his wrath on the production, like has been put forth by more than one politician in our barely functioning democracy.

However, the more I roll the events around in my head, the more I go back to what we hide and what our society is starting to force us to reveal.

While it was vanity and fear that drove *Come Knocking* to create massive effects that were dangerous in the wrong hands, it was hidden pain that drove the leader of Who's There. There was more than a little conspiratorial thinking and love of the "LOLs" that drove the internet community of Who's There to create an enemy in their mind, an enemy that was pure evil and needed to be vanquished, but it was one man's need for companionship that added accelerant to their fire. It was pain and shame that stopped Reilly Pegg from putting an end to his quest for retribution, but it was others that pushed him further than he wanted to go. And it was escalation that turned a prank into a crime and a crime into a bloodbath, on both sides of the ledger.

Quickly, I fear the above paragraph is going to make it sound like I hold both sides equally at fault, and that is not my position. Who's There was, by far, the aggressors and its members, particularly Reilly Pegg and Joanna Proctor, who were at the helm in the control room, are responsible for the largest amount of mayhem, pain, and death. But there is blame to go around, which brings me to my final story.

Several weeks before this book was to go to the editors, I was contacted by an employee of *Come Knocking* in Los Angeles. This person wished to remain anonymous, and I was able to verify his or her records as an employee but not their presence on March 14. This person gave me the following paragraph to print and for all of us to consider by way of testimony.

March 14 wasn't a surprise to all of us. The Discord server that housed Who's There was open to almost anyone and most of us found the whole conversation amusing. One person told me if a bunch of "keyboard warriors" actually did something violent it would be the first time in history. I brought up half a dozen examples of speech leading to violence and this employee laughed. "This isn't that bad." "It's funny to read." The warnings were there. Collectively, we chose to laugh at them.

That last statement has kept me up at night. As a journalist and as a person navigating through our world, I try to live by the mantra that "when someone tells you who they are, believe them" but does that even work anymore if nothing is to be believed? Have we reached a "post-truth" age where we can no longer believe anything people write or say? Are you someone completely different online than you are in real life? If so, what does that do to you as a person, as a citizen, as a member of an audience?

I believe the answer is "nothing good." And I think the shifting sand around our feet has made us all jumpy.

Or, to put it another way, underneath the mask a lot of us are scared and a lot of us are arrogant, myself included. If you are scared long enough and if you believe yourself to be infallible long enough, very few of us are going to be lucky enough to end our lives overlooking the British countryside, cocktail in hand. Most of us will bleed and suffer for that fear and that arrogance. And, while keeping "the mask" on isn't the solution either, I worry that fear and arrogance are entrenched. I worry we are eager to show others how angry we are and, in doing so, how selfish we are as well. I worry that we have tipped over into a situation where not much can stop the torrent of fear of the other, fear of loss, fear of not being superior.

I hate to end it this way, but I'm left no other conclusion.

The masks appear to be off.

Please plan accordingly.

—Adam Jakes